Mom looks at me finally. Her lips compress and flatten like it's hard for her to even look at me. "You can't go back to school."

"What? I don't—"

"Let me finish." She takes a breath like she's preparing to dive into deep waters. "You've been uninvited." Her lip curls at this last bit. Everton Academy never *expels* students. They "uninvite." As though the gentle euphemism could mask the reality of what being uninvited means.

I slide a step back. My hip bumps into a table holding an assortment of framed family photos. One hits the floor with a loud crack. I don't even move to pick it up. Shaking my head, I whisper, "Why?"

It's Dad who responds, his voice biting deep with words that will change everything forever. "You have the kill gene."

BOOKS BY SOPHIE JORDAN

The Firelight Series

*Firelight*

*Vanish*

*Hidden*

*Breathless* (a digital original novella)

*Uninvited*

*Unleashed*

# UNINVITED

SOPHIE JORDAN

HARPER TEEN
An Imprint of HarperCollinsPublishers

HarperTeen is an imprint of HarperCollins Publishers.

Uninvited

www.epicreads.com

---

Library of Congress Cataloging-in-Publication Data
Jordan, Sophie.
Uninvited / Sophie Jordan. — First edition.
pages cm
Summary: When seventeen-year-old Davy Hamilton tests positive for Homicidal Tendency Syndrome, everyone believes it is only a matter of time before she murders someone.
ISBN 978-0-06-223364-6
[1. Science fiction. 2. Genetics—Fiction. 3. Psychopaths—Fiction. 4. Murder—Fiction.] I. Title.
PZ7.J76845Un 2014 2013015448
[Fic]—dc23 CIP
AC

---

Typography by Torborg Davern
14 15 16 17 18 PC/RRDH 10 9 8 7 6 5 4 3 2 1
❖

First paperback edition, 2015

*For Catherine and Luke*

# PART ONE

# CARRIER

# NEWS RELEASE

For immediate release:
Contact: CDC Press Office

March 15, 2021

*Surgeon General releases new report on HTS.*
*More than 19,000 registered carriers.*

A new report on Homicidal Tendency Syndrome shows that cases are more dangerous and widespread than originally thought. The data illustrates a predisposition for extreme violence in HTS carriers and a clear correlation between the HTS gene and convicted murderers. This information, coupled with the rise in capital crime, calls for increased testing protocols and more severe measures to protect our citizens against HTS carriers. . . .

# ONE

I ALWAYS KNEW I WAS DIFFERENT.

When I was three years old, I sat down at the piano and played Chopin. Mom claims I heard it the week before in a hotel elevator. I don't know where I heard it. I just knew how to place my fingers on the keys . . . how to make them move. Like one knows how to walk, it was just something I knew. Something I did.

Music has always been my gift. That thing I was good at without having to try. First piano. Then the flute. Then violin. It never took me long to get the hang of a new instrument. All my life I heard words like *gifted. Extraordinary.*

*Blessed*. When everyone discovered I possessed a voice to rival my skills with an instrument, I was called a "prodigy."

These talents aside, I had the normal dreams, too. When I was six I decided I would be an archeologist. The following year, a race car driver. There was also the requisite princess fantasy in there. I spent hours in my room, building fort castles, only to have my brother knock them down. I just pretended he was a dragon and rebuilt those castles.

I had all these dreams to become something. Someone.

No one ever said I couldn't.

No one ever said *killer*.

Closing my eyes, I savor the sensation of Zac's lips on my throat. He inches toward the sensitive spot right below my ear and I giggle, my body shaking in his arms.

"Zac, we're at school," I remind him, arching away and shoving halfheartedly at his shoulder.

He levels brilliant green eyes on me, and my breath catches.

Two freshman girls pass us. They try to avert their eyes, play it cool, and look straight ahead, but I can see it's a battle for them. A battle they lose. Their gazes slide over Zac admiringly. He's in his gym shorts. An Everton rugby shirt stretches tight over his lean torso. When he lifts an arm and props his hand on the locker behind me, his shirt rides up to reveal a flat stomach, sculpted from long hours at the gym. My mouth dries a little.

The girls walk away, whispering loud enough for me to hear: "Freakin' hot . . . so lucky . . ."

He's oblivious to them. "But don't you like this?" He leans in, backing me against the lockers, and places a lingering, tender kiss at the corner of my mouth. "And this." He kisses my jawline next.

My stomach flutters and I'm about to give in, forget that I have Mrs. McGary and tons of calculus homework waiting, and surrender to making out with Zac outside the orchestra room, where Anthony Miller is less than successfully warming up on the drums. One of the only instruments I don't play, but I'm sure I could still play better than Anthony.

Zac pulls back with a sigh and gives me one of those smoldering looks that I know he thinks is irresistible. Only because it is. Only because every girl at school trips over herself when he bestows that smile on them.

But he chose me. My heart swells inside my chest and I let him kiss me again even though I'm already late for practice and Mrs. McGary hates it when I'm late. She constantly reminds me that I'm supposed to be the example for everyone.

Tori walks up to us with a roll of her eyes. "Get a room, you two." She pulls open the orchestra room door and the sound of the drum solo inside murders my ears.

She holds the door open for me. "Coming, Davy?"

Zac frowns at her. "She'll be there in a minute."

Tori hesitates, staring at me with that whipped puppy-dog look on her face. "Are we still studying tonight? I thought you wanted me to help you with your calculus."

I nod. "I do." Calculus. The bane of my existence. I barely made an A the last six weeks. And that A was mostly due to

Tori and her endless patience with me. "We're still on."

She smiles, looking mollified.

I smile back. "I'll be there in a minute. Save me a seat."

Tori disappears inside the orchestra room. Zac blows out a breath.

I smooth a hand over his firm chest. "Be nice."

"She's always interfering."

I make an effort to divide my time between Zac and Tori equally, but it's a balancing act. I never manage to satisfy either one of them. "Have I said that I can't wait until next year?" I ask. It's the only thing I can think to say in moments like this when he complains about Tori.

He stares at me knowingly. He has a way of looking at me. So deeply. Like he can see right to my very soul. He knows I'm trying to distract him with the promise of our future. Fortunately, it works.

His fingers thread through my hair. He loves it when I wear it down, loves touching it. Touching *me*. Yeah. I'm kind of addicted to my boyfriend. It's getting harder and harder to stop ourselves these days.

"Yeah. And you know the best part of it all?" His eyes hold mine. "Our very own dorm rooms."

I laugh. *Next year.* The dream of it tantalizes me. Me at Juilliard. Zac at NYU. I know I shouldn't be excited at the prospect of my best friend attending college hundreds of miles away from me, but it'll be nice not having to worry about hurting Tori's feelings all the time.

My phone rings. I squeeze out of his arms to see who's

calling me. With a quick glance at Zac, I mouth, *Mom*.

He lifts an eyebrow. My mom is usually still at work this time of day.

"Hello?" I answer.

"Davy, I need you home."

I hesitate before answering. Not because of her demand but because of the tremble in her voice. So unlike Mom. She always talks fast, her words spilling out in a rush. Hours spent bossing people around at her design firm, I guess.

"I have practice—"

"*Now*, Davy," she cuts me off.

"Is everything all right?" Silence meets my question and then I know everything isn't all right. "Is it Dad?"

"Your father's fine. He's here."

*Dad's home, too?* He's more of a workaholic than Mom. "It's Mitchell," I announce, dread pooling inside me. "Is he okay?"

"Yes. Yes. He's fine," she says hurriedly, that nervous tremor still there. Maybe even worse than moments before. I hear the rumble of voices in the background and the phone muffles, like Mom's covering the receiver with her hand so I won't hear. Then her voice returns to my ear. "Come home. I'll explain everything when you get here."

"Okay." I hang up and face Zac.

He stares at me sympathetically. "Mitchell?"

I nod, worry knotting inside me for my brother. *What's he done this time?* "Let me just let Mrs. McGary know." I stick my head inside the orchestra room. Mrs. McGary is at her desk in the corner talking on the phone. I motion to her but she shakes her head and holds up a finger for me to wait.

Seeing me with Zac in the doorway, Tori heads over. The orchestra room has always been a "no Zac zone," and I know she likes it that way. "What's going on?"

"My mom called. I have to go home."

Frowning, she touches my arm. "Is everything all right?"

"I don't know." I bite my lip.

She angles her head, her eyes bright with concern. "Mitchell?"

I shake my head. "I don't know."

Her hand moves up and down my arm in a consoling manner. "It'll be all right. He's just going through a phase. He'll get it out of his system."

If that's the case, my older brother has been going through a phase since he was thirteen. And now that he's twenty-one, I am not convinced he's going to grow out of it anytime soon.

"You'll see." Tori nods with certainty. "He's a good guy."

"Thanks." A quick glance reveals Mrs. McGary still on the phone. "Look, will you let her know—"

"Of course." Tori gives my fingers a comforting squeeze. "Go. I'll head over when practice ends. Want me to pick you up a smoothie on the way? Watermelon?"

"Thanks, but I better pass. I don't know what's going down at home."

"C'mon." Zac takes my hand. I grab my backpack, and together we head upstairs to the classroom level. We pass several friends. Zac keeps us moving when they try to stop us to talk.

Zac's best friend is the only one who succeeds. A consummate flirt, Carlton never lets me slip by without a hug. "Hey, gorgeous."

I step back from his embrace. "Hey."

Carlton bumps fists with Zac. "Doing weights today, man?"

Zac tugs me back to his side. "Nah. Gotta get Davy home."

Carlton winks at me. "Cool. See you guys later."

"Hey, Bridget," I call out to the sophomore girl who sits beside me in orchestra. She's second-chair violin. She jerks to a sudden stop, her hand clutching the railing as she stares at me in almost wonder.

The sophomore nods rapidly, holding still even as we keep climbing. "Hi, Davy." Her gaze slides to Zac and her cheeks grow pink. "Hey, Zac."

He looks back at her with a blank look. "Hey."

I smile a little.

"Why are you smiling?" he asks as we reach the first floor. "You don't even know her name."

He wraps an arm around my waist and pulls me closer against him. "I know *your* name."

I laugh. "Oh, really? Just my name?"

His gaze slides over me, and it's a hot look that makes me all fluttery inside. "I know a few other things about you, too."

"You'd *like* to know a few other things," I tease.

"I will." He grins, so sure of himself. So sure of us.

He gets the door for me and we leave the Academic Building behind, walking along the pebbled path toward the parking lot. There's a nip to the late afternoon—what consists of a Texas winter making its final stand. Soon it will be so hot that shirts stick to skin, and the air feels like steam.

I'm looking forward to New York. I've only seen snow once, ten years ago. It melted almost immediately, just sticking to the rooftops for the day. My brother and I scraped what we could off the lawn into snowballs and stuck them in the freezer, hoping to save them. They resembled dingy, brownish balls of ice with twigs and dried leaves sticking out of them. Mom threw them away before we ever got a chance to recover them from the freezer.

My gaze skims the brown-green hills etched against a sky so blue it hurts your eyes. The headmaster's white-pillared mansion looks down on us from the top of the hill as we pass the refectory where we eat. A perfectly manicured expanse of green stretches to our left. In the distance, flags slap in the wind, mingling with the soft drone of a golf cart driven by the head of campus security as he rolls toward the practice fields. Everyone calls him "Snappy" because he likes to snap his fingers to get your attention. My brother coined the nickname years ago as a freshman. Snappy busted Mitchell on more than one occasion.

We descend the hill toward the parking lot. Seniors get the best spots. It's one of our privileges at Everton, in addition to having our very own senior lounge replete with couches, TV, and soda and snack machines. Zac's parked in the front row beneath a crape myrtle tree in full bloom. Tiny white blossoms decorate the hood of his car.

"Someone needs to cut that thing down."

"It's pretty."

He squeezes my hand. "Not as pretty as you."

I roll my eyes, but still smile. He unlocks his BMW and walks me around to the passenger side. I love that he still does this. Even six months into our relationship, he makes me feel special. Like every day is a first date.

Before I can get in the car, he stops me. Placing his hands on either side of the car, he traps me between the vehicle and his body. My heart speeds up. I smile up at him, thinking he's going to kiss me again. But he doesn't. His vivid green eyes drill into me with unusual intensity.

"Davy. You know what you do to me, how you make me feel. . . ."

I touch his chest, flattening my palms against him. "You make me happy, too."

"Good. Because that's all I ever want, Davy. To make you happy."

"You do," I assure him.

He nods but he still doesn't move. He stares at me like he's memorizing me.

I angle my head, wondering at his odd seriousness. It's not like he goes around declaring himself all the time. "Zac?"

"I love you," he murmurs, the words falling slowly.

Everything inside me tightens. He's never said those words before.

My heart clenches and the ache there is so sweet. It's a perfect kind of agony. I suck in a sharp breath and then release it in a rush. Words are impossible. They stick inside my closed throat.

His gaze darts around and he almost looks nervous. "I didn't know I was going to say that here. Right now. In the parking lot. I mean . . . I've known for weeks that I love you. You're all I think about—" He grins down at me. "I'm babbling."

"I noticed that."

He kisses me. We've shared some amazing kisses before but nothing like this. *Zac loves me. He. Loves. Me.*

He breaks for air and mutters against my lips, "God, I've been trying to get up the courage to tell you that. Sorry it wasn't someplace more special."

I swat him on the shoulder. "Why would you be afraid to tell me that?" *Probably the same reason I've been afraid to say the words, too.*

His expression sobers and his arms tighten around me. "I don't know if I can handle you not loving me back."

I touch his face. Place my fingertips against his jaw. It's a little bristly. My fingers move over his skin, reveling in the texture. "Well, that's not possible. I think I loved you before you ever even asked me out."

Relief washes over his face. He kisses me once more, sweet and lingering, before we finally move and get inside the car.

It's a short drive to my house. I sit there in a daze, absorbing the sensation of his hand holding mine between us, and everything it means. *Me. Zac. Forever.* That's what it feels like. I know I'm just seventeen, but why not? Why not forever?

We're at my house in ten minutes. In this instance, I wish I didn't live so close to campus. Wish we could stay in our little world longer.

Two extra cars sit in the circular driveway. I don't know who they belong to, but my gaze drifts to Dad's Range Rover. Home in the middle of the week in broad daylight. That never happens.

Zac gets out with me. He quickly reclaims my hand. We've barely reached the wide rock steps leading to the double front doors when one of them swings open.

Mom steps out and I stop.

She looks pale, her normally smooth complexion drawn tight. Mom's key to looking young is to never get in the sun. As in—*never.* She only swims in our pool at night. But right now, even those efforts seem lost.

"Davy." She says my name on a breath, staring at me in an intense, devouring way that makes me want to touch my face and check that I haven't broken out in a rash suddenly.

Her gaze skitters to Zac. She nods at him. "Thanks for dropping her off." The translation is clear: leave. My parents adore Zac. If I didn't already know something is wrong, I do now.

Zac gives my hand a squeeze and locks his impossibly green eyes on me. The concern is there—the *love.* I'd seen it before but now it has a name. Now I know. "Call me."

I nod.

With one last look, he walks back to his car.

Then it's just Mom and me. She looks over her shoulder

and I can hear the voices drifting out from somewhere in the house. I recognize Dad's baritone and not just because it's familiar. It's the loudest.

"Mom? What's going on?"

She motions me inside.

I drop my backpack in the foyer. We walk across the dark wood floor into the living room. I inch inside warily, toeing the Oriental rug.

Immediately, I see Dad, standing, pacing. His arms and hands are all movement as he talks. No Mitchell though. My gaze sweeps the cavernous room. I recognize my headmaster, Mr. Grayson. He rises when we enter. He's never been to our house before, and it's strange seeing him here and not on campus. As though the only place he belongs is at Everton.

And there's another man. I've never seen him before. He's dressed in a cheap suit. The cuffs stop well before his hairy wrists and the fit is all wrong, too loose at the shoulders. I've been taught to appreciate good suits. Dad wears Caraceni and Gucci. The stranger stays sitting, looking almost bored.

Mr. Grayson tucks one hand inside his suit pocket. He addresses Dad in a placating voice, "Patrick, listen to me. My hands are tied. There's protocol— "

"Wasn't there protocol with Mitchell, too?"

Mitchell graduated three years ago. He's always been in trouble. Drugs. Failing grades. Nothing really improved when he started college, either. He came home first semester and currently lives in the guesthouse. Dad keeps pushing him to work at the bank. An "internship," he calls it. It sounds better than saying, "My son's a teller at the bank I own."

Hamilton Bank has been in my family since my great-grandfather founded it. It looks like that legacy will die with Dad. Mitchell's not cut out for it, and I have other plans.

Dad waves an arm wildly. "I wrote a check then. A fat donation and everything was fine. Why not this time? This is Davy! She's a damned prodigy. She sings and has been playing God knows how many instruments since before kindergarten. . . . She even performed for the governor when she was nine!"

I blink. Whatever this is, it's about me.

"This is beyond my control." Mr. Grayson speaks evenly, like he's rehearsed what to say.

Dad storms from the living room, passing me without a word.

Mr. Grayson notices me then. His entire demeanor changes. "Davy." He claps his hand together in front of him. "How are you?" he asks slowly, like I might have trouble understanding.

"Fine, Mr. Grayson. How are you?"

"Good!" He nods enthusiastically, reminding me of a bobblehead. *Weird.*

His eyes, however, convey none of this cheer. They flit nervously over me and then around the room—as if sizing up all possible escape routes. Marking the French doors leading outside, he shifts his gaze to the man on the couch.

The headmaster motions to him. "This is Mr. Pollock."

"Hello," I greet. "Nice to meet you."

He doesn't even respond. He looks me over with small, dark eyes set deeply beneath his eyebrows. His mouth loosens, the moist top lip curling in a vaguely threatening way. The thought seizes me: *he doesn't like me.*

Ridiculous, of course. He doesn't even know me. He's a stranger. How could he have formed any opinion of me at all?

In the distance, I hear the slap of Dad's returning footsteps. He enters the room breathlessly even though he didn't walk far. Even though he plays raquetball every week and is in great shape. His face is flushed like he's been out in the sun.

He brandishes his checkbook as he sinks into a chair. With his pen poised, he demands: "How much?"

Grayson exchanges a look with the stranger. He clears his throat, speaking almost gently now. "You don't understand. She can't come back tomorrow."

I cut in. "Come back where? What's going on?"

I move farther into the room. Grayson takes a notable step back, his gaze flying almost desperately to Pollock.

Staring down at his checkbook with fixed focus, Dad shouts, "How much?!"

I jump, my chest tight and uncomfortable. Prickles wash over the skin at the back of my neck. Dad never yells. He's too dignified for that. Everything about this is wrong.

My stomach churns. I look at Mom. She hovers at the edge of the room, her face pale. Her mouth parts and she moistens her lips as though she's going to speak, but nothing comes out.

Mr. Pollock rises from the couch, and I see just how short he is. His legs and torso appear almost the same length. His square hands brush over his bad suit. He takes a long, measuring look around our living room, his gaze skimming the furniture, the floor-to-ceiling bookcases, the heavy drapes, and the grand piano in the corner that I've played ever since I sat down in front of it at age three.

Dad lifts his gaze now, watching Pollock almost with hatred. And something that resembles fear. Although obviously not. Patrick Hamilton fears nothing and no one. Certainly not this man with his beady eyes and ill-fitting suit.

Watching Dad, I marvel at the harsh glitter of his gaze . . . the heavy crash of his breath. A part of me wants to go to him and place a hand on his tightly bunched shoulder. For whatever reason. Maybe to just make *me* feel better. Because Dad like this freaks me out.

Mr. Pollock stops before Dad and looks down at him. My father rises, still clutching his checkbook in his hand, crushing it.

Pollock jerks his head in my direction. "You can't buy her way out of this."

I stare, at a total loss. What did I do? Fear crawls up my throat in hot prickles, and I fight to swallow.

"Dad?" My voice is a dry croak.

He turns to me, the whites of his eyes suddenly pink, shot with emotion.

Mr. Grayson moves to leave. He gives me a small, sympathetic smile as he passes, lifting a hand as though to pat my shoulder and then dropping it, changing his mind.

Then it's Mr. Pollock before me, so close I can smell his

sour coffee breath. He flips out a small card. "I'll be your caseworker. I won't come here again. From now on, we meet at my office. Be there tomorrow at ten sharp."

The unspoken words *or else* hang in the air.

My thoughts jumble together. I glance down at the card but can't focus on the words.

Then the men are gone. It's just me and my parents.

I spin to face Mom. "Why do I have to see him tomorrow? I have school—"

"No," Dad announces, slowly sinking down into a chair. "You don't."

Mom moves inside the living room, her hand gliding along the back of the couch as though she needs the support of something solid under her fingers.

Dad drags a hand over his face, muffling his words, but I still hear them: "Oh, my God."

Those barely there words shudder through me.

I wet my dry lips. "Someone please tell me what's going on? What did that man mean when he said he's my caseworker?"

Mom doesn't look at me. She fixes her stare on Dad. He drops his hand from his face and exhales deeply, shaking his head. "They can't do this."

"Oh, Patrick." She shakes her head as if he just uttered something absurd. "They've been doing it all over the country. What can we do?"

"Something," he snaps. "This isn't happening. Not to my daughter!" He slams his fist down on the desk and I flinch.

My eyes start to burn as apprehension curls through me

sickly. Part of me feels the irrational urge to run. To flee from whatever horrible truth has my parents acting this way. Find Zac and hold him, bury my face in his chest and listen to him tell me he loves me again.

Mom looks at me finally. Her lips compress and flatten like it's hard for her to even look at me. "You can't go back to school."

"What? I don't—"

"Let me finish." She takes a breath like she's preparing to dive into deep waters. "You've been uninvited." Her lip curls at this last bit. Everton Academy never *expels* students. They "uninvite." As though the gentle euphemism could mask the reality of what being uninvited means.

I slide a step back. My hip bumps into a table holding an assortment of framed family photos. One hits the floor with a loud crack. I don't even move to pick it up. Shaking my head, I whisper, "Why?"

It's Dad who responds, his voice biting deep with words that will change everything forever. "You have the kill gene."

U.S. Department of Justice • The Federal Bureau of Investigation • Criminal Justice Information Reporting Division

United States Crime Analysis

| YEAR | POPULATION | HOMICIDES | HTS HOMICIDES |
|---|---|---|---|
| 2017 | 320,494,019 | 102,209 | 59,212* |
| 2019 | 322,320,103 | 181,717 | 98,052* |
| 2021 | 332,012,992 | 234,020 | 196,015** |

**HTS testing yet to become protocol in many state-level jurisdictions.*

***HTS testing fully realized at every state-level jurisdiction.*

# TWO

I CAN BARELY RECALL WHEN THEY TESTED US FOR HTS at school. It was at the start of the year. Before the leaves started to fall and calculus made my head hurt. Before Homecoming. Before Zac asked me out.

The Everton Board of Trustees decreed that all students needed testing. Not such a surprise. Everyone in the country is being tested these days. Dad even started requiring it of all employees at the bank. That's some bitter irony now.

All advisory periods were sent to the nurse's clinic. For me that meant leaving the orchestra hall and missing practice time. I think I remember that the most. Being mad about that.

One quick cotton swab in the mouth and it was done. My DNA stuck in a tube.

I think someone joked about Albert Adolfson obviously being a carrier. The Swedish kid is the star of our wrestling team and has serious anger issues. I always suspected steroids, but then the joke became HTS.

*Now the joke is me.*

Once everyone finds out. That bit of realization makes it hard to breathe. I don't stay long in the living room with Mom and Dad. I can't. Dad's anger. The weird way Mom looks at me. It makes terrible sense now.

And Mr. Pollock with those small, mean eyes . . .

He makes sense, too. He's part of my life now.

Images fire across my mind. One after another. An endless flash of killers in their prison jumpsuits. And the victims, the grieving people left behind. The media loves to zoom in on them. I never turn on the television anymore.

I flee to the sanctuary of my room and stare at the pictures of Zac and my friends all over my dresser mirror, wondering how they'll react. Of course, I'll have Zac and Tori, but what about the others? Will they still be my friends? I pace, humming an aimless tune, searching for my peace, my solace. Ever since I was a child, music has lived inside me. It lulls me to sleep at nights and calms me whenever I feel anxious. Lyrics and notes trip through my head as I wait for the terrible tightness in my chest to go away. For the calm to come. For the panic to fade.

But no matter how much I hum, no matter how much

the music plays in my head, it doesn't happen.

I open my laptop and search for HTS.

I can't ignore it. *I can't ignore me. No.* Not me.

Not me, whatever some stupid DNA test says. My stomach rolls, rebelling at the idea. They might say I am. But it's not true. It's not.

It can't be.

My search lasts only a few minutes. The first thing that pops up is footage from the *20/20* feature on HTS. Death row inmates are interviewed by Dr. Wainwright. I listen as they share the horrific accounts of their crimes with the stoic-faced man. Some of them smile weirdly as they recount their transgressions. Those curving lips make my skin crawl. A breath shudders from my lips. *I'm not them.*

I punch fiercely at the keyboard and move to another site. A video of some extremist group brutally assaulting three men . . . *three HTS carriers.* From the comment feed below, everyone thought they got just what they deserved.

It's too much. My already churning stomach pitches. The laptop falls from my lap as I dive for the bathroom, retching until my stomach is empty.

After that, I stagger back into my room and pick my laptop off the floor. Logging off, I set it on my desk and drop back on my bed.

Gradually, sunlight fades from behind my blinds. My phone rings and I glance at it. Zac. I can't talk to him right now. Not yet.

I roll on my side and close my eyes, pressing a hand to my

lips, smothering the cry that rises up in my throat and seeks escape. But there is no escape. No running from this.

After a while, I breathe normally again and feel like I can face my parents. I have to. I can't pretend nothing happened. I need them to tell me everything is going to be okay. I need to know the next step. The plan. Sucking in a breath, I open the door. As I descend the stairs, I stop at the sound of Dad's voice.

"She's not a carrier. We would know something like that! You've seen those monsters all over the TV. The Minneapolis Bomber . . . the Atlanta Day-Care Shooter. We'd know if our daughter is like them!"

I flinch and ease down one more step.

"The kill gene," Mom says. "That's what they call it. It can be dormant until something triggers it. They don't all start out as monsters. . . ."

I sink down on the step and hug my knees, unable to face them after all.

It sounds like Mom believes I'm this . . . *thing*. A monster waiting for darkness to come so that I can leap out.

I bury my face in my knees. My shoulders shake but I don't cry. Don't make a sound. I'm not a killer. Although if I believe the propaganda, I'm going to become one. It's just a matter of time. That's what being an HTS carrier means. At least that's what everyone says. Apparently, even what my parents believe. Or at least Mom.

"No. It has to be a mistake." *Yes!* I latch onto these words. It is a mistake. It *is*. I hear the clink of glass and guess that Dad is pouring himself a drink.

"Patrick." Mom says his name sharply. "You heard the headmaster. He had them double-check the DNA. That's why it took so long to get the results from the fall. We can't live in denial. We have to deal with this."

Dad doesn't respond. After a few moments, Mom adds, her voice clipped and efficient, "I'll take her to her appointment with the caseworker tomorrow."

"Yeah, you do that." Even from where I huddle on the step, I don't miss the edge to his voice.

Mom doesn't miss it, either. "You blame me? Is that it?"

"She certainly didn't get this damned gene from my side of the family."

"So this is my fault?" Mom's voice is a snarl. "It's recessive. It took the both of us for this to happen! You always have to blame someone anytime anything goes wrong. You blame me for Mitchell and you might as well blame me for our daughter turning out to be a sociopath."

I gasp.

There's a loud crash. Dad's glass hitting the wall or floor.

My hands grip the edge of the step, needing something to hang on to, something to keep me from splintering apart. A fingernail cracks under the pressure.

In the distance, I hear the faint ring of my cell phone in my room. Zac calling again. Or maybe Tori.

Mom's raspy voice drifts to me, quieter now, subdued. "Feel better?"

"No. I'll never feel better again, Caitlyn. Should I? I just lost my daughter."

I bow over, clutching my waist, the words a painful blow. I cover my mouth so that no sound escapes. I want to shout that I haven't *gone* anywhere. I'm the same girl I was yesterday. I'm no different. But somehow I am. To them, I am. I'm lost. Tomorrow the world will know that, too.

I hear the creak of the French doors followed by my brother's voice. "Hey, what's for dinner? I'm starved."

"We haven't cooked," Mom snaps. No. No dinner. We forgot about food. "There are leftovers from last night." I hear glass rattle and guess that she's digging through the fridge. "Lasagna. Some garlic bread. I'll warm some up. Sit down. We need to talk. . . ."

I rise and lightly tiptoe back to my room, not wanting to hear the inevitable conversation.

When they tell Mitchell that his sister's not who they thought she was. That girl is gone and never coming back.

Sleep eludes me. Zac stops calling around midnight. I lie in bed, a song whispering through my head, fingers laced over my stomach as I stare up at the ceiling. My eyes are dry as bone. Strangely, I haven't cried even though it feels like I lost everything. My head spins against the backdrop of an aria, thoughts racing through everything that's happened, everything that's going to happen. *Zac will still be there. My real friends*. They won't change because they'll understand that *I* haven't.

Anxiety gnaws at me as I try to process how everyone will react. I remind myself that it's just a few months until graduation when everything was going to change anyway. But then that leads to thoughts of the future, college. I've been expelled. What now? Will my new HTS status prevent me from going to Juilliard? I groan and rub my hands over my face. I don't know. Don't know anything anymore. Except what I am. *What I'm not. Not a killer.*

A knock sounds at my door and it pushes open. My brother stands there. "Hey."

He looks like Mom. Brown eyes and dark hair. I've got the eyes but lighter hair. Like Dad. My father is mostly gray now, but when he was younger he had blond hair. Mom met him when he was lifeguarding at the country club. She said he looked like a young Brad Pitt. Whoever that was.

Mitchell wears his hair long and shaggy. Not because of any style he's going for. He's just too lazy to care. Staring at him now, I know Mom told him. He knows.

I force a smile. "Guess you're not the family troublemaker anymore, huh?"

"Shut up," he says without heat. He digs his hands into his pockets and walks into my room. Dropping his slender frame down on the bed beside me, he announces, "It's crap. You know that. No one can predict the future. *Your* future."

Sitting up, I cross my legs and drag a pillow into my lap. "There's something to it. Why else are they testing people? You see the news? Some states even have special camps—"

"Yeah. Like ass-backward states. Not here." He shakes his head. "You'll see. In a few years, they'll say HTS is all bogus. Some doctors will come up with something to discount the validity of it and all that." He waves a hand like he's swatting a fly. His gaze captures mine.

I want to believe that. Really I do. That in a few years, maybe even sooner, all this will be a bad memory.

He leans onto his side. "There are a lot of bad people out there, Dav. These are dangerous times. People are scared. And when people are scared they need to feel in control. HTS lets people feel like they still have control against all the bogeymen out there." He squeezes my arm. "No way are you one of them. Anyone can take a look at you and see that."

I nod, his words feeding me hope. "In the meantime, I'm uninvited from Everton."

"Everton sucks. I tried to get kicked out of that place but Dad kept getting me back in."

I roll my eyes and laugh. It feels good.

He gently nudges my shoulder. "Hey. You'll be fine. Everyone loves you. You're, like, perfect—"

I sigh. "Mitchell. I'm not."

"I'm serious." His brown eyes look earnestly into mine. "This will all blow over."

"I just want my life to stay the same," I mumble into my pillow. "Or at least continue according to plan."

It was a great plan, too.

"I know." He rolls onto his back and stares up at the ceiling. "But nothing ever stays the same, Davy. You just have to adapt. . . . Show them this HTS is all a load of shit." He laughs brokenly. "I mean, if anyone in this family is a carrier, it should be me. I'm the screwup."

Suddenly, my phone rings again. I stare at it for a moment, waiting for it to stop ringing. I guess Zac isn't ready to give up on me yet. Hopefully, that won't change once he knows the truth.

"You're going to have to tell him. Better if he hears it from you anyway. He'll understand."

I nod and squeeze my pillow tighter like I can crush all my fears and the ugly reality of this day. "I know. Tomorrow."

---

**Text Message**

6:45 p.m.

Tori:

Hey thgt we were studyin 2night u coming over?

8:11 p.m.

Tori:

U there??? I'm starting to worry

10:58 p.m.

Tori:

What's wrong??? R U mad at me???

11:34 p.m.

Tori:

Pls answer ur phone

# THREE

MOM DROPS ME AT THE FRONT DOOR WHILE SHE hunts for a parking space. She's paranoid I'm going to be late. Like the police will appear if I'm one minute late or something. It's the "or something," the not knowing anything anymore, that makes her nervous. The ground hasn't just shifted beneath our feet; it's been ripped away entirely.

I feel groggy from lack of sleep. A dull ache throbs at my temples. I still haven't talked to Zac. I sent him a message saying I was sick and not to pick me up for school. I figured that might also offer some explanation for my ignoring him last night. It's a reprieve. For now at least.

A receptionist sits at a desk in the lobby of the Wainwright Agency. Very utilitarian. Like most government buildings. Behind her, the first floor stretches into a labyrinth of cubicles. Phones ring. Voices hum in a low drone.

I give her my name and she motions for me to take a seat on a row of chairs lining a wall.

I move numbly and sink into hard plastic. I tuck my hands under my thighs and stare ahead with dry eyes. Even though I ignored Zac's calls, I listened to his voice mails, letting the sound of his voice bleed into my heart. I'll have to tell him today, and even though I know he'll still love me, I can't help worrying he'll look at me just a little bit differently. The way Mom does.

There's an older guy waiting several seats down from me. I slide him a furtive glance, wondering if he's a carrier, too. Wondering if he's like me . . . an identified carrier who clearly isn't dangerous. It hits me then that before yesterday I believed it all. That every carrier was . . . *is* a danger.

He's wearing a faded army-green jacket that makes him look faintly military. Or at least like he once might have been in the service. He's too scruffy-looking to be currently enlisted. He catches me looking, setting cold eyes on me, and then I'm convinced that he's not like me at all. He's a *true* carrier. Alarmed that I'm staring into the eyes of a killer, I quickly look away.

And then my throat closes up, thinking that to the world I'm no different from him. I'm someone who must be monitored. That's why I'm here.

Mom joins me just before Mr. Pollock appears and motions

us to follow him. It looks like he's wearing the same suit today. Just a different tie. We zigzag through a path created by the labyrinth of cubicles and sink down into the two chairs in front of his desk. I can hear a woman talking on the phone on the other side of the partition. Her voice is monotone as she warns someone that if he doesn't come in for his next appointment she will issue a warrant for his arrest.

"All right." Pollock opens up a crisp manila folder and surveys it for a moment. Without any warning, he picks up a narrow black device. A tiny blue light glows at its center as he leans over his desk and swipes it through the air once in front of my face.

"What's that?"

"Face scanner," he replies brusquely.

I glance to Mom. Her fingers lightly worry her pearls. He sets down the scanner, makes a mark in my folder, and returns his attention to his monitor, clicking the keyboard a few times.

Finally, he looks at us. "I've already alerted your local public school. They're expecting you tomorrow."

"Keller High School?" Only fifteen minutes away, it's closer to the city. I've never been there. My world has been Everton since kindergarten.

He looks at me with those small, dark eyes, totally emotionless. "You're seventeen. You're required to attend school. You're lucky. Some states don't even allow carriers in public school anymore." The way he says this, the way his head nods, makes me believe he agrees with the policy, that we should be doing it here, too.

He looks at Mom and I can't help noticing his eyes are a little less icy when he turns his attention on her. He probably feels sorry for her . . . pities her for having a daughter like me. "You'll have to take her tomorrow, Mrs. Hamilton, to complete all the necessary registration. Keller already has a few HTS carriers, so they have a protocol in place."

I shift in my chair.

"In the meantime . . ." He hands me a card. "This is your HTS identification. Keep it with you at all times." Then he hands me a heavy packet. "Familiarize yourself with current HTS regulations."

I thumb the stapled papers, looking back up at him when he says sharply, "Ignorance of the rules is no excuse. If you commit an infraction, break a law, justice will be swift."

These words make my chest pull even tighter. "Rules?" I echo.

He lowers his elbows to his desk and steeples his fingertips. "I'll do you a favor and explain one now. Maybe the most important thing you can take away from this meeting." He lifts one finger and holds it ominously before him. "You get one chance. One shot. The first time you hurt someone or behave in a threatening or violent manner, you're imprinted." He taps the side of his neck. "One infraction from you, one word from me, and you wear the H. I'm sure you've seen it."

Not up close. Never up close. We live in a good neighborhood. I go—*went*—to a good school. Only hung out at *good* places. If there were carriers around, they weren't the imprinted kind. I only saw those kinds on TV. Usually cuffed and being led out of a courtroom. Or walking the streets of some crime-ridden area. They were to be feared.

"Of course, if your infraction gets you arrested, then you're imprinted *and* you end up in jail." Pollock leans back in his chair. "You're out of my authority at that point."

I nod. "That won't happen," I say.

He smirks. "You all say that."

My lungs swell at the unfairness of it all. I've never even been in a fight. Not even in elementary school. It's ridiculous to imagine *me* committing one of these infractions he describes. I want to scream: *Look at me! I'm not bad! I'm not a monster!*

Pollock returns his attention to the monitor and taps the keyboard a few more times.

The fiery indignation fades away and numbness slides into place, envelops me like a blanket. I wrap myself in it to keep from shattering. He rattles off more information. *Protocol.* He drops that word a lot. He offers more papers. Mom takes them. I can't move. Can't speak.

I watch Pollock's mouth move, but the words are a jumble in my ears. I tune him out and sink inside myself, listening to the music weaving in my head.

Pollock stands and I realize the meeting is over. Mom rises, too. She looks down at me with wide eyes that just don't seem to blink anymore.

I move sluggishly to my feet, arms crossed, hugging myself. Suddenly, I'm cold. So cold. Inside and out, I'm chilled to the bone.

"I'll see you next month. Hopefully, not before." Pollock snaps my file shut and slides it aside on his desk. My fingers itch to snatch it and read for myself the words that say I'm this terrible thing that must be watched and monitored like a bomb waiting to blow. Like there will be something there I can point at and say, *Aha! That's not true. I can prove it. I'll show you.*

I nod, not knowing what to do or say. I turn to follow Mom from the cubicle but pause as someone else steps inside the small space. Saunters really.

My gaze moves over him unevenly, jerking along the long body. The legs, waist, chest. He's more muscular than Zac. And taller. *Fighter's build* floats through my head.

I glance up at his face, survey the strong lines. Even if his face isn't the perfection you see in the movies or on magazine covers, there's no doubt that he's hot. His brows are thick over deeply set eyes. The nose looks like it's been broken. His hair is too long, almost to his shoulders, and I suspect he himself might have hacked the dark blond strands framing his face.

He's got that confidence that always attracts females. Features carved from stone, but a body relaxed and at ease. Suddenly, I remember a line from *Julius Caesar*. As my gaze crawls over him, the words come back to me: *a lean and hungry look . . . such men are dangerous.*

Without being told, I know he's a carrier.

"Mr. O'Rourke, nice of you to show." Pollock glances at his watch. "Only an hour late. This is unacceptable. We're going to have to discuss this."

O'Rourke shrugs. An intricate ink design creeps up his muscular bicep and disappears beneath the sleeve of his gray T-shirt. My gaze lifts, collides with his. His eyes are smoky blue, the irises rimmed with a blue so dark it appears almost black. He looks me up and down appraisingly.

Heat bursts over my face at his speculative look. Me. *Here.* It doesn't take a rocket scientist to figure out why. I already deduced the same about him.

Except *he* looks the part.

His hard features remind me of the faces that flash across the television screen—criminals found guilty for committing some horrendous crime, all proven HTS carriers. This guy's fathomless eyes hold secrets, shadows where light can't reach.

He doesn't even acknowledge Pollock. His deep voice rumbles across the air, turning my skin to goose bumps. "Hey, princess."

I shiver. And then I see it. The proof. I missed it before, too mesmerized by his body, his face, his eyes. His neck bears the mark. The H trapped inside a circle set within a wide ink band that wraps his neck. And maybe it was just that I didn't expect to see it. Even here.

Mom must see it, too—must be filled with my same fear, the same curiosity over what he did to get imprinted. She grips my arm like she's hanging on for life.

"Sean." Pollock says his name sharply, motioning to the seat. "Sit."

After a long moment, the boy looks away. He drops in his seat, shaking his hair back from his face, the imprint even more visible now. Like he doesn't care who sees it.

Mom's hand slides down my arm to my hand. She gives it a hard tug. I barely hear her whisper, "C'mon."

She leads me from the cubicle. Still, I glance back over my shoulder at the boy sitting in the chair. I stare at the back of his head, at the dark blond hair my friends would spend ridiculous money for in a salon. I doubt he does anything except shampoo it. It's rich brown underneath the sun-gold strands. Maybe he works a lot in the sun cutting lawns or something. I can't imagine my parents hiring him to mow the grass.

He sits so at ease in the chair. Does he care where he is? And why? Did he lose sleep over that imprint on his neck? At his corrupt DNA?

Pollock has already opened his folder and is stabbing his finger threateningly as he talks. I turn around and let Mom pull me away.

As we leave the building, I'm only sure of one thing.

I'll never wear that mark.

Conversation between Dr. Wainwright and the United States chief of staff:

**SWITZER:** At this time, the president is not prepared to take such measures.

**WAINWRIGHT:** Oh? Instead, he wants the homicide rate to keep climbing? He wants to quarantine another city? I hear you've already lost Phoenix.

**SWITZER:** We have the situation in hand—

**WAINWRIGHT:** How is it you can even say that with a straight face? The power to test and identify carriers does nothing except tell us who the monsters are. It doesn't stop them. The president needs to grant me more authority.

**SWITZER:** What you're suggesting is impossible.

**WAINWRIGHT:** It's not a suggestion. I'm telling you. If you want to keep the country from going under . . . then give the carriers to me.

**SWITZER:** . . . I'll talk to the president. . . .

# FOUR

ZAC COMES OVER STRAIGHT AFTER SCHOOL. HE must have skipped rugby practice. I hear the familiar purr of his car drive up and rush to the window to confirm that it's him. Peering out, I curse under my breath and jerk back as though the blinds sting my fingers. I look around my room as if I can hide somewhere. Ridiculous, I know. It's my fault I put this off so long.

Shaking my head, I bound over my bed to my dresser mirror and pull loose my ponytail. I run a quick brush through my long hair and then flip my head, hoping to get some body back into the dark-blonde mass. Slapping my brush on the dresser, I hurry downstairs and answer the door before he can push the bell. I don't want Mom to answer it. Don't want him to see her face and think someone died.

She took the rest of the week off. I guess she thought she needed to be here for me. Which is kind of funny since I've been in my room all afternoon and she's been in hers. Ever since we saw that boy, she's been even more distant. Like he's the manifestation of everything she fears I will become. But that will never happen.

I close the door behind me, clutching the knob at my back like a lifeline. Zac's steps slow as he advances, his gaze locking on me. A breeze ruffles his brown hair. The sides are cut close, but he's always had a good inch or two on top. Enough for me to thread my fingers through.

I smile, a lump rising in my throat.

He steps up on the porch and stops before me, frowning, and I know he's mad that I've been ignoring him. "What's going on? Are you okay?"

Exhaling, I lean in, press my cheek against his chest and wrap my arms around him. His arms envelop me, holding me. I need this. So much. His arms. His love. Right now when everything is falling away, he's here. Holding me together.

"Why haven't you answered my calls? Were you really sick?"

The sensation of his hands on my back is like a drug. It feels good . . . tempts me to forget. And I want to forget. Only I can't.

"Davy? What's wrong?" he presses, his voice a soft croon in my ear.

A hundred different excuses burn on my tongue. Lies all. But what would be the point? He has to know. We'll get through this. *We love each other.*

I peel my face away from his chest, from the pleasant thump of his heart against my ear. His bright green eyes dazzle me. I moisten my lips. "Do you remember when they tested the students for HTS earlier this year?"

He's caught off guard. Like he doesn't know what that has to do with anything. With me. His eyes swing to the right, searching his memory. "Uh, yeah. Think so. Why?"

"The results came back. I have it. I tested positive." I say it quickly, let the words tumble free as though it won't sound so bad because I'm talking so fast.

He pauses and then laughs. "Yeah. Right."

"Zac." I gaze into his face, waiting for him to see that I'm serious.

Everything in him tenses. Except his face. His features go lax with shock.

Several moments pass and he doesn't move. I watch him intently, desperately, waiting for him to speak, to say the words I need him to say.

My voice shivers from my lips. "Zac?"

"The kill gene?" he whispers.

I wince, hating that. HTS sounds more vague . . . clinical but harmless.

I nod and his arms drop from around me. He takes a step back, staring at me with wide eyes. Eyes that don't blink—just like Mom's.

I follow him, holding out a hand, trying to reach him, touch him. He drags a hand through his hair, out of reach from my seeking fingers. Bowing over, he tugs on the strands like he wants to rip them free. His face twists and he looks as though he's in physical pain. He stares down at the porch, like he can find something there in the stamped concrete. A truth, something to explain away what's happening.

I say his name again. Louder.

He looks at me then, and my heart seizes inside my chest. Because it's not him. Not Zac. Not like I know him. The warmth is gone. The craving, the need for me. His green eyes are brighter than ever but filled with bewilderment . . . horror. Grief.

He lifts his arm like he's going to swing. Hit something. He holds it in the air for a long moment. A growl erupts from him as he curls his hand into a tight, bloodless fist. I flinch.

"I'm still the same person," I say desperately. "I'm still the same girl you loved yesterday. That hasn't changed."

He drops his hand from his hair and shakes his head. "I—I know. I just don't . . ."

Not an outright rejection but it feels like it. Suddenly, it's hard to breathe. The air feels thin, but I nod like I understand.

"Yeah. Okay." The words stumble from my lips.

He turns. His graceful loping strides are gone. He's almost running to his car. I watch, shaking, trembling so badly that I can't stand. At the door to the car, he hesitates and looks at me. He's conflicted. I can tell from his body. Part of him leans forward like he wants to come back to me. And God, I want him to. I need him to. I need this—*us*—to still be all right.

Then he's inside the car, slamming the door shut after him.

I fall back against the front door and slide to the porch as he peels out of the driveway.

I squeeze myself, hugging my knees to my chest so tightly I can hardly breathe. Tears run hotly down my cheeks, and my mouth opens with a silent, breathless sob even as I know his reaction is . . . normal. *Expected* even. He didn't know what to say, what to do. . . .

Understandable. Neither do I.

**Text Message**

8:42 p.m.

Zac:

Can u come over?

8:55 p.m.

Tori:

Sure. What's wrong?

8:56 p.m.

Zac:

Everything

9:00 p.m.

Tori:

Is Davy w/u?

9:02 p.m.

Zac:

No

Need 2 talk. Can't b alone right now

9:10 p.m.

Tori:

On way

# FIVE

I REPORT TO KELLER HIGH SCHOOL AT EIGHT SHARP. Amid the packet of information from Pollock were the bolded instructions to arrive at eight and depart at three in order to avoid fraternizing with the general population. My first clue that even at Keller things were going to get worse.

Although it's hard to imagine that. After Zac left yesterday, it took me a long time to pick myself up and go back inside. Even longer for the tears to stop. The tight, aching twist in my chest? That still hasn't stopped.

My phone sat quietly on my nightstand all night. I had hoped Zac would call after he had time to process. No call.

Not even a ring from Tori. I could only guess that Zac told her. Or he told someone who then told her. It only takes one person to get gossip rolling. *Davy Hamilton is a killer.* That kind of gossip would be too juicy to keep quiet.

I shake loose the crippling thoughts and focus on getting through this first day.

The building is gray—from the outside brick to the flat carpet and chipping paint inside. Idly, I wonder if gray is the school color. It's doubtful I'll be attending any pep rallies to find out.

We enter the office and get behind a student waiting for a tardy slip to class. The secretary's smile slips from her face when Mom tells her who we are. Humming lightly under my breath, I scan the office as they talk. A student aide gawks at me as she staples papers together behind a desk.

I arch an eyebrow at her and she quickly looks away.

Mom signs her name to a few papers, not even pausing to read anything. It's like she can't get out of here fast enough.

"Here's your ID. Wear it at all times." The receptionist slides a neon-orange tag across the counter that already bears the picture Pollock took of me yesterday. I take it and loop it around my neck.

"The orange identifies your carrier status," she announces, loud enough for everyone in the office to hear. A woman on the phone in the corner stops talking and stares.

The secretary nods with approval at the ID dangling in front of my chest, letting me know I have no chance of staying under the radar. I glance at the student aide. Her badge is white. Yeah. No chance.

My eyes burn. I blink back tears, refusing to cry, refusing to let this small thing break me. I've been through worse than this in the last forty-eight hours.

She continues, "The counselor, Mr. Tucci, will take you to the"—the secretary pauses, catching herself and correcting whatever it was she was going to say—"your classroom."

Mom faces me.

I stare at her, hollow inside, nothing there except the lyrics of an old Beatles song: *Hey, Jude, don't make it bad, take a sad song and make it better*. It doesn't help much because I want to grab her and hold her and beg her not to leave me here, but it won't do any good. She's shut herself off. Her eyes are dull—like she's beyond feeling anything.

She squeezes my shoulder. "Have a good day, Davy."

Like that's possible. I nod and watch her walk away. Leave me in this strange, horrible place.

"Sit there." The secretary directs me to a chair against the wall. "Mr. Tucci will be with you soon."

Hugging my sack lunch, I drop into the seat, not bothering to slide off my backpack. A sack lunch is another requirement. Carriers aren't allowed to eat anything from the cafeteria. Too much chance of mingling with the general population. I sit at the edge of the seat, my body taut, waiting, watching as people come and go through the office.

It's nine thirty before Mr. Tucci appears. The secretary murmurs something to him and motions in my direction. He advances on me, sizing me up with a mild expression. I stare back. He's dressed well in a pressed polo and slacks.

Something my dad would never wear to work, but still.

"Welcome to Keller, Ms. Hamilton." He extends his hand for me to shake. I stare at it for a moment, thinking he's joking. He can't want to touch me.

His expression softens. "I know this is hard, but if you stay out of trouble, you can finish out your senior year here with no fuss." Leaning down, he whispers for my ears alone. "Prove them wrong."

A ragged sigh escapes me. His words remind me of Mitchell and for a flash of a second I don't feel so alone. *Prove them wrong.* A lump forms in my throat at the unexpected kindness from this man. Maybe it won't be so terrible here after all.

A moment passes before I nod, fighting the lump down in my throat. "I can do that."

"Excellent." He smiles broadly. "Follow me."

He leads me from the office and down a deserted hall. We pass lockers. Teachers' voices drift from inside the classrooms. His shoes clack over the linoleum floor. We descend a set of stairs and walk until it feels like we're in the very bowels of the school. We are long past any classrooms. We pass the gym. The stink of the weight room greets me well before we pass its open doors. A quick glance reveals a few sweaty guys working out inside.

There are no windows. No sunlight. Just the buzz of a fluorescent bulb every few feet. I see that the wide corridor dead-ends ahead.

My pulse skitters nervously. "Where are we going?"

He shoots me a disarming smile. Instead of answering, he

says, “There are five others. Like you. You won’t be alone.”

I swallow. He means five other HTS carriers. And me. Until graduation. I’m not sure I wouldn’t prefer to be alone.

“You’ll get to know them well, I’m sure.”

Before the end of the corridor, he turns left and stops in front of a set of steel double doors. Opening the right side door, he steps inside. I follow, but don’t go much farther. The space is too small, occupied by a single desk. A teacher sits there, reading a magazine. He’s young, looks barely out of college. He quickly stands when he sees us, dropping his magazine.

“Ah, Mr. Tucci. Good morning. Is this the new one?” He nods in my direction, tugging on his waistband as though his wind pants need adjustment.

“Yes, Mr. Brockman, this is Ms. Hamilton. I’m sure you’ll show her the ropes.”

Mr. Brockman looks me over, his gaze crawling, and I suddenly feel exposed before him. “Not a problem, not a problem,” he says.

I cross my arms. As if that might help to shield me from his measuring look.

“Very good.” With another smile for me, Mr. Tucci departs. I wince as the heavy steel clangs after him.

And I’m left with Mr. Brockman and the others, HTS carriers whose stares I feel boring into me.

Mr. Brockman motions behind him. “Welcome to the Cage.”

“The Cage?” I echo.

He chuckles. “Yep. That’s what the kids call it. The name

kind of stuck. Even the staff calls it that now." He nods to the wall of chain link behind his desk.

It makes terrifying sense. What better way to remove us from the general population than to stick us down here with only ourselves for company? And beyond isolation . . . we're confined.

"The Cage" consists of chain link stretching from floor to ceiling. On the other side of the chain link there are about ten desks. Only four students occupy the desks, all staring at me with varying expressions. Maybe Mr. Tucci was wrong about the number. Or maybe number five has done something bad and is in jail.

Immediately, I see that the gate-like door is the only way in or out. Mr. Brockman moves to open it. "It'll take them a while to round up your assignments. You'll just have to amuse yourself for today."

The door squeaks as he pulls it open.

I pause at the entrance, reluctant to move inside, to take the first step that will officially make me one of them. I look back at him, unnerved at how close he's standing beside me, still looking me over in a way that makes me feel like a piece of meat.

"So you don't actually teach us?" I ask for clarification, scanning his attire. He looks more like someone on his way to the gym than a real teacher.

"No. Call me a glorified babysitter. I started as a part-time sub, but they hired me full-time last year. I just turn your work in to your teachers on the outside."

*On the outside.* Teachers I'll never even meet. I realize this now.

I peer inside the Cage, eyeing the others. Three boys and one girl. She's no longer looking at me, concentrating instead on carving something into the desk with her pen.

"That's Coco." He takes one more step, bringing his body closer. The soft bulge of his stomach presses against my arm. "Bet she'll be glad for some female company. Just been her in here with the boys since last year."

There's something in his voice that makes the tiny hairs on my nape prickle, and suddenly I'm not sure what I'm more afraid of: the Cage and the supposed killers inside—or Mr. Brockman on the outside.

"Course you don't have to go in just yet." His voice falls close to my ear. "If you want you can stay out here a bit with me."

Then I *know* what frightens me more. At least right now, in this moment, the answer is clear.

In the Cage, I notice Coco's pen holds still. Her attention remains fixed on her desk, but I know she's attuned to me. To Brockman. Her alertness reaches me, folds into my own veil of awareness.

Squaring my shoulders, I step inside the Cage.

---

Office of the Attorney General

*Department of Justice ORDER NO: 3109-09*

---

By virtue of the authority assigned to me as attorney general, I, Samantha Jinks, hereby direct that all United States citizens be tested for Homicidal Tendency Syndrome, otherwise known as HTS, within thirty days of the issuance of this command. Persons who fail to comply will be taken into custody where they will submit to HTS testing standards accorded within their own locality. . . .

# SIX

I SIT NEAR THE FRONT NEXT TO THE GIRL, COCO. IT'S the obvious choice. I'm not ashamed of my predictability. Two of the boys huddle together, their desks close. It looks like they're playing some kind of card game. One boy sits by himself, his slight shoulders hunched over his desk. He's small, hardly big enough to pass for a freshman. Face buried in a book, his long, spindly legs stretch out far beneath his desk and he reminds me of a puppy that hasn't quite grown into his limbs and paws. Hard to imagine he's a carrier. Maybe he's like me. Maybe they made a mistake.

Coco doesn't look up from her desk as I lower into a desk

near her. She carves intently, her expression focused. A quick peek at her work reveals an elaborate geometric design.

No one gives my presence much reaction. Several minutes pass and I begin to think this won't be so bad. Boring, yeah. But not bad. Certainly not dangerous. And then I hear a chair scrape the linoleum floor. My skin tightens, the back of my neck prickling, but I don't turn to look. I stare straight ahead, pretending I don't sense someone approaching. As though pretending he doesn't exist and is coming my way will make him not real.

Coco moves from geometric angles to swirls now. Her pen works faster on her desk, whirring on the air, the pitch reminding me of an aria I sang last year at the bank's Christmas party.

"Hey." The word hits the back of my neck in a hot gust of breath.

I jump a little. Masking my fear, I look over my shoulder. It's only one boy. He occupies the seat behind me, his body dwarfing the desk. He's wearing a vintage-looking gray shirt with green sleeves that fits him tightly. He smiles. It's totally insincere though.

His companion watches with interest from his desk. Suddenly, I feel like a lot weighs on this moment, on how I react. I wipe sweaty palms on my jeans. Like a new inmate who has arrived in prison, I'm being evaluated on all sides.

"Hey," I return.

"Where you from?"

"Does it matter?" For some reason I hesitate to tell him

where I live. I don't want to come across as the spoiled little rich girl that's fallen low. Even if I am.

"I suppose not." He smiles widely. "Nothing matters anymore. Our life is this Cage."

"Maybe yours," I return.

His smile vanishes. "Oh. You think so? You think you're special?"

"This is only temporary. Few more months and I'll graduate—"

He laughs and I stop talking. "Stupid bitch. You think I just mean this room? We'll be in a cage for the rest of our lives. Whether it's this one or another one. Graduation?" He shakes his head. "You think that's going to save you? You think you're going to get a great job or something? Go to college? Right now, the only thing that's going to help you is how many friends you can make in here." He looks me over, his cold eyes assessing. "You any good at making friends?"

Friends? As in becoming *his* friend? Something twists sickly inside me. I don't answer, but he keeps talking anyway.

"You're dead to your old friends. You're swimming in a different pond now. You'll need new friends. Carriers. Like you." He leans back in the seat and crosses his thick arms over his chest. He doesn't say it out loud, but his words hang there. *Like me.*

I open my mouth, but can't think of a proper response, too disgusted with the idea that I am somehow the same as him. That carriers everywhere are all the same. Even if that's how we're treated. Even if that's how everyone views us. I'm different.

The exception. It's arrogant thinking, but all I can cling to.

He smiles, clearly satisfied that he's put me at a loss for words. Leaning forward, he runs his hand along my arm, his fingers soft as moths' wings. I slap it away. A mistake. His smile fades and he grabs my offending hand, giving my fingers a hard, cruel squeeze. My heart gallops in my chest, stunned that he's even touching me like this . . . hurting me.

I glance quickly at Brockman. He's reading his magazine. I try to wiggle my fingers free, but he holds tightly, twisting my fingers until they're bloodless. Until I have to clench my teeth to keep from crying out. I debate calling for help, but he clicks his tongue at me, drawing my attention. "Hey, don't look at him. I'm talking to you. We're going to be spending a lot of time together. There are a lot of things that can happen to you. When Brockman leaves to use the bathroom. When he falls asleep at his desk. Hell, even right now. So let's get off on the right foot."

I swallow back my whimper and hold his gaze, searching for some scrap of emotion in eyes as glassy and dead as a mannequin's.

"Leave her alone, Nathan," the little guy interjects.

I'd forgotten about him.

"Shut up, Gil," Nathan snarls at him, his face instantly contorting into something mean and ugly. "Keep your nose in your book and I might forget you exist for the rest of the day."

Gil doesn't look away. He glares at the bigger boy. "You mean until he gets here."

Nathan releases me and lurches from the desk. In two

strides, he's at Gil, pulling him up by his collar. He backhands him once, the sound a startling crack on the air.

I jerk in my seat at the blatant violence. Brockman lifts his head up from his magazine, looking into the Cage, his expression mildly concerned but mostly just annoyed. At Everton, teachers intervene at the slightest whiff of a fight. With a pronounced sniff and swipe at his nose, Brockman goes back to his magazine. I gawk. He's not going to do anything.

"He's not here now, wimp." Nathan gives him a shake. "Or every morning, for that matter. If I were you, I'd watch your mouth. Plenty of chances for you to get a pounding. He can't protect you every minute of every day."

That said, Nathan flings Gil back into his desk. The boy's hip crashes into the top of the desk. He winces as he falls awkwardly into his seat. He folds into himself, pulling his thin frame close.

Then Nathan looks at me, evidently remembering my existence. "You better learn how things work around here quick." Those dead eyes slide off me as he returns to his desk.

I glance over at Gil. His breath is a wheezy little rasp as he clutches at his hip.

"You all right?" I whisper, convinced more than ever that he's like me and in here by mistake.

"Yeah. Stupid ape." His eyes widen. "Oh, not you—"

I smile. "I know." I shoot another glance at Nathan, engaged in his game of cards again.

"He's right, you know. You should try and make as many friends as you can. Allies are important."

I glance around the Cage. My choices aren't exactly overflowing. So far, Gil looks like the only candidate. He must read that conclusion in my face because he starts shaking his head. "I won't exactly help your rep. I'll just get you beat up or . . ." His gaze lowers, skimming my body before quickly looking away.

He doesn't need to finish his sentence. The sudden flush in his cheeks says it all, and I understand. A shiver rolls over me. Ironically, being labeled a dangerous individual has left me a target for violence. How messed up is that?

"Really. For your sake. We shouldn't talk. Find a friend that can actually intimidate guys like Nathan and Brian back there." His head jerks slightly in the direction of the boys playing cards behind us.

He returns to his desk, leaving me to stare at his profile as he picks up his book.

"Listen to him."

I snap my gaze to Coco. The first words out of her mouth, but it's like she never spoke. She's not looking at me. She's still hard at work carving up her desk. She's back to geometric patterns. No more angry, fast-spinning swirls.

Not a glance. Not another sound from her. *Listen to him.* That's her advice? That's it? Frustration wells up inside me as I sit. Alone. Ignored. And realize that it might not get any better than this.

I must have dozed off. I lift my head from my arms at the sound of the Cage door opening. My heart leaps. For a moment, I think that this horrible day is over and I can go home. A quick glance at the clock reveals I still have hours to go. My heart sinks.

I look up as another student enters the Cage. A boy. Mr. Tucci hadn't been wrong apparently.

There are six of us.

I don't have time to wonder at his tardiness because I get my first good look at his face and everything inside me seizes hard, like a car locking up on its brakes.

My gaze shoots to the tattoo collar around his neck. The sight of the circle H transfixes me. It's familiar. And not because I've seen it on some news feature calling for greater involvement from the Wainwright Agency. I saw this specific one yesterday in Mr. Pollock's cubicle.

The same sun-streaked hair brushing his shoulders. The smoke-blue eyes beneath thick, slashing eyebrows several shades darker than his hair. *Sean O'Rourke.*

He tucks a lock of hair behind his ear as he moves inside the Cage, his stride loose and confident. It's like he doesn't care that he's advertising himself as a carrier for everyone to see. It's like he's comfortable with what he is. Not a hint of shame to him.

He hasn't seen me yet. I don't breathe, facing forward, watching to see where he sits, expecting him to sit with Nathan and his buddy. He doesn't. Instead, he takes the first desk he reaches, close to the door, close to me.

He slides into his chair, his frame almost too large for the desk. And that's when he looks up at me. Heat crawls over my face, but I can't look away from the recognition lighting his eyes. His expression doesn't change. He remains stoic and unaffected.

After a moment, he arches one eyebrow—and I realize I'm gawking like some middle school girl drooling over her first crush.

With a small gasp, I snap my gaze straight ahead. A quick glance reveals Coco still doing her thing like nothing has changed. Like a confirmed carrier hasn't just walked into our midst. Gil glances at me. I only get a brief look at his face, but it's enough. He gives a slight encouraging nod and I know he's telling me that this new arrival is the type of "friend" he thinks I should have. It dawns on me that Sean O'Rourke must be the "he" that Nathan said couldn't protect Gil forever.

He must be joking. Sean O'Rourke . . . a *good* guy? The evidence is there. On his neck. He can't be. My insides heave and tremble at the thought of approaching him. How does one even befriend a carrier? An *imprinted* carrier? And just to remain safe? It seems a bit of a contradiction. And one I'm not about to put to the test.

The bell rings at two thirty and I anxiously start gathering my things, stopping when Brockman's voice rings out.

"Not yet, Davy. That's for the regular kids." My face burns at being singled out—and the reminder that I'm not a "regular" kid. "Ya'll leave in thirty minutes after the halls have cleared out."

I sit in my chair and face forward, blinking eyes that

unaccountably sting. After everything, this shouldn't get to me. This shouldn't make me want to cry.

But it does. *Regular kids.* Which I'm not. None of us in here are.

My gaze sweeps around me. Sean is looking directly at me, his expression still that blank nothingness. I make the mistake of wondering what he's thinking as he stares at me with those deeply set eyes. Because my mind immediately wonders if it has something to do with gags and hacksaws.

I spin back around. Only a couple more months of this. I slip down in my chair, fortifying myself with that reminder. In the grand scheme, a couple months won't amount to much.

The minutes drag by. Finally, Brockman announces, "Okay, you can get out of here. See ya tomorrow."

I'm the first out of my desk. I fly past Sean as he rises, casually stuffing a notebook into his backpack. Like someone announced the building is on fire, I move, swing my backpack on my shoulder, and truck it out of the Cage.

Even thirty minutes after the bell, a few students loiter in the halls, but fortunately none point at me like I'm some sort of freak show. The newest addition to the killers on campus. I cross my arms, tucking the colored ID flapping against my chest out of sight. Just in case. No need to call undue attention to myself.

I'm almost to the parking lot—Mom and I took separate vehicles so I could get home on my own—when I realize I left my purse in the room. Everything is in it. My wallet and phone. My keys. *Stupid.*

Groaning, I spin on my heel and head back into the building. I pass Gil. His eyes meet mine, widen for a moment, and then jerk away as he scurries past. I don't see any of the others on the way back down, and count my blessings.

When I arrive at the Cage, it's empty. Brockman's no longer at his desk. Guess he was as eager to leave this place as we were.

My bag is under the desk where I left it. Just to be safe, I give it a quick inspection to make sure everything is still there.

And that's when I hear a sound. Like someone . . . crying.

I glance around, confirming I'm alone in the Cage. Thinking someone might be hurt, I inch forward, scanning the room. The door to the storage closet is shut, but as I near it I hear the noise again. A muffled whimper. Louder this time. I close my hand around the knob, my heart thumping hard against my ribs.

I turn the knob and push open. The door swings soundlessly. A path of bright fluorescent light spills into the dim room directly on two people.

It takes my mind a moment to register what my eyes are seeing. Coco pinned between Mr. Brockman and a rack of basketballs. *Kissing.* His back is to me, but one of his hands grips her shoulder. The sight of that hand on her shoulder snares my attention. His nails are jagged and shorn to the quick like he spends a good portion of every day chewing them.

I absorb it all in an instant. With a quick, horrible scan of my gaze.

Brockman doesn't see me, but Coco's eyes are open. The heavily lined eyes fall on me. They glitter through her ragged bangs, locking on me. Rage lights up their depths. The venom there stabs me. She tears her face free. "Get out! Get out of here!"

Brockman swings around.

I gasp and slam the door shut, unwilling to watch another moment. I hate that I saw what I just did. Just as much as I hate that they saw *me* seeing them. If I could erase the image from my corneas I would.

This time I run.

---

911 Transcript

**911 DISPATCHER 3026:** Operator 3026, what is your emergency?

**MARIE DOYLE:** This is Marie Doyle at 1919 Elmwood in Boerne. I have a carrier living down the street from me.

**911 DISPATCHER 3026:** (typing) D-O-Y-L-E. 1919 Elmwood.

**MARIE DOYLE:** Yes.

**911 DISPATCHER 3026:** Okay, ah, yes, ma'am. Um, has the carrier done anything specifically—

**MARIE DOYLE:** She's a carrier! That means she's a killer.

**911 DISPATCHER 3026:** But she hasn't assaulted you in any way—

**MARIE DOYLE:** Are you kidding? (loud slam) Are you a mother? I have two small children. How am I supposed to let them play outside? We moved here because it's supposed to be a safe place. . . .

**911 DISPATCHER 3026:** I understand your distress, ma'am, I do, but unless she threatens you or your family, I can't help you.

**MARIE DOYLE:** Great! You'll come when I'm dead then? Fantastic! Good people like me shouldn't have to live in fear. This is wrong. Carriers should be behind bars. I watch the news. That's where they're headed.

**911 DISPATCHER 3026:** I understand, ma'am. But for now you're going to have to sit tight. Stay vigilant. If she makes the smallest threat, please . . . call us back. . . .

# SEVEN

MITCHELL FINDS ME IN MY ROOM. I'M STILL IN MY bathrobe, my hair a wet, unbrushed snarl. I showered as soon as I got home. As if I could wash away the day. The Cage. The sight of Brockman and Coco in that storage closet. I guess I understood now why Nathan left her alone . . . and why Gil thinks I need an ally.

He catches me tuning my guitar, singing lightly to myself as I adjust the pegs and test the strings. "Hey." He drops down on my bed, tucking a pillow under his head. "How was it?"

I set my guitar down and whirl to face him on my chair, tucking my hands beneath my thighs. They're still shaking. I haven't stopped shaking since I ran to my car. "I can't go back."

"C'mon. It's just until May. And Mom said it would look good with the Agency if you finished out the year at school. . . . Show them that you can function in the real world—"

I just look at him. I know my expression is bitter. Because last week I was functioning in the real world. I was better than functioning. But now I have to prove it?

"You know what I learned today? That they don't want anyone with HTS to *function* in the real world." I air quote the word *function*. "They keep us isolated. I'm stuck in a cage with a bunch of other carriers and some pervy teacher."

He sits up. "What do you mean, 'pervy'? What happened?"

I shake my head. "Nothing." If I tell him, he'll tell Mom and Dad and then what? In the last forty-eight hours, I've discovered just how little influence my parents truly possess. There's no point going to them for help. They can't do anything.

He stares at me for a long moment before finally saying, "You're better than this, Davy. I know you can handle it."

Shaking my head, I groan in frustration. "Why are you so sure?"

"Because you're *you*. You can do anything. When you were three years old you sat down at the piano and played like you'd been doing it all your life. And as if being a music prodigy isn't enough, when you were four years old you walked into my room and finished the puzzle that had been kicking my ass for the past week."

I smile. "I don't remember that."

"Yeah. Well. It pissed me off. It hasn't always been easy having a little sister who's better at everything than you are."

My smile slips. "Sorry."

He drops a fist on the bed. "Don't apologize for being smarter than I am. I got over it. Basically, I'm . . . I'm just proud of you. And this crap doesn't change that. It doesn't change *you*."

My phone chimes. I pick it up and read the message. My stomach dips. "It's Zac."

"Told you he'd come around."

"He's outside."

He hesitates for a moment. "Well, you better get dressed. I'll let him in."

I wait for Mitchell to leave and then change into jeans and a T-shirt. I'm attacking my hair with my brush when there's a knock on the door.

"Come in."

Zac sticks his head in first. He's never done that before. Usually, he breezes in like he owns the place. "Hey."

I wave him inside.

He steps in. "How are you?"

"Okay," I say, because I'm not going to burden him with the kind of day I had. Even if I wasn't embarrassed—which I am—I wouldn't want him to know just how different I've become. Just how far apart we suddenly are.

He sits on the corner of my bed. "I—I miss you."

My chest lightens and I finally feel like myself for the first time in days. This is me. Here with Zac. "I miss you, too." It takes everything in me not to cry. My eyes burn, swollen and unbearably tight, but I keep it in.

He moves, drops onto the carpet, and crouches on his knees before me. "I'm sorry I was such a jerk." He slides his arms around my waist and looks up at me. "I shouldn't have run off—"

"No." I hold his face in my hands. "Anybody would have been freaked out."

"I shouldn't have been. I mean, it's you. . . . I know you're not some killer. No matter what others—"

His voice fades and his eyes flare a little, like he's worried he said too much. *Others?* Does he mean what the world in general thinks? If the media is to be believed, people believe the Agency should have more control than it already does—that carriers should be *more* than identified and monitored. That we should be locked up. Better safe than sorry.

Or is he talking about our friends?

I kiss him. Mostly just because I don't want to talk about it anymore. I don't want to think about what my friends are saying. I don't want to think about *me.* HTS. It's all I am anymore. Everything. My new reality even though I'm not a monster.

I want to have something it doesn't touch. Even if it's only pretend.

The kiss is slow and sweet. Maybe even hesitant. Like we're new to each other again. It's definitely not the hot, fumbling desperation of before. We've come close to going all the way several times lately. Zac's been pressuring and I'd been considering it more and more. But now it feels like we've lost ground.

When we break apart, he doesn't say anything about killers anymore and how I'm definitely *not* one of them, and for that I'm glad. It's almost like he's convincing himself when he does that.

It's just his smiling eyes on me. "I have to get back home. Are you free tomorrow night?"

I nod.

"Good. Carlton is having a party."

Something inside me sinks. I assumed it would just be the two of us. Recovering ground. The idea of being around all our friends . . . my old friends. The kids I no longer go to school with. Tori hasn't even called since I told Zac. I tried calling her yesterday but she didn't pick up. He has to have told her. Everyone must know by now. Their silence tells me all I need to know. Everything has changed. But Zac wants me to hang out like nothing has.

I force a smile and lie. "Sounds great."

I'm all about being something I'm not, after all. A carrier. A killer. In this instance? Pretending like everything is okay? I'll have to get used to that.

I take careful measures to be on time, but not too early, the next day. I don't want to be caught alone with anyone. Definitely not Mr. Brockman, but not any of the other students, either.

Sean, of course, I know, won't arrive until later. For

whatever reason, that's his pattern. I keep my head down, eyes averted as I slide into my desk. It doesn't matter though. I eventually have to look up, and the first time I do it's like Coco has been waiting. Her heavily lined eyes stare at me, unblinking. I feel the blood rush to my face.

*I'm sorry,* I mouth to her, not really knowing what to say except that.

She looks at me dully before shaking her head and looking away, like I somehow disgust her.

I wish I could rub out the image of her with Brockman from my eyes . . . erase the knowledge from my mind. I haven't allowed the horror of it to fully sink in. Maybe the horrors of the last few days have numbed me to something so horrible and shocking.

An hour into the morning, and an office aide drops off some manila folders.

Brockman enters the Cage to hand them out. The pair in the back sigh heavily as they take their folders. He stops by my desk and holds out my folder to me. I'm paranoid about looking Brockman in the face. I've been dreading it. I try to take the folder, but he doesn't release it, holds it hostage until I look up at him.

His gaze is intent. "Doing okay, Davy?"

I nod. The grapefruit-sized lump in my throat prevents me from speaking.

He continues, "Settling in? Everyone treating you well?"

I can only stare. He leans down and it takes everything inside me not to arch away. I guess it's my innate politeness—drilled into me ever since I could tie my own shoes. Ironic. I'm here because of my inherent dangerousness, but it's my inherent politeness that makes me put up with this. With him.

He grasps my shoulder, squeezes. And I see that hand as I saw it yesterday. Nails blunt-tipped, chewed up to the quick. My stomach rolls. Bile rises in my throat.

"I'm here for you . . . if you ever want to talk. I've got your back." He smiles. It's patronizing at best. What I really see lurking in the curve of his lips is his smug knowledge that I know that I'm at his mercy.

I dismiss the idea of reporting him. I know enough to know that I lack any credibility. My word won't matter. I remember my conversation with Mitchell. It's like he said. I just have to make it through May. After that, I'll figure out what comes next. Clearly it's not Juilliard anymore. Everton will notify them of my expulsion. That dream is dead. But not every dream. Zac flashes in my mind. No. Not all of them.

I find my voice. "Thanks. But I'm fine."

He angles his head and sets my folder on my desk. "Really?" The single word carries doubt.

I lift my chin, determined to convince him that I'm fine and will never have need for his particular type of friendship. "Everything is good. I like it here." Maybe I went a bit far with that last part, but it's almost worth it to see the flicker of surprise cross his face.

He lets go of my shoulder and straightens. "I see. Well. Good. Good."

He didn't believe me for a second. There's a glint of annoyance in his eyes before he turns away and moves on to Gil. I almost smile.

Until I see Coco, twisting around in her chair. "You think you're so smart?" she whispers and, even though she's whispering, her voice falls hard.

But there's something in her eyes. A vulnerability, a fear, that gives me pause. I shake my head. "No. I don't—"

"Keep your paws off Brockman."

"You don't seriously think I would let him touch me?"

Her dark eyes flash and I know I offended her. Hot color creeps up her caramel-hued cheeks. "Oh. You're so good, aren't you? Better than me, is that it?"

"No—"

Her knuckles whiten where they clutch the desk. "We'll see what you think after a month in here. Just remember what I said. Stay away from Brockman. Find someone else."

Before I can respond that I don't need anyone, she faces the front again.

What happened to her to make her think she needs to surrender to Brockman? My jaw locks. Whatever it is, I vow to never let that happen to me.

Opening the folder, I try to focus on my assignments, letting the chorus of AC/DC's "Back in Black" weave inside my head. Right now, I could use some serenity. A wadded ball of paper hits me in the head. Touching my hair, I turn around and glare. Nathan blows me a kiss and throws another paper ball that I jerk to the side to avoid.

With a huff, I turn back around in my desk and study the assignments. They're a far cry from my usual workload, but I still need to get them done. The goal is that diploma. Even if it's from the wrong school.

Even if I'm living the wrong life.

---

**Text Message**

4:07 p.m.

Tori:

Don't bring her

4:32 p.m.

Zac:

Told u I have 2

# EIGHT

I FINISH MY ASSIGNMENTS BEFORE LUNCH AND take my work to Brockman as I've watched the others do. I stand at the Cage door until he motions me through. He takes my manila folder from me and I stand there as he flips through my work like he knows what he's looking at. Like he's a real teacher.

"You work fast." He hands me the folder. "I hope you did it all correctly."

I take it, unsure what I'm supposed to do with it now. He's supposed to turn my work in for me so that the regular teachers, teachers I'll never even meet, can grade me.

"You can turn that in to the office."

This surprises me. "I can walk around on my own?"

He doesn't answer right away, just stares at me like he would like to say something else. Something more. "Classes are in session right now. Just hurry back. Don't talk to anyone."

Who would I talk to? Nodding, I walk out into the corridor, through the haze of stink—the perpetual sweat that hangs in the hall. I can hear the squeak of shoes on the gym floor and know there's at least one class going on down here now.

I don't pass anyone as I head up the stairs to the school's main floor. It's a straight shot to the office. The same receptionist is there. For a moment, I think she's going to say something about me being loose in the halls. Out of my cage.

Her lips just tighten like she's holding her breath. Afraid to breathe around me. She snatches the folder and turns her attention back to her monitor. It's still strange . . . wounds me. I'm the kid everyone likes. Teachers. Parents.

I *was* that kid.

Dismissed, I step back in the hall. A couple of students walk past me into the office. They don't notice me. Specifically, they don't notice my special badge. And I'm relieved . . . which makes me feel like a coward. Like I'm happy to hide. Like I *need* to hide.

Feeling a little bit disgusted with myself, I stride down the hall, letting my shoes strike the floor loudly. Like I can make up for my cowardice by injecting force into each stride.

At the top of the stairwell, there's a trio of students. Two girls. One guy. It's the guy who catches my attention. He leans back against the steel railing, relaxed. The girls flank him, talking, moving their hands animatedly with every word. They remind me of butterflies ready to launch into air. It's a scene I've seen countless times. When girls are around Zac. They're so obvious in their attempts to impress.

And the boy is none other than Sean O'Rourke.

*Sean*? They're not frightened of him at all. I slow my steps and watch, thoroughly baffled. If I didn't have to—*before I became one of them*—I would never deliberately come into contact with a carrier.

As I approach, the girls' voices register in my ear. I recognize the pitch, the cadence as perfect as a C-sharp. They're *flirting* with him. An HTS carrier who's been imprinted? He's proven himself dangerous and they're *into* him.

One of the girls reaches out and toys with his orange badge. They must be some type of masochists, I decide. They get off on the danger and potential pain a carrier like Sean can inflict on them.

I give them as much berth as possible as I near the stairs. But just the same, I gawk at them like some kind of tragic car accident. I can't *not* look.

Sean's elbows are propped back on the railing. He holds a can of soda loosely in one hand. He's wearing a gray-and-black graphic T-shirt. HONEST BEES is written across the front and I wonder if it's a cool band or edgy hot spot in the city that I've never heard of. I pretty much stick to a ten-mile radius of my house. Everyone I know does. The streets aren't safe.

Even the streets you know. No sense roaming the streets you don't know. And there's a curfew anyway. That always keeps me from staying out too late. Well, that and my parents. The few times I stayed out late I was always with Zac . . . and no more than a couple miles from home.

His gaze fixes on me. He shakes the sun-streaked hair back from his face as if to see me better with those deeply set eyes. My hand closes around the rail, and I pause, staring back, seeing what they see in him. Confidence. Edge. The sexy, dark, misunderstood hero you see in movies or read about in books. Only this is real life. And he's no hero. The tattoo around his neck proclaims that.

The girls notice his attention straying. They look over at me, assessing, critical. The blonde one with dark roots asks, "Who's that?"

He doesn't answer. His face registers nothing. It's like he doesn't even hear her. Just watches me as I begin to descend, but I can't help wondering what he would say. Who am I? What am I to him?

And why should I care?

I try to pretend I don't hear the Cage door opening. The clang of steel. The rattle of the latch. The solid tread of feet. The whisper of clothes as he slides into his seat a few desks behind me. I fill my mind with the lyrics of "Casta Diva." It usually focuses me. The notoriously difficult aria flows through my head. I race along with the high notes, grasping for them, but it's no good.

I still see Sean in my mind. His image fresh from half an

hour ago. That's how long he stayed upstairs, talking to those girls, I guess.

The cool smoke-blue eyes. The hair shielding a face that begs for an extra look. Even with that too-long hair, the imprint encircling his neck can't be hidden. Yes, a turtleneck offers temporary cover, but they're not standard in Texas. And anyone could just tug it down to see, anyway.

And that's the point. Imprints can't be denied. Just like bad DNA.

The ink-black band almost an inch wide. The circled H. It reminds me of a cattle brand. Dark. Deep. Permanent. Once you see that, it's the *only* thing you see. Not the person. And that's the purpose.

The person doesn't matter.

It's no longer who. It's *what*.

My back tingles, and I wonder if it's him. Looking at me. Or is it just my imagination? My fear knowing he's there, here, close, watching.

My mind strays to that imprint on his neck again. What did he do to get that? Was it one thing? A series of transgressions until Pollock finally ordered the imprinting? I shake my head and press my pencil tip harder into my notebook where I'm spelling out my name: *Davy Hamilton*. Again and again and again.

As if that will keep me sane. Keep me *me*.

Because him. Behind me. Will never be me.

"I'll be back in two minutes," Brockman calls from the back of the Cage.

I start a little at the realization that he's leaving us alone. Together. A room full of carriers, one of whom probably belongs in prison. My skin tightens sharply. This strikes me as a bad idea. The door clicks shut behind him. Too late for me to object.

Immediately, Nathan and Brian are on their feet. They laugh low under their breaths, practically tripping over themselves to get out of the Cage. A quick glance reveals that everyone else is watching, too. Gil, Coco. Even Sean is turned.

The two boys speak in rushed tones, scanning Brockman's desk, their expressions giddy.

"What are we going to do, man?" Brian anxiously asks.

Nathan points. "His chair."

"Yeah, yeah. Let's unscrew the bolts." Brian nods stupidly, bending to tamper with Brockman's chair.

Nathan drops a hand on his arm, stalling him.

He lifts his face, looks straight at Sean. For permission? Approval? I'm not sure which. Maybe both. But it's clear to me these two guys don't make a move in the Cage without considering Sean O'Rourke first.

Sharp prickles break out over my skin. I'm almost disappointed. I don't know why. Did I somehow think he was better than Nathan? I have no basis for that conclusion. If anything, the imprint on his neck should have told me otherwise. That he's worse. More dangerous than these other boys.

I watch Sean, wait for his reaction. It's the barest motion. Just a dip of his head. Then he turns around and faces front again. My chest squeezes to find myself directly in his line of vision. I spin around, too alarmed to look into those cold eyes.

I listen to Nathan and Brian as they loosen the bolts on Brockman's chair and scurry back inside the Cage, laughing like hyenas.

What does it mean when the guy who crushed my hand in a death grip, the one who backhanded poor Gil, whose eyes gleamed when inflicting pain . . . answers to Sean O'Rourke?

Brockman returns. I don't dare turn around. Instead, I sit waiting. Listening.

He crashes to the floor with a yelp. We all turn to look then. Nathan and Brian laugh, slapping their desks as the teacher pulls himself to his feet, cursing and red-faced. Even Coco giggles behind her hands. Gil grins.

Huffing and holding his back as though he's injured, he faces us through the chain-link wall. "Go ahead and have your laugh, you little bastards. We all know where you're going to end up. All of you!"

The laughter fades as Brockman storms from the room, still cursing under his breath.

Nathan wipes the tears of mirth from his eyes. "God, that was classic." He looks over at Sean. "Did you see that, O'Rourke? Priceless."

Sean turns in his desk, silent and unsmiling. Even though he sanctioned the little prank, he doesn't look amused, and I wonder if it has something to do with what Brockman said. *We all know where you're going to end up.*

I don't know where I'm going to end up. It's hard for me to imagine that I would ever end up in the same place as Nathan and Brian and Sean O'Rourke.

And yet here I am now. With them.

Another office aide comes down toward the end of the day. Brockman enters the Cage and rouses everyone.

"Okay. New assignment."

This is met with several groans. I don't think we're all in the same grade and I wonder what assignment we all have in common.

"This is for your Community Awareness."

If possible, the groans only get louder. Even Gil reacts. "Those assignments are such a joke."

I've never heard of a Community Awareness class and wonder if it's something unique to this school. I glance at the sheet of paper Brockman drops on my desk. A quick glance at the paper clears things up. The Wainwright Agency is identified in the header. This is some kind of assignment specifically for carriers then.

"According to my instructions, you have a week to complete the project."

A project? I sit up a little straighter. Even if it comes from the Wainwright Agency it sounds like this might be real schoolwork. Close enough anyway. My inner geek perks up. Anything to break up the monotony of sitting in this room. To tide me over until I can escape this place and return to my real life. Zac and the party tonight. When I can be myself again.

"You will need to pair up."

At this, my enthusiasm wilts. Everything inside me tenses. I have to work with someone in this room.

Obviously, Nathan and his better half in the back will pair up. They don't even have to move desks.

But what about the others? Who does that leave me with?

I don't get a chance to decide for myself. Coco gets up and moves to the empty desk beside Gil. Leaving me to pair up with Sean O'Rourke.

*Fantastic.* The back of my neck itches, the skin crawling as if something swarms beneath it. I look down quickly, stare at the paper on my desk, eyes feverishly moving, scanning the blur of words. I expect him to move in. Like the predator he is. *Like all of us in this room are supposed to be.* Only I'm not. My being here is a mistake. I'm not like them at all. Maybe if I was, I wouldn't feel so uncomfortable. So afraid.

Brockman leaves us. The door clangs. I can hear Gil and Coco talking in low voices. I guess they've begun to discuss the assignment. I toy with the corner of the paper, waiting for him.

He never comes.

Finally, I take a breath and stand, pen and paper in hand. As though he senses me, he lifts his head. His eyes settle on me, his expression mild, empty. How does he do that? How does he look as though there is nothing going on behind the façade? Not a dark thought . . . not a thought at all. A blank slate.

Squaring my shoulders, I approach and drop into the chair

before him, turning so that we're facing each other.

I flex my fingers very deliberately around the paper so that it crinkles. "I guess we have to do this."

"I guess so." His deep voice washes over me, and I realize I've hardly ever heard him speak. Except when he called me "princess" in Pollock's office. It's deeper than I expect. It makes him seem older somehow.

Clearing my throat, I force myself to read the work sheet. Difficult, considering he doesn't do the same. Instead, he continues to watch me with those absorbing eyes. Finally, I process the instructions. Dread sinks likes rocks in the bottom of my stomach.

"We have to interview each other." My lips move numbly. "Write each other's biographies."

"Uh-huh." His lips twist. Almost a smile but not quite.

Why would the Wainwright Agency want us to do this type of exercise? What's the point?

As if he can read my mind, he says, "They're trying to train us in humanity. You know. Because we obviously lack empathy for others." He says this flatly with no inflection, and I can't tell if he's joking.

I wave to the Cage we're trapped inside. "Then maybe they shouldn't treat us like animals in a zoo."

He angles his head, staring at me intently, his face that perpetual blank slate. It's impossible to tell what he's thinking. He probably thinks that I'm getting bent out of shape over nothing. This is the life he's accustomed to, after all. My gaze strays to the tattoo on his neck, before jerking quickly away. I don't want him to see me looking at it.

"Okay." I suck in a breath. "You want me to start?"

"Sure."

"Name?"

"Sean."

"Sean?" I prompt even though I know his last name.

This time he actually smiles, and I know he's amused because I'm taking this so seriously.

I go through the rest. Birthplace. Birth date.

"Parents' names?"

"My mother's name was Cecily O'Rourke."

*Was.* My pen hesitates for a second before scrawling her name down. "Father?"

"Don't know."

I try to show no reaction at his blunt response, but it takes me a moment to gather my thoughts and move to the next question. *Who doesn't know the name of their own father?*

"Siblings?"

"None." He shrugs one shoulder. "Just foster ones—"

"Oh?" It's something, and I'm beginning to suspect there's not a lot he's going to volunteer. I'm sure there's a lot more to him . . . more than I'll ever know. More than he lets anyone know. But for now, I need to fill out this work sheet with something. Even if it's just empty facts. "So you live with foster parents? What are their names? How long have you been with them?"

I don't look up from my notes, but I feel his eyes on me.

"I have a foster mother. Martha Delaney. She's taken in

five of us. At least the last time I counted."

A joke. I didn't think he had a sense of humor.

I nod, still writing. "Uh-huh." Cocking my head, I read the next question: "What's your favorite hobby?" I try not to cringe at the totally inane question. Does this guy have a hobby? He doesn't strike me as the kind of guy who knits or plays the violin. Maybe he likes video games. The zombie-killer kind. Those are plenty violent.

He leans forward, both his arms relaxed on his desk. His fingers lightly tap the surface, just at the tips. "No hobbies."

"Something you do in your free time . . . something you enjoy . . ."

"I know the definition of 'hobby,'" he replies, and I feel justifiably dumb.

"Of course." I scrawl *N/A* next to the question.

"I have a job . . . but I wouldn't call washing dishes at the Golden Palace six nights a week a hobby."

Before I can think, I ask, "Then why do you do it?"

It's the wrong thing to say. I know this immediately. I see that as his features harden, looking even more carved, more like granite. I don't have time to explain what I meant, which was: Why does he work that *particular* job?

"God, you're so sheltered, aren't you? It's how I make a living. Martha isn't big on allowances. She puts a roof over our heads, cooks and feeds us, and collects a state check for fostering six kids no one else wants. There's not a lot left over after the bills are paid." He smiles enough to reveal teeth. Even and startling white against his complexion.

He continues, and it's the most I've heard him speak, even if every word drips scorn. "If I want socks, a pack of gum, gas money for my piece-of-crap truck that's always breaking down . . . I have to earn it." His gaze scours over me. "But you wouldn't know anything about that, would you, *princess*?"

I flinch, feeling shamed. Just like he intended.

But then something happens. I start to get mad. Anger warms my face, creeps over my ears in a stinging wash of heat. "A princess in a cage?" I cock my head. "I've never heard of that particular fairy tale. You don't know anything about me. I might have had certain advantages, but I'm still in here with you. Don't judge me."

He laughs lightly, the sound low and deep. "Don't judge you? That's funny. You better get used to the world judging you. You're a carrier now. That's all there is."

"I won't ever get used to that." I shake my head, vowing this to myself.

He considers me. "You're going to have a hard road if you can't accept what you are."

"Like you do?"

He nods.

I press a hand to my chest. "I'll never accept it."

He looks at me strangely, almost curiously, his eyes less flinty. There's a glint of something in his gaze as he looks at me. For a moment, he doesn't seem so harsh, so ruthless. Which unnerves me almost more.

I snatch the work sheet off the desk and storm to my seat in a huff, deciding I've had enough for one day. We have a week to complete the project. I'll finish the interview when I'm less pissed. Or maybe I'll make it all up. Who's to know? I doubt he'll care.

I don't know what the Agency hopes to accomplish by having us get to know each other. Maybe they hope that we'll dislike each other so much that we'll turn on one another. Kill each other off so that the world doesn't have to worry about carriers anymore.

Only it dawns on me as I sit there that I don't dislike him exactly. He scares me—yes. No denying that. But a part of me admires him. This boy who walks around almost proudly, like he doesn't care what the world thinks of him. Even imprinted, there's nothing beaten or cowed about him.

The scathing way he called me "princess" rings in my ears. I'm sure he dislikes me though. And that, for some reason, bothers me.

The female carrier should be considered no less a threat purely because of gender—or because of her small subset within HTS carrier population. Her anomalous existence begs careful consideration. In a manner, she is more complicated than her male counterpart. Without DNA testing, she would likely be entirely unidentifiable. Her actions are less predictable and she should, ergo, be viewed as extremely dangerous and treated with extreme caution. . . .

*—Lecture from Dr. Wainwright to the National Center for Analysis of Violent Crime at Quantico*

# NINE

LATER THAT AFTERNOON, I RISE FROM MY DESK and approach the Cage door. From the left corner of my eye, I try to see what Sean is working on. It looks like a work sheet. I could probably turn my head to get a better look. It's not as though he would catch me looking and mistake my interest for . . . well, interest. He's oblivious to me, not even looking up as I pass him.

Brockman motions me through the door.

"Davina. What can I do for you?" That he insists on using my full name grates on my nerves. Like he's somehow this mature, responsible grown-up who doesn't go around molesting young girls.

I glance back into the Cage. Just a quick look and, sure enough, Coco is watching us, her dark eyes alert and wary.

I face him again. "Can I use the bathroom?" He takes a long moment before answering. Making me wait uncomfortably in front of him. I shouldn't have consumed so much water at lunch. I'll have to quit doing that if it means having to ask him to use the restroom every afternoon.

Leaning forward over his desk, he scribbles a pass for me. Tearing it off, he hands it to me. When I reach for it he pulls it back. "Don't be long," he warns, and I know he gets off on this—on demonstrating his power over me. *Jerk.*

"I want to go, too!" Nathan shouts from his desk.

"Shut up, Nathan," Brockman replies mildly, finally letting me have the pass.

Nodding, I turn and push open one of the heavy metal doors. It bangs shut behind me, echoing off the narrow corridor. I hurry past the workout room, not even looking inside. The sound of male voices and the clang of weights tells me there's a group in there working.

The girls' bathroom is small, just two stalls. I'm in the second stall when the door creaks open. I finish but hesitate inside the cramped space. I don't know why. Maybe because this time of day, there don't seem to be any girls down here. It was just the sound of guys in the workout room, and I imagine the girls' locker room has its own bathroom.

Standing, I listen, lightly resting my hand against the cold, graffiti-riddled door. Straining to hear something, I lean forward, waiting for the sound of running water in the faucet. Or the door in the neighboring stall swinging open and shut. Normal sounds of someone in here simply doing her business.

Nothing.

I know someone's here though . . . imagine that I can hear the soft fall of their breath. I lean forward a bit more now. Peek through the stall crack.

Maybe Brockman let Coco go to the bathroom. Somehow, the thought of this doesn't make me feel any more at ease.

"I know you're in there. Come out."

The sound of that voice jars everything loose inside me. I shouldn't hear this person here. Of all places, I should be safe from him in the girls' bathroom.

"Come out or I'll come in."

This threat sends a hot streak of panic racing through me. I fumble for the lock and step out.

Brockman waits with his arms crossed over his chest, his pose relaxed.

"What are you doing in here?" I manage to get out.

"I thought we should have a word about what you saw yesterday."

I cast my eyes downward and move to the sink. Turning on the faucet, I wash my hands, desperate to have something to do other than look him in the face.

"I didn't see anything."

He doesn't reply and I look up in the mirror, biting back

a gasp to see he's moved behind me.

"Come on. Let's not pretend."

Instead of denying what I saw again—clearly, he's not going to accept that—I shut off the water and lightly shake my hands over the sink. Having no choice, I turn.

"You're in the girls' bathroom. Someone might come in here," I tell him, gratified to hear that my voice is steady. Especially as all I can see when I look at him are his fingers with their chewed-to-the-quick nails clenched around Coco's small shoulder. The image is burned into my memory and fills me with rage and disgust and the overwhelming urge to slap him.

"Girls' PE doesn't start until seventh period."

"Anyone could walk in."

Smiling, he rips me a paper towel from the dispenser. "The arrangement I have with Coco isn't exclusive to her, you know."

I think I'm going to be sick.

"There's room for you, too. A girl like you is going to need protection."

Yeah. I need protection from the likes of him. And what does he mean, "a girl like me"? Somehow I think he just means: a girl. Period. But then I think of Nathan slapping Gil. That easily could be me. He already squeezed my hand hard enough to hurt—and that was just in the first two minutes after I met him. Since then I'd caught him looking at me several times, bending his head close to Brian and then laughing in my direction. Jokes at my expense. And maybe something more sinister. Who knows? Maybe he has a nasty plan for me. The thought has been there, lurking in the shadows, but I refuse to let that cow me into accepting Brockman's particular brand of friendship.

"No, thanks." I move past him, careful not to touch him as I drop my paper towel into the trash.

"Just think about it," he calls as I push open the door.

But it fails to swing out all the way. It stops. Thuds against something. Someone. I move back. The door swings and Sean steps inside. I stare, trying to reconcile the sight of him here. In the girls' bathroom. The small space suddenly feels claustrophobic. It's like all the air and energy are sucked up inside him.

His face is stoic as ever, but his eyes . . .

I swallow at the sight of them. His eyes are like frosted glass, that outer ring of dark blue starkly prominent as he looks from me to Brockman.

"O'Rourke. Why aren't you in the Cage?" Brockman's voice is different. Not so silky.

I stand between the two of them, feeling trapped. The teacher suddenly doesn't look so relaxed. He plants his hands on his hips and tries to look stern . . . older than the five years or so he has on us. Maybe he's even going for strong and formidable, but that's a stretch when he's a foot shorter than Sean and nowhere near as muscular.

"You're not going to do this," Sean says softly—vague words but with an underlying steel to them.

Brockman's face flushes and his chest puffs out. "You don't come in here and—"

"Davy," Sean interrupts him, "go back to the Cage."

I bristle, resenting him telling me what to do. But then he looks at me. The icy frost still chills the blue-gray of his eyes, but something else gleams there, too. It gives me pause.

He steps to the side, his voice quieter. "Go on."

I nod. Quite simply, I don't want to be in the bathroom with either one of them. I don't look at Brockman. Just move. Hurry out of the bathroom as quickly as I can.

Once in the hall, I pause to look over my shoulder. What just happened? I frown, certain Sean just *helped* me. That the indefinable something I had seen in his eyes was . . . concern. For me? Why? How? He is a carrier. A true carrier . . . with an imprint. He's not a mistake. He's the real thing.

Utterly confused, I turn and walk back inside the Cage. The others are waiting for me.

"Did you see O'Rourke? Is he with Brockman? Is he kicking his ass?" Nathan bounces on his desk like a four-year-old who consumed too much candy. He beats the surface. "Man, I've been wanting to kick that guy's ass."

Clearly, everyone knew that Sean had come after Brockman—and that Brockman had come after me. I wince.

Nathan pumps a fist in the air. "Sweet. I hope O'Rourke stomps all over him."

Gil rolls his eyes and then looks at me, his light brown eyes deep with worry. "You okay?" Again, I'm struck with the fact that this boy is supposed to be dangerous. A killer?

I nod, letting the door clang shut behind me.

His gaze moves beyond me. "Where's Sean?"

I motion vaguely behind me, uncomfortable elaborating

on the fact that he followed Brockman and me into the bathroom.

I sink down in my chair and slide my hands beneath my thighs. Sitting on my hands, I fight the urge to watch the door for Sean. I remind myself this day will be over soon, and then I'll be with Zac tonight, living the life that really belongs to me. Not this.

Coco suddenly drops down in front of me. "What happened?"

I blink.

She cocks her head to the side, her gaze sharp. "With you and Brockman?"

"I—nothing."

Her dark eyes narrow. "He mess with you?"

I shake my head, not wanting to talk about this. Especially with her. The last thing I want is to get warned off Brockman again.

The door clangs shut and I can't help myself. I look up as Sean lowers into his desk. His gaze holds mine and the air suddenly becomes too thick. Or my lungs too small. Either way, I can't breathe.

Brockman's back, too. He sits at his desk and flips open a magazine, not glancing at us. I study him carefully, looking for any evidence that he and Sean had an altercation, but he looks totally normal.

"Sean's a good guy."

I look at Coco with surprise. She uttered the words so

softly I wonder if I heard her right. I study the way her dark eyes settle almost wistfully on Sean.

"A good guy?" I echo, trying to wrap my head around this. It's not something I had even considered before. Not something I *let* myself consider. Although if me being here is a mistake . . . then maybe it is a mistake for others, too. Okay, not Nathan, but I had already decided Gil couldn't possibly be a bad sort.

Coco's gaze snaps back to me. "When I first got sent here, he tried to help keep Brockman away." She shrugs as if it were nothing. Just a dim memory.

I shake my head. "Why didn't you let him?"

She snorts. "He might be tough, but he doesn't have any real power. He might be able to handle Nathan and Brian, but in the end, who's gonna help me in this school? The teacher? Or another carrier?"

I just stare at her.

"I do what I have to." She looks me over. "And you will, too. Eventually." Her gaze shifts. I don't need to follow her gaze to know she's looking at him again. "There won't always be a Sean around."

She gets up then and moves to her desk. I watch as she opens her backpack and starts rifling through it, hunting for something. I study the slim line of her bent neck, the curly hair pulled up in a messy knot on her head, wondering what about this girl is so dangerous . . . so deadly. What lurks inside her?

What has she ever done, or Gil—or me, for that matter—to deserve ending up down here?

*What did Sean O'Rourke do*?

I gnaw on the edge of my thumb through the remainder of the day, eyeing the clock, willing the hour hand to move. It's starting to get to me. The chain link, the space that feels like it's shrinking, closing in. The long stretch of soundless hours. I can't wait for tonight when I can pretend none of this exists.

Every time I glance behind me to check the time, my gaze collides with Sean's. Those pale eyes bore into me. When I look, it's like he's waiting for me . . . like he knows I'm going to turn around.

When we're finally dismissed, I'm the first out of my seat. I'm careful to leave nothing behind. Not my satchel or purse. I sling both over my shoulder and bang out of the Cage. My feet race without quite running down the narrow hall. I don't cross paths with anyone, and I reach the parking lot without incident. All of this makes me feel like I made it. Like I escaped.

Sliding behind the wheel, I drag a deep breath of stale, warm air inside my lungs. It's not home, but close enough. It's my car, my space, my sanctuary. Air releases in a loud shudder from my lips. I wrap both hands around the steering wheel like I need something to hang on to.

Suddenly, someone raps the glass next to me. Not very loudly, but a bomb might as well have dropped outside my car. I jump. A yelp escapes me, and both my hands fly over my mouth.

Gil stands there, hands buried in his pants. I haven't started the car yet, but I need to in order to roll down the window. He waits, watching me patiently through the glass as I fumble with the keys and start the engine. I hit the button for the window. It slides down with a purr.

"Nice car," he murmurs, his gaze sliding over the plush interior.

"Thanks."

Silence hangs between us for a moment. It's strange seeing him outside the Cage. His hair seems darker against the bright light of day. His eyes glint behind the frames of his glasses.

"You okay?" he finally asks. "You flew out of there so fast."

"I'm fine. Just can't stand being in there a moment longer than I need to be."

He nods but looks unconvinced.

My gaze drifts. Across the parking lot, Sean moves toward his truck, his strides unhurried. He doesn't glance at us. Simply stares straight ahead as if nothing in the world can touch him.

"Davy?" I jerk at the sound of my name, almost forgetting Gil still stands next to my window.

Gil's head angles and he looks over at Sean. His shrewd eyes narrow behind his lenses. "Are you and he—"

"No!" My voice comes out harder than I intend.

"Sorry. He went after you when Brockman followed you . . . and he hardly talks to anyone inside the Cage. Even me. And I try talking to him all the time. All I get is monosyllables out of him. Guy's like a wall. Guess that's what happens when you've been treated like a deviant all your life. Can you imagine? When you're just a kid? A toddler?"

I watch Sean back his truck out, thinking about this. Thinking how Sean had known he was a carrier practically forever. As a foster kid, he had to have been one of the first groups tested.

I slide my gaze back to Gil. "How long have you known you're a carrier?"

He pushes up his glasses on the bridge of his nose. "Since last summer. I applied for a position as a camp counselor. Everyone had to get tested." He shrugs as if it should have been nothing. A formality. Only for him it had been the end of everything. I understood that too well.

"You're a nice guy, Gil," I say suddenly. I have Mitchell to tell me that, but I don't know if Gil has anyone to tell him. I hope he does.

He grins and then sighs. "Yeah? Well, tell that to the rest of the world."

I smile, and the curve of my lips feels brittle and every bit forced. "Are you headed home?"

"No, work."

"Need a lift?" I offer before I have time to consider whether I should. He's a carrier, but it makes no sense how this boy could be dangerous. I'm not dangerous, and I don't want others to judge me without proof. They do, of course, but I don't have to be like them.

He nods to the street bordering the parking lot. "It's not a long walk."

I shrug. "I don't mind. Get in."

He grins widely and walks around the front, sliding into the passenger seat.

He directs me out of the driving lot, and he's right. It's not far. We travel maybe five blocks before I turn left into a gas station.

I pull up front. "You work here?"

He nods. "Stocking and cleaning. Can't be trusted for much more." He rolls his eyes. "I used to get paid well for tutoring but no one will hire me now."

"What did you tutor?"

"Math, computer science . . . your geek subjects." He grins again. "I used to dream of going to MIT. Maybe work for the CIA someday." He snorts and waves around him. "Funny, right? It's a long way from this."

"No. Not funny," I murmur, shaking my head. "I had dreams, too." I flex my hands on the steering wheel and look forward again, oddly in no hurry to leave.

"You want to come in and get an ICEE? I don't start for another half hour."

I smile at him. It suddenly feels right to be here with him. Better him than an empty house. "Sure."

Turning off the car, I follow him inside.

He waves to the woman behind the counter. "Just getting some drinks."

She smiles, eyeing me curiously.

We take our drinks outside and sit on the curb away from the door. The cold cup sticks to my palms.

I swirl the straw around the frozen red slush. "I don't think I've had one of these since I was twelve."

"You're kidding!" He looks at me in horror. "That's criminal. I can't get through a week without one."

"You might have a problem."

He shrugs as if he's known this for a long time and it doesn't faze him. He slurps long and deep from his straw. "You could come here anytime. After school. You shouldn't wait another five years until your next ICEE."

"Yeah. I shouldn't let that happen again," I agree, feeling oddly content beside this boy who I hadn't even known existed a month ago. He smiles as he stares out into the parking lot, and I'm suddenly glad to have made at least one friend in the Cage. My thoughts drift back to Sean and how he followed Brockman when he came after me. Maybe I made more than one.

The party is in full swing when we arrive. Zac holds my hand, and I cling to his just a little bit too hard. Like I'm afraid he'll let go of me this first time around all our friends again. Or maybe I just need to feel his hand around mine, holding me after the day I've had.

*Our friends?* They are more Zac's friends than mine or they would still be calling and coming around. Zac's the only one. I shoot him a glance, my heart aching and swelling at the same time. I'm beyond glad he's proven himself loyal, but what does it say that none of my other friends have? I attended Everton Academy since kindergarten. Many of these people have been my friends for that long.

We climb the porch steps of Carlton's house. His parents are at their lake house. They practically live there full-time now, leaving Carlton to finish out senior year. His mom is scared to be this close to San Antonio. And she's not totally off base. Our little suburb is hardly crime-free. Just like the rest of the country, crime is on the rise.

As I step over the threshold, I wonder what Carlton's mom would think if she knew a carrier was inside her house. I almost smile as I imagine her swooning in a dramatic faint.

The living room is crowded. Bodies press close together in tight groups. Conversation is loud, but the music louder. No one stops and points at me. There's no outright gawking, but the awareness of my arrival is palpable. Sly glances turn my way. Heads shift subtly to examine me. It's impossible to understand anything in the deafening mash of words, but I'm sure I've become the topic.

A few of the guys approach Zac, their hands slapping one another in that guy way. These are boys I've known for years. They're strong, good-looking. Confident in themselves and where they're going even in this uncertain world. They're at the top of the social hierarchy. Just like Zac. If I wasn't dating him, I'm sure I'd be dating one of them. Carlton, with his blue eyes and lashes so long any girl would kill for them. Josh, with his matching dimples.

They always hugged me. Teased and flirted with me in a way that would make Zac get all huffy.

"Hey, Davy." They greet, smiling down at me almost with

embarrassment. It's mutual. My cheeks burn. The whole situation is awkward. I'm sure if I said boo they would jump. Ironic, considering they both top me by almost six inches.

None of the girls approach. They hang back, pretending not to watch. Except Tori. She doesn't hide her stare. I stare back at my best friend. I start to move toward her but Zac stops me. A deliberate move, I know. His gaze flits uneasily between us.

"C'mon. Let's get a drink." He laces his fingers with mine and leads me to the keg. Away from Tori.

Carlton follows us. The two guys talk about rugby as I pretend to drink from the Solo cup. I hate beer. Zac knows it, but it's never stopped him from handing me a cup. It's the thing you do at these parties. Everyone drinks in order to make it okay to act dumb and do things you'll regret later. I know the game, but I don't feel like playing it tonight. Not after the day I had. I just wish Zac and I could be alone together. I wish we could talk. I wish I could hug him and share all the horrible things that have been happening to me.

I spot Tori pushing through the crowd to reach the keg. But I know it's really not the keg she's after. Her gaze is bright and glittery, fixed on me. A quick glance at Zac, and I see he hasn't noticed her advance. He's too busy chatting with Carlton.

She stops in front of me. "Why are you here?"

"Am I not supposed to be?" I ask carefully, hoping somewhere deep inside, maybe in that part of me that's delusional and still believes in the tooth fairy, that Tori and I can still be friends.

Zac tenses beside me. "Tori?" His voice is full of warning . . . and something else: an easiness and familiarity that I've never heard in his voice when talking to her. They hardly ever talk. She annoys him. He calls her clingy. I'm the one always mediating between the two of them. This reversal of our roles, that Zac is now the mediator between us, is just weird.

She holds up a hand as if to stop him from saying anything. "No, Zac. I told you not to bring her here."

She told *him*? Like they somehow have a relationship now? A friendship? As though Zac listens to her? Since when?

*Since you got labeled a carrier*. I ignore the voice, refusing to give it validity, refusing to admit that I'm any different than I was last week. These are my friends. I'm still me. Not a monster. They should see that.

"She needs to go."

"Who are you to decide where I can and can't go?" I demand, the emotions I held in check seeping out.

Her gaze is back on me, withering and sharp, and I can't help wondering where my friend went. Tori couldn't pick out lip gloss without getting my opinion first. At that moment, I realize how much I had enjoyed being in control of our friendship—how gratifying it felt knowing my best friend couldn't win over my boyfriend. And yes, I knew she had wanted him. Like so many other girls, she had stared longingly after him. But winning Zac was something I alone had the power to do. Secretly, that had pleased me. Petty, but there it is. I swallow my suddenly constricted throat, not liking this insight into myself.

"You don't go to our school anymore." Tori flips her hair over her shoulder.

"This isn't school. It's a party."

"You're not one of us anymore." For a moment, I hear the hurt in her voice. The accusation. As though getting identified as a carrier was somehow a betrayal. Like I failed her. I see it in her eyes, too. For a moment they glimmer wetly like she might cry. Then she blinks and the hint of tears vanishes.

Gradually, I become aware of the lack of conversation around us. It's just the pump of music from the speakers. I glance at the faces of my old friends. There's no comfort, no reassurance in their eyes. Carlton stares down into his cup as if it's the most fascinating thing in the world.

Zac looks pissed. He shakes his head at Tori. "I told you not to do this tonight."

And that's when I fully understand that they have been together . . . discussing this. Discussing me. At length. Tori knew I would be here tonight. Zac told her he was bringing me and she had objected. My best friend, who couldn't even bring herself to call me, didn't want me here. She didn't want me around at all. And Zac had never mentioned any of this to me. Not even when I asked him about Tori.

"I told you not to bring her," Tori retorts, tapping her head. "Not smart. Try using your *brain*." Her gaze scours him and there's no missing her meaning. She thinks he's using another part of his anatomy.

A slow hiss escapes me. "How can you treat me like this?"

She crosses her arms. "I'm only glad that we found out. Before you hurt one of us."

I tremble from the shock of her words. *She actually thinks I'm dangerous?*

"Leave Zac alone. I know you think you would never harm him, but all carriers think that at first. And then they snap. It's always family and friends that get hurt. It's just a matter of time. . . ."

*Before you snap.* She didn't finish the sentence, but the words are there as if she had uttered them aloud.

I'm tempted to throw my drink in her face, but instead I tighten my fingers around the cup. That would only prove her point. That I'm some volatile person about to go off the deep end. Instead, I laugh. It's a brittle sound and Zac looks at me uneasily. "Since when did you become an expert on . . . anything, Tori?"

It's mean, but I'm feeling mean. And angry.

Her eyes narrow to bright little slits and I start to suspect that *she* is going to throw her drink on *me*.

"Come on." Zac pulls me after him. At first, I think we're leaving, but he steers us up the stairs, his strides determined, his steps resounding thuds on the limestone.

I glance quickly behind me. Tori's face is flushed, splotchy like it gets when she works out.

"Where are we going?" I ask when we clear the top.

"Carlton's room. We can have some privacy there."

A relieved breath rushes out of me. We can finally talk about everything and figure stuff out. We need to come up with a plan if we're going to make this work. I catch myself. Something pinches sharply in the center of my chest. I've never thought in terms of *if* before when it came to us.

Obviously, we've hit a hurdle. We no longer attend the same school. Our friends aren't our friends anymore. That will make being together a struggle—but not impossible. Not as long as it's what we want. And Zac must want us to work out. He's here. I'm here. We're together now. He came back after the shock of learning that I'm a carrier.

I step inside Carlton's room. It's full of rich browns. A mahogany dresser and bed. A desk with a built-in case behind it that overflows with rugby and diving trophies. On the paneled wall hangs a photograph of our entire senior class at our fall retreat. I'm on Zac's shoulders, waving for the camera. That day seems very long ago.

I turn around to face him, to explain to him how much it means to me that he's standing beside me when none of our friends are. But he's there. In front of me, sliding his cool palms along my cheeks, delving his fingers into my hair, pressing his mouth over mine and drowning out any chance for words.

For now, this is enough.

Seventy percent of all violent crimes are committed by offenders known to the victim. This figure jumps dramatically—to 90 percent—when the perpetrator is female, with the most common targets being significant others and family members. . . .

*—Lecture from Dr. Wainwright to the National Center for Analysis of Violent Crime at Quantico*

# TEN

FOR WHAT SEEMS LIKE FOREVER, ZAC KISSES ME long and deep, nearly smothering me. I hold his wrists, loving that this is the first thing he does. Almost like he has to do it. Like he can't wait. After the ugliness of downstairs, it's a stamp of affirmation. I'm the only thing that matters to him. Not the opinions of others. Not my carrier status. Just me.

He nudges me back and we fall on the bed, bodies tangling together. I laugh lightly against the insistent press of his mouth, but even that sound is quickly swallowed up in his anxious lips.

The heavy weight of his right leg curls over my hip, pinning me. He's heavy. Solid. I press a palm against his firm chest, reveling in the feel of his heartbeat, strong and swift.

I break from his lips to speak, to get out the words I want to say, *need* to say, but he quickly captures my mouth again. His hand flows along the slope of my thigh, pulling me in closer to his body.

"Zac," I gasp.

"Davy," he returns, still kissing me. Not stopping.

I push both hands against his shoulders and force him up. "Zac, can we take a minute?"

"For what? We're finally alone." He brushes a strand of hair back from my face and tucks it behind my ear. His brilliant green eyes pin me. "I've missed you, Davy."

"I've missed you, too, but I thought we should talk."

"About what?"

"Everything, Zac. Everything has changed. I'm not even welcome here."

"Carlton doesn't care—"

"I'm not talking about Carlton. I'm talking about everyone. Tori—"

"Please." He rolls his eyes. "I can handle Tori."

And this irks me. She's *my* best friend—*was.* He shouldn't be the buffer between us. Talking to her. Talking to me. Being pulled in two directions. And maybe there's the fact that I know she's always wanted him for herself. And if not her, there are others. Other pretty girls at Everton, waiting in the wings, who are a better fit for a guy with everything going for him.

His head dips to kiss me again, but I press a hand to his

mouth, stopping him. His eyes gleam with frustration.

"Okay. What about our plans? Or future? I can't go to Juilliard anymore." A heaviness sinks inside me as I acknowledge this out loud. "That's not going to happen for me." I slide my fingers from his lips. "How can we make this work? You'll be at NYU in the fall. I'll be . . . here. . . ." That's a safe guess. I can probably go to the local community college. Get a job at Dad's bank.

I wait, eager to hear the words that will make me feel better.

Make me believe in him . . . in us. I need something to hang on to. Something to believe in. Something that won't go away, vanish down the drain in a whirl with everything else.

"Do we really have to talk about this now, Davy? Can't we just enjoy being together?"

His coaxing voice, his melting gaze. All of it gets to me. This time I don't stop his head from lowering. We kiss. His hands roam and mold to me. Our breathing grows harsh, air passing from his mouth to mine.

His fingers trail down. Lifting my shirt, he grazes the sensitive skin underneath. He seizes the snap on my jeans and pops it free with an easy flick of his hand. The zipper is loud on the air, a discordant rip over the crash of our breaths.

My hand flies to his, closing over him. It's an instinctive move. One I've been executing for months now.

He stills. Looks down at me with slightly dazed eyes. "C'mon, Davy," he pleads, kissing my jaw. I feel the tip of his tongue there and shiver. "You said we would. . . ."

I look up past his face to the blur of the fan blades above, not wanting to debate the point that I had not actually agreed to sleep with him. I had been considering it. On the verge, true. But I hadn't agreed. Yet.

"I just . . ." My voice fades. I don't know what to say. Before, it had felt right. A definite likelihood. I'd felt ready. But now. Now . . . everything about this feels wrong. Here. In this room. With people downstairs who think I'm some sort of deviant. It's wrong.

"I need this, Davy," he whispers against my ear.

*This*. Not me.

He doesn't need *me*.

"I can't," I announce. This time the words fall with no reluctance. No regret. I *know*. I can't do this.

He lifts up to peer at me, evidently recognizing from my tone that I'm not in a place where he can sweet-talk me. He stares hard at me for a long moment, his expression varying, shifting from frustration to anger. "Why not?"

I sit up and re-snap my jeans. "This isn't how I envisioned—"

"Have you envisioned it?" he demands. "At all? Because I'm beginning to wonder."

I look at him, baffled at his tone, at his seeming anger. It's not as if I haven't told him no before. "Why are you so upset with me? I just don't feel—"

"I've waited for months, Davy. And you just keep teasing me with promises. You should be grateful that I'm the kind of guy who's patient . . . especially now."

I angle my head, my flesh suddenly prickling. "Why *especially* now?"

He looks away briefly before turning back at me. His lips compress as if he's holding something in.

"Why?" I stab him in the chest with my finger. "Why should I be especially grateful *now*?"

I wait, my chest swelling with the aching hope that I'm wrong. That he won't say it. That he will say something to erase all the horrible things running through my head. I desperately need confirmation that he's not as bad as the rest of them. That he doesn't see me as damaged.

I wait, hungry to hear him say that he didn't bring me here tonight expecting some kind of reward for sticking with me.

The words never come.

He crosses his arms over his chest as he faces me, his expression odd. It's almost like he's a stranger staring at me, his eyes dull and somehow less green. His mouth unsmiling. "You know why."

I suck in a sharp breath.

And he's right. I do know why. I understand.

In that instant, everything about him—about who I thought he was—dies a quick death. Grief swallows me as I blink at my boyfriend. Looking at him, I only see another disappointment. Another loss. Another piece of me gone and crushed to tiny bits.

Turning, I open the door and flee the room.

"Davy, wait!" His steps pound after me. Before I reach the top of the stairs, he grabs my arm and forces me around.

"Where are you going?"

I look at him evenly. "I'm going home."

"You're mad at me," he announces.

"And you're observant."

He drops his hand from my arm. "Why are you being like this?"

Why am *I* being like this?

"You know why," I say, deliberately echoing his words.

His face hardens and he crosses his arms, reminding me of a spoiled little boy. "We just got here. I'm not ready to go home."

I stare at him for a moment, still reconciling this Zac with the boy I thought I knew. The boy I loved.

What did I know anymore about anyone? About anything? If I'd been so wrong about him, what else am I wrong about?

White-hot panic hums through me. *I've got to get out of here. Escape.*

"I'm leaving." My feet move swiftly down the steps. I don't look back to see if he's following. I hope he's not.

The loud pulse of music vibrates up my legs from the floor as I push through the crowd. When I burst out onto the porch, it almost feels like I've emerged from underwater. I suck in a slightly frigid breath and brace a hand against the limestone post. I stare out at the dark street lined with cars. The late March wind folds over me. It's still cold in the evenings. I know I need to enjoy this weather while it lasts. Soon, the days will be scorching.

But enjoying anything anymore seems the most implausible thing.

I brush fingers to my lips, still tasting Zac there. Familiar. But no longer exciting or comforting. The memory of him doesn't make me warm and tingly inside. There's only hurt. Betrayal and bitterness.

It took losing me—the death of the old Davy Hamilton—to meet the true Zac. To learn what the world is really like. A hard lesson, but now I know at least.

Shaking my head at the gnawing ache in my chest, I descend the wide porch steps.

"Davy, stop!"

I don't know why, but I do. Turning, I watch as Zac jogs down the steps. Several of our friends—his friends—spill out onto the porch, like vultures scenting blood. They love a good scene.

Squeezing my hands into fists at my sides, I vow not to give them one.

He stops before me, releasing a breath.

I wait, bracing myself for his coming apology, telling myself that I can be dignified and accept his apology, but that it won't change anything. I can't be with him anymore. Now that I know how he really feels. He'll gladly use me. Sleep with me. But he doesn't want me. Not really. I'm ruined in his eyes.

He turns his face slightly, looks behind him, aware of our audience standing on the porch. Tori pushes to the front, her arms crossed in a hostile pose.

Zac looks back at me. I wait, saying nothing. He stopped me, after all.

"Davy," he begins, "I want my sweatshirt back."

I blink, uncomprehending.

"The NYU one," he prompts, as if I might not know what he's referring to.

He stopped me for this? Not an apology. He wants his sweatshirt back?

I gawk at him. He flicks a quick glance over his shoulder. Several of the kids on the porch laugh. Tori smiles, satisfied. Even Zac smiles . . . just a hint, but those lips that had kissed me only minutes ago curve ever so slightly.

Then I understand. He's doing this for their benefit. Dumping me in front of them. Making sure they all know that *I* didn't walk out on *him*. That a girl with the kill gene didn't leave him high and dry. There's no apology coming. There never was.

My hand shoots out. Before I even realize what I'm doing, my palm connects with Zac's face. Gasps ripple through the kids assembled on the porch. Even in the night, I can detect my white handprint against his cheek.

Tori thunders down the steps. "See? See? Get out!" She's practically shrieking at me, waving a hand in the direction of the road.

I back away, horrified. I gave them a scene. I gave them the evidence they wanted that I was someone dangerous and violent. That I don't belong with them. It didn't matter that I was justified. Any other girl could have reacted this way. Any girl but me.

I don't belong with them. This much is true, I realize. With any of them. And surprisingly, this doesn't fill me with even a shred of sadness. Outrage burns through my veins, keeping me warm against the wind as I turn and walk past rows of cars lining the circular driveway.

It's going to take forever to hoof it home, but I'm not going back to that house for anything. Tonight's misery quota has been met.

I've only covered a few yards before headlights flash behind me. Zac's car rolls up beside me. I shoot him a cursory glance and keep moving. He sticks his head out the window. With one hand propped on the steering wheel, he drives slowly, keeping pace with me.

"Davy, get in the car."

I bristle at his tone. "I can walk, thanks."

"It's going to take you an hour on foot."

"I'll be fine. Besides . . . are you sure you'll be safe with me?"

He makes a sound, part grunt, part sigh. "Stop it."

"I'm just saying. You're sporting a nice handprint on your face there."

He glances at the road, turning the wheel a bit to avoid someone's recycling bin that's still in the street. "I picked you up. I'll take you home."

A little laugh breaks loose from me. "Trying to be a gentleman now, are we?"

"Damn it! Get in. I'm responsible for you. Come back to the house with me. Or let me take you home. What if you're caught out here? You know there's a curfew."

I snort. "Like we always obey that."

"Yeah, that was before. What's gonna happen if they find you wandering out here, a carrier . . . ?"

Of course everything comes back to that. I whirl to face him. "Just stop! Go! I'm not your concern, Zac. We're done. I absolve you, or whatever."

"Fine. Walk," he bites out, ducking his head back inside the car. "I tried. Just remember that. I tried."

And he's not just talking about me getting into the car. He's talking about us. He actually thinks he tried to keep us . . . *alive.* I laugh out loud, the sound harsh in the night, making me feel a bit like a madwoman.

"Is that what you think? Does it make you feel like less of a jerk to believe that? You need to believe you didn't quit on us just because of some stupid DNA test, but you did!"

"I'm not a jerk!"

"Ha! You're the worst kind because you don't even know it. It would have been far kinder to just break up with me instead of dragging this out. At least that would have been honest."

For a long moment, he says nothing. There's just the purr of his engine and the gleam of his eyes from within the dark interior of his car. And then: "You're right. I should have broken up with you," he confesses. "I wanted to. Guess I was too much of a coward."

His words shouldn't wound me, but they do. My chest

tightens, and it hurts to breathe.

I fight past the lump in my throat to say more. "Consider it done then."

He nods, the motion rough and jerky. I can't make out his expression in the dark, but I sense his relief that it's done. That we're done.

"Good luck, Davy." He floors it and the car shoots ahead into the night, turning the corner at the far end of the street so fast that it fishtails before righting.

Then he's gone. And I'm all alone.

TEXAS ORDINANCE NO. 12974B (MODIFYING TITLE II: POLICE ACTION OF PERSONS UNDER THIRTY-FIVE YEARS OF AGE)

WHEREIN the State concludes there has been an increase in violence and crime by persons under the age of thirty-five, resulting in a broad variety of offensive behavior, including vandalism, breach of the peace, and assaults on citizens . . .

WHEREIN persons under the age of thirty-five are chiefly susceptible to engage in dangerous and unlawful activities . . .

WHEREIN the offensive actions of persons under the age of thirty-five are not easily controlled by existing law . . .

HENCEFORTH a curfew for those under the age of thirty-five will be in the interest of public safety and welfare and will facilitate and promote public safety for the citizens of Texas. . . .

# ELEVEN

I'VE BEEN OUT PAST CURFEW BEFORE, BUT NEVER alone. Never walking the streets. Even in a nice area like this, where the houses sit far back from the road, draped in oak trees, it's not completely safe. The most dangerous criminal behavior is reserved for the cities, but some of that element spills over. All I need to do is flip on the television to remind myself of that—or think about why the Wainwright Agency even exists, wresting more and more control from the government.

Plenty of police patrol the area, issuing citations, and even arresting people for being disruptive. Or just suspicious. Their presence used to make me feel safe. Now I feel hunted. Like they're out to get me, waiting for me to make a mistake. Someone like me, a carrier . . . it wouldn't have to be a big mistake. It could be something small.

*Like getting caught out after curfew.*

I move swiftly along the street, past manicured lawns. There are no sidewalks out here. Simply large, acre lots with curving roads intersecting them. The vast carpets of rolling green look so inviting. I want to lie down on them. A sprinkler chugs, and the sound reminds me of a distant train.

Mom always says we're lucky to live where we do—outside the city, where local law enforcement keeps strict vigilance. The majority of the crime happens in town. Not just in Texas but across the country. Some cities have been abandoned entirely to the indigent and criminal. *To carriers.* The police never even set foot in those places—even parts of San Antonio are lost.

Still, considering that I'm now a perpetual suspect, I wouldn't mind a little less diligence on their part.

As I hum lightly, my gaze scrutinizes every car that appears in the distance, trying to detect if it's a patrol or just a random vehicle hurrying home before ten. A quick glance at the lit screen of my phone reveals I have about half an hour left.

As much as I hated Zac's reminder, he's right. If I'm caught out past curfew, it won't be a simple ticket. I'm in the HTS database. They'd take me into custody. I remember that much from the packet Pollock had given me.

A car approaches in the night, and it looks like it has a

light bar on top. Even though it's not yet ten, I panic and dive into a yard, tucking myself behind a hedge of boxwood edging the driveway.

The car passes me and I see it's a simple luggage rack on top. My breath eases and I shake my head. It's not even past curfew. How jumpy am I going to be when it's after ten and I'm still walking the streets?

Rising from behind the hedge, I watch as the car turns into a driveway and disappears into a three-car garage. The doors rumble shut and the neighborhood is silent again.

My heart slows but still doesn't resume its normal pace. Suddenly, I feel foolish. I should have just let Zac drive me home.

Pulling my phone from my pocket, I quickly punch in Mitchell's number. After a few rings, it rolls to his voice mail. He's probably at some bar where he can't even hear his phone.

I debate calling my parents, wincing as I imagine the questions that will be fired at me. Mom was so thrilled that I was going out with Zac. At least one part of my life appeared unchanged. Even if it's just my love life. Funny . . . they always thought Zac and I were too serious. Now that's changed along with everything else.

Sucking in a deep breath, I dial her, loathing that she will now know just how much life has changed. That I've lost him, too. Her phone goes to voice mail. I punch END harshly, punishing my phone.

Shaking my head, I scroll through my contacts. All friends that I can't call. Or I could. But they wouldn't come. I cringe, imagining the scenario. I've already had enough humiliation for one night. I'm not up for more.

Perhaps this more than anything else alerts me to how terribly wrong my life has become. When you're stranded and in trouble and there's no one to call, you've hit rock bottom.

I stare at my phone, considering my lack of options. Well, one option teases at my mind. But it's ridiculous. Even possibly dangerous. The goal right now is to avoid danger, avoid getting into trouble. And calling him definitely spells trouble.

Another car approaches. The headlights blind me for a second. My pulse jackknifes against my neck until it passes.

"Enough," I mutter, and dial information. Stranded out here, I don't have a better choice. I wait as the operator connects me.

A woman answers, the din of voices and dishes ringing behind her, "Golden Palace."

"Yes. Could I speak with Sean, please?"

"Sean busy," she snaps sharply into the phone.

"Wait. This is his sister," I lie, hoping the woman doesn't know that he only has foster brothers.

"No calls at work," she barks into the phone.

"Please. It's an emergency."

She grunts and mutters something in another language, and then, "Hold on."

The sounds of the restaurant hum into the phone as I wait, still walking along the dark road . . . watching for cars. There are no streetlights. The only light is the occasional glow from an elaborate entrance gate or distant porch light.

Finally, a deep voice comes on the line. "Hello?"

I open my mouth, but nothing passes from my lips. The words strangle in my throat.

"Hello?" he says again, a ring of impatience to his voice and I can tell he's about to hang up.

"Sean," I blurt his name. "It's me. Davy. From school." My words tumble free in a rush.

Silence stretches between us and for a moment I wonder if I lost the connection. Then I hear his breath, just the faint rasp of it.

"I'm sorry to call you at work." I realize I'm pressing the phone hard into my ear and peel it away from my face before I accidentally end the call.

"Why are you calling?" To the point. No emotion.

"I didn't know who else to call." My voice cracks a little. To admit this to a veritable stranger, to an imprinted carrier . . . someone I can't figure out. Someone probably dangerous. Yes, dangerous. He rules the Cage, and Nathan clearly has all the makings of a sociopath. His HTS status is spot-on. So what does that say about Sean? And yet . . . he stepped in and helped me with Brockman. He can't be all that bad.

*So you think he'll go out of his way to help you again?*

I press my fingertips against my lips, a hot ball of anxiety twists inside me. It's a horrible sensation. I shake my head. *No.* "I'm sorry. I'm fine. I shouldn't have called—"

"Where are you?"

I blink at the abrupt question. I thought he would have slammed the phone down by now. "What?"

He repeats himself, enunciating each word firmly in his deep voice. "Where are you?"

I glance at the street sign and nearest house. "3412 Red Mulberry Lane. Boerne."

"I'll be there soon. Stay out of sight. It's almost curfew," he warns.

I release a shuddery breath. "I know." I start to add a thank-you but the line goes dead.

I chafe a sweating palm against my thigh. He's coming.

Which is why I called him in the first place, but it doesn't stop the ball of nerves from forming in my stomach.

There's an SUV parked not too far down a driveway and I hide behind it, waiting. My palms feel clammy and I continue rubbing them against my thighs, glancing between the street and the house, making sure no one notices me lurking next to the parked car.

I tell myself I'm only worried about getting caught. And not the boy coming to my aid.

The minutes slide by. It's after ten now. I'm officially out past curfew. I hear another car, and this time it's a police cruiser. It was inevitable. They make the rounds several times a night in this neighborhood. Mine too.

They don't notice me where I crouch. I squeeze my eyes in a tight blink and wait for the sound of the engine to fade. I tremble long after the car is gone and the sounds of crickets fill my ears.

When I hear another car, I take a peek. It's an old truck, moving slowly. The driver comes into view. Even in the dark

I recognize the fall of his hair, the ends brushing the back of his neck.

I stand fully and hurry down the driveway. The truck stops. I hover uncertainly at the driver's door.

He rolls the window down. We stare at each other for a moment, several feet separating us. Even in the shadows, I can make out the thick band encircling his neck, the bold, circled H.

"Get in."

I move around the truck and open the door. It swings wide with a groan. I ease myself carefully onto the passenger seat and shut the door after me, flinching as it clangs harshly.

I brush the hair over my shoulder nervously and lean back against the worn upholstery. "Thank you."

He starts to drive. "Where do you live?"

I give him my address. "It's only ten minutes away."

We drive in silence. I stare straight ahead, hands clasped around my knees. It's somewhere to rest my hands. Some way to try to contain my shaking. An insane urge to laugh bubbles up inside me. Nerves, I know, but it just strikes me as suddenly unbelievable that I had started the night on a date with Zac and now I'm in a truck driving through the dark with Sean O'Rourke.

"You can't do this."

I jump at the sound of his rumbling voice. My gaze skips to him. He's staring at the road, one hand draped loosely over the wheel. It's almost like he hasn't spoken at all, except his lips move as he adds, "If they catch you after curfew—"

"I know." My voice sounds tired even to my ears.

"Do you?"

"That's why I called you." *I was desperate enough to do that.*

"I can't look out for you."

I bristle. "I just need a ride. Not a bodyguard." But then I see him in the bathroom when he walked in on me with Brockman, and my words lack the desired punch.

He laughs hollowly. "You need a bodyguard in the *worst* way." The way his voice says "worst" . . . with such emphasis and conviction, rubs me the wrong way. Probably because it's true. I can't even name a friend who would pick up the phone for me anymore.

He continues and it's salt on the wound. "You have no clue how the world outside your little bubble works." He motions to the sprawling houses we roll past.

"I'm a quick learner." I squeeze the words past my tightening throat, thinking that I've already got the gist. This last week has been the worst of my life. I hardly feel secure inside a bubble.

"Yeah? Well. You're going to have to be."

"And were you a quick learner, too?" I lash out. "Is that how you got imprinted? I guess you didn't get things figured out fast enough, did you?"

The moment the words slip out I wish I could take them back. I can't believe I flung that in his face.

The interior light casts enough of a glow that I see his square jaw tighten. A muscle feathers along the flesh there. Suddenly, he's pulling over, yanking the truck to the side of the street.

Panic shimmies up my chest to clog my throat. I'm struck

again with the knowledge that I'm in a vehicle. Alone. With a carrier who has proven himself to be a violent offender. For a moment, I had let that fade from my mind. I provoked him like he was just an ordinary guy. Like *I'm* an ordinary girl. A girl who, a week ago, could get away with anything.

He shifts into PARK and turns to me. All my doubts about him return. I forget that he cared enough to help me with Brockman. I just see the tattoo on his neck. I scrabble for the door handle, seize it, and shove it open.

"What are you doing?" he growls, and slides across the bench seat, reaching around me for the handle. His hand squeezes over mine, crushing my fingers as he swiftly slams the door shut.

He's draped over me. His left hand is folded over mine on the handle while his other arm stretches along the back of the seat. My chest heaves, pushing against him. I'm consciously aware of every inch of him plastered to me.

He's not built like Zac. He's stronger. More muscular. Like he's accustomed to hard labor and fighting with his fists. I feel his power and imagine it used against me. Grinding me into nothing. A scream rises in my throat and starts to leak free. He quickly slams a hand over my mouth.

My chest rises and falls against him as I struggle for breath. I stare at him, afraid to blink, and my eyes start to ache. We're so close I can see the dark ring of blue rimming his irises.

"You're going to get us both in trouble. Trust me. You don't want that to happen. You think it's bad now. You have no idea how bad it can get." There's an edge of desperation to his voice.

I shake, trembling uncontrollably. In my mind, all the news footage I've ever seen highlighting the gruesome damage wrought by carriers flashes before me.

He mutters a curse and I flinch. "Look, I don't get off on hurting girls. I'm not going to harm you." His hand softens on my face, his fingers lifting up ever so slightly, allowing me to breathe better. "Okay?"

I nod.

"I'll lift my hand, but unless you want to get us both arrested, for God's sake don't scream." His gaze flicks to the street, assessing.

I nod again, relaxing somewhat. Able to think again.

Of course. Coco certainly wouldn't have called him a good guy if he was into hurting girls. And he wouldn't have helped me out with Brockman.

My gaze drifts to his neck. The deep band and circled H. He isn't into hurting girls. So what did he hurt then? He didn't get that imprint on his neck for nothing.

"Stop looking at it," he hisses, giving his head a little shake. The roughly shorn, gold-streaked strands brush the planes of his face. He looks at me beneath hooded eyes. Something flashes in those pale pools of blue. "Look at *me*." A glimpse of real emotion. Not anger . . . but something else.

His hand lifts off my mouth now, hovering over my face, ready to cover my lips again if I start to cry out.

"I—I'm sorry," I whisper, almost convinced I can feel the thud of his heart through his chest into mine.

"You've got to get a grip on all this. I know you probably

think nothing could get worse, but it can." He moves off me then and falls back on the seat with a sigh.

I nod. That's exactly what I had been thinking. That I'd hit rock bottom. "I'm sorry I'm so jumpy around you."

"You . . ." His voice fades and he fists his hand on the steering wheel. He shakes his head fiercely as if stopping himself from saying what he wants to say.

"What? What were you going to say?"

He turns, studies me with his head angled. Like how an animal curiously examines something it's never seen before. "I was going to say you shouldn't be sorry. You *should* be jumpy around me. Around every carrier there is. Nathan and Brian. Even around Pollock. Anyone with the Agency. Everyone. It's smarter to be cautious. Distrustful. If you want to stay in one piece."

*Everyone?* That is my life now? An island unto myself? Always alone?

He continues, "You shouldn't have called me. And I shouldn't have come."

"But you did," I say, hoping that he's wrong. That there's something good in others. In him. That I'm not alone. I can't be. *I don't want to be.*

"Next time I won't." He pulls the truck out onto the street again.

His words inexplicably wound me. It's not as though I count him as a friend, but he's the only one tonight who came when I called. If I can't have a friend among my own kind—and I have to accept that I'm one of them now—then what's left for me?

An oncoming car lights up his face for a brief moment, and I don't miss the unyielding set to his jaw.

"So you're telling me to trust no one." I cross my arms over my chest.

"Remember that and you might survive." Nodding, he slides me a measuring glance. "You're soft. You need to toughen up."

I can't help thinking that telling an HTS carrier that she needs to toughen up is ironic. Presumably, carriers are already tough. Sociopaths waiting to snap.

He slows in front of my house. Like most homes in this area, it sits far back from the road. He pulls up to the gate but doesn't drive all the way down the driveway to the porch. Probably a good idea.

I open the noisy door and stick one leg out. "Thanks for coming to get me."

"Be more careful."

Because he won't bail me out again. He doesn't say those words, but he doesn't need to. He already did. He made his point clear.

As I walk down my drive and beneath the covered portico, I fish out my keys, resisting the temptation to peek behind me. I haven't heard him drive away yet. The glow of headlights bathes me in white as I unlock the door.

*Is he still watching me? Making sure I get safely inside?* That seems a little too courteous for a carrier who just vowed to never help me again.

As I punch in the alarm code and step inside, he reverses

and drives away. I lock the door behind me. The house is dark and silent. My eyes adjust to the gloom. I inhale, smelling the aroma of fresh-cut flowers on the foyer table.

I move into the living room, not bothering with the light. I know my way well. Especially toward the piano, the first instrument I ever played. I push back the lid and sink onto the bench. I don't need sheet music. I lightly poise my fingers, curling them softly. They're elegant and slim from long hours of practice. My fingertips sink down on the smooth, well-loved keys. A soft swell of music rises from the belly of the piano as I play something I wrote a year ago. I still remember it even though I haven't composed lately, too busy with school and voice lessons and Zac. Now all those things are gone. Lost to me. My body sways slightly with the harmony. At least I still have this.

I finish playing half an hour later. The last note hangs, reverberating in the silent room, fading into space until the only sound is the faint whir of fan blades from above.

With one last caress for the keys, I rise and head upstairs. Usually, Mom or Dad wait up, but they must have gone to bed. Light spills into the hallway from my parents' bedroom, a bright puddle of yellow on the bloodred runner. I have to pass the open door on the way to my room.

I pause and peer inside. Mom's asleep in bed, a book forgotten next to her. A relieved breath shudders past my lips. At least I don't have to lie to her and tell her I had a great time with Zac. I'll have to tell her the truth soon enough and dash her dreams that Zac is sticking by me through all this.

Even across the room, I can detect the dark smudges beneath her eyes. Her lamp is still on and I'm contemplating turning it off when the empty space beside her registers.

I frown. It's not like Dad to work this late on a Friday. Usually, he and Mom share a bottle of wine and watch a movie together.

I can't help wondering where he is and if it has anything to do with me. It has to be because of me. Mom's been the calm one, practical and accepting. Dad's been angry, storming around the house. Slamming doors. At first, it made me feel better. Proof that he cares. He may not have been able to stop all this from happening to me but at least it made him furious. And that gave me hope that maybe he could do something. Figure something out to save me. Typical daddy's-girl thinking.

At night, I hear him fighting with Mom through the walls. They never used to fight. I don't feel good about that. That I'm the reason.

I move from the doorway, wondering where he is . . . why he isn't fighting with her now. Have they moved on to avoidance? In some ways I wish he was in there, his voice raised in anger. That's better than this silence.

Walking into my bedroom, I can't help thinking that this is my life now. I drop onto my bed and pull one of my pillows close to my chest, hugging it tightly.

No one to trust. No friends. A life of silence broken only with music.

---

Inscription on page 21 of Davy's eleventh-grade yearbook:

*To my best friend! The sweetest, most brilliant girl ever!!! Looking forward to our senior year together! We'll be unstoppable!*

*Love you to the moon and back!*

*Your BFF,*

*Tori!*

# TWELVE

"DAVINA, COME UP HERE."

At the sound of my name, I stand and head to the front of the Cage. I pass Sean. He arrived an hour ago. I don't look at him. At least I don't turn my face in his direction. From the corner of my eye, I observe him writing something in his notebook. He doesn't glance at me.

Since Friday, I've taken his advice. I haven't talked to him. I've tried not to look at him at all. Other than a few words exchanged with Gil, I haven't said anything to anyone at school. Brockman is the only one I talk to and just because I have to.

Every afternoon, Brockman has either Gil or me take our class's completed assignments to the office and collect any new work. By Wednesday, I know the drill. I guess today it's my turn.

"Here you go." Brockman hands me several manila folders, barely glancing at me. This has been his manner since the bathroom incident with Sean. No inappropriate remarks. He doesn't so much as brush hands with me when he passes me the folders.

"Come right back." He says that every time. Like I have a choice. Like I have anywhere else to go.

I nod and start to turn but stop at his "Oh, wait." I watch as he digs some spare change out of his pocket. "Why don't you get me a soda, too. Big Red."

I hold my hand out for the money. He drops the coins into my palm. I slip the change into my jeans pocket and hurry away.

The athletics hall, ripe with the ever-present aroma of sweat, is familiar by now. Sometimes I pass boys or girls heading into one of the gyms or weight room. They often notice my ID badge and look me over like I'm sort of a freak. Like they're not accustomed to coming face-to-face with a carrier. I can't imagine I look very threatening.

Three boys emerge from the locker room. They're dressed in their gym clothes, black shorts with gray T-shirts. A hawk, the school mascot, is emblazoned across the front, its wings stretched in flight.

Their loud voices compete with each other. One of them nudges the guy next to him when he spots me, and soon all three fall quiet, assessing me with eyes that move rapidly, taking special note of my orange ID badge.

One whispers something to the boy beside him and they laugh. It's a mean, dirty laugh and it makes my skin crawl.

I walk as close to the wall as possible, clutching the folders, bending them away from me in my hands.

"I thought they were supposed to keep them in lockdown," one of them says in a distinctly loud whisper.

*Lockdown*. Like I'm a prisoner. A captive.

I hurry past them before I can hear more. Before one of them gets the courage to actually address me. At least there's that. They don't outright confront me. Too uncertain of the girl with the kill gene.

I find a bathroom on the top floor. I prop the manila folders down on the tiny shelf in front of the mirror and stare at my reflection. I hardly recognize the pale girl looking back at me. The fear in my eyes is as unfamiliar as my surroundings. I guess I'm uncertain of the girl with the kill gene, too.

I turn on the faucet, pump soap into my palms, and wash them together, letting the cool water run over my hands and down the drain. If only everything else wrong in my life could disappear as swiftly.

Brockman grunts a thanks when I return with his soda and set it on his desk. There were no new assignments waiting for us. This actually makes me kind of disappointed. It's going to be a boring afternoon with nothing to do.

I hesitate a moment before I open the Cage door. Suddenly,

I'm overwhelmed with longing for my old school. My classrooms. People to talk to, teachers who actually give a damn and want to teach us.

Sinking into my desk, I pull out a notebook and start writing. Composing. I hum under my breath as I jot down notes, toying with varying pitches and combinations in my head. I'm so absorbed I don't hear him approach.

"What are you doing?"

I jump and slam my notebook shut.

Sean stands over me, holding a spiral notebook. It looks small in his large hands. Even the pencil looks fragile, as if he might accidentally break it in his grip.

"N-nothing." I want to ask him why he's talking to me. I thought we were finished with that. With him talking to me . . . helping me. I got his message loud and clear. I'm in this alone.

"What were you drawing?"

I shake my head, not about to explain that I was composing a piece of music. "Just doodling."

He eases into the desk in front of me and turns to face me. Using my desktop, he opens up his notebook and pulls out a work sheet tucked inside there. "Thought we'd finish that assignment."

"The one from last week?"

He nods.

I angle my head. "You want to write my biography?"

"That's the assignment," he replies, his voice even, his gaze unflinching.

I didn't think he cared. He'd hardly been a willing subject when I posed the questions to him. "Okay," I say slowly.

"Name?"

"Davy Hamilton."

"That's not your full name." He stares at me steadily, his eyes serious. He's always so serious. I've never heard him laugh. Never seen him smile.

"Davina Evelyn Hamilton."

And then I see it. The corner of his mouth lifts ever so faintly.

"What's so funny?"

"Nothing. Just sounds like the name of someone's great-great-aunt."

"They were my grandmothers' names . . . on both sides."

His pencil scratches the paper. "Of course," he murmurs softly beneath his breath.

"Parents?"

"Patrick and Caitlyn Hamilton."

"Siblings?"

He asks the rest of the questions. All basic stuff. I rattle off answers.

"Hobbies?

I hesitate. He looks up at me. "Come on. You have them." He sounds almost amused at the idea that I would try to deny this.

"Debutante training?" he suggests. "Tennis at the country club?"

I glare. "Funny. No. Music," I snap.

"Music? You like listening to music?"

"No. I play. I sing."

"What do you play?"

I sigh. "Piano. Violin. Flute, guitar. A few others . . ." My voice fades.

He lifts his pencil from the desk and looks at me squarely. "You play all those instruments?"

I nod, waiting for him to make a remark, to poke fun at me.

He returns his attention to his paper. "That's really cool." The comment is mild enough, but from him it feels . . . I don't know. Important somehow. I've impressed him. For some weird reason this warms me. I doubt much impresses him.

"Is that why you're always humming?"

"I don't always hum," I deny.

"Yes. You do. You're really quiet, but you do."

"I don't think so." At least I don't think I *always* do it. "No one has ever pointed that out to me before—"

"Then they aren't paying attention." He gazes at me as he says this with that serious expression of his, his smoky eyes shrewd in a way that seems older than his years.

His words resonate in me. *They* aren't paying attention. But *he* is.

My face heats beneath his gaze. I tuck a strand of hair behind my ear, feeling suddenly self-conscious.

He breaks eye contact with me and goes back to scrawling on the paper. After a moment, he asks, "Boyfriend?"

"What?"

"Do you have a boyfriend?" He spaces each word out as

though to help me comprehend.

"What does that have to do with anything?"

He looks up, his expression almost bored—like the question and my answer mean little to him. He motions to the paper. "You're what, seventeen?" I nod. "Just figure it's a relevant question for the biography of a teenage girl."

"No. I don't have a boyfriend," I say after some moments. I wait but he doesn't ask any more than that. I don't have to say anything else, but I hear myself confessing, "We broke up. The night you picked me up. That's why I left. I got mad and stormed off."

He considers me. His eyes deep, absorbing. There's no judgment there.

"He couldn't handle it. None of my friends can."

He looks down at the tip of his pencil. He starts to pick at the thin splinters surrounding the lead. "So he let you walk off? After curfew?"

"I didn't give him a choice."

"He had a choice."

"No. Really. We had a fight and then I refused to get in the car." I wince, unable to confess the slap. Even to him. I regret that slap. Regret losing control.

"I would have convinced you."

I release a short, breathy laugh, and look away, my face hot at the idea of what this boy would have done if he were my boyfriend. An unlikely scenario. I shift uncomfortably in my chair.

"Think I have enough." He stands abruptly and moves

back to his desk. I blink and look straight ahead. For a minute there, things had felt . . . friendly. Like he wasn't a carrier. Like he hadn't warned me to keep my guard up around him and everyone else in my life.

Like I wasn't so alone.

---

**Text Message**

2:37 p.m.

Tori:

R U coming???

2:40 p.m.

Zac:

Don't do this

2:42 p.m.

Tori:

Fine. Will go w/o u. Carlton agreed 2 come. Others 2. There were plenty witnesses

2:44 p.m.

Zac:

She used 2 be ur friend

2:47 p.m.

Tori:

She slapped u. She's dangerous. It's the right thing 2 do. Meet us there

2:55 p.m.

Zac:

I provoked her

2:57 p.m.

Tori:

Listen 2 urself. U still luv her

2:59 p.m.

Zac:

. . .

3:00 p.m.

Tori:

U don't even deny it

3:15 p.m.

Zac:

What time r u meeting there?

# THIRTEEN

THEY COME FOR ME THE FOLLOWING DAY.

I'm writing an essay, using this week's assigned vocabulary words—determined by some anonymous teacher I will never meet. I turn at the sound of voices and spot Pollock instantly. I haven't seen him since the meeting in his office and my reaction is almost visceral. My body tenses and panic claws up my chest, closing my throat.

He's with Mr. Tucci and another man I've never seen before. Brockman rises, his expression alert, his eyes blinking awake. He's such a phony, pretending to look attentive when anyone can glance at his desk and count the dozen magazines and candy bar wrappers littered there.

I spin around, clutching the edge of my desk. My gaze lands on Gil. He's rotated in his chair and stares at me, eyes wide, unblinking, questioning. My heart skips a beat and I know somehow. This is because of me.

Or maybe I'm just paranoid. I haven't done anything. I glance around the room and catch Coco looking at me. She quickly turns away, goes back to working on her desk. Nathan sits up, his eyes worried. No doubt he's done any number of things that could have brought them here.

A quick read of the clock confirms that Sean won't be here for another forty-five minutes. For some reason, I wish he was here. Not that he could do anything.

I slide my gaze back to the men at the front of the Cage. Their voices rumble low and deep. Mr. Tucci talks to Brockman, but it's Pollock who holds all my attention. He moves in front of the Cage door, squares himself directly center with it, arms crossed, expression set, determined. A man on a mission. And I know. I'm the mission.

His small, dark eyes settle on me and he crooks a finger, motioning me forward.

Mr. Tucci avoids my eyes as he leads us to the front door of the building. Pollock walks to my left and the other man to my right, flanking me. Like they're afraid I might bolt.

"Where are we going?"

Pollock stares straight ahead, not replying.

My breath falls fast. I take several swallows and try to

slow my racing pulse.

Tucci doesn't step outside with us. I glance back at him through the glass doors, but he's already walking away.

"Does my mother—"

"We don't need to contact your parents." Pollock opens the passenger door of a white, nondescript van. "You're under the supervision of the Wainwright Agency."

I hesitate, staring at the dark blue interior. It's just another cage. Wire mesh separates the front of the van from the back. I inch away.

"Get in." The other man shoves me, and I stumble forward. My hands catch on the floorboard.

"Now, Webber." Pollock clicks his tongue. "I'm sure Ms. Hamilton isn't going to give us any trouble."

I look over my shoulder. Pollock cocks his head at me. "Are you?"

Webber rests a hand on his belt, and I'm sure he means to look imposing . . . threatening.

"No." I climb up inside and settle my backpack on my lap, hugging it close like a pillow. The door slides shut behind me with a reverberating slam. Pollock and Webber get in the front. They don't speak as we pull out of the parking lot. We're soon on the highway. It only takes me a few moments to realize we're not headed toward the Agency office. We're heading even farther away from the city. North toward Fredericksburg. The highway winds through hill country. We pass an occasional gas station and rest stop. A few houses dot the sloping, mesquite-covered hills, isolated and safe from the city.

"Where are we going?"

They exchange looks.

Pollock glances back through the wire. "We'll explain when we get there."

A sinking sensation starts in my stomach. I ease my hand inside my bag, searching for my phone. Pretty certain they're not going to approve of me using it, I peek inside and start to compose a message for my mother.

Pollock has me don't know where he is tak

"Hey! What are you doing?" Pollock's voice cuts through the silence. "Damn it! Pull over, Webber!"

The van jerks to the side of the road. I gasp and send the message, hoping it's enough.

Pollock hops out and yanks open the back door. He grabs my bag off my lap. The phone is still clutched in my fingers.

"Stupid," he mutters, ripping it from my hand. I don't bother resisting. He scans the message I just sent.

His body relaxes and he glances to Webber. "She just texted her mother. We're good."

Who else did he think I texted that might not have been *good*? I wish I knew. Wish I had their number.

"I want to call my parents," I say hotly. "I have rights! You can't just take me from school—"

"We can. We did." The vein in Pollock's forehead bulges. "When are you going to get it? You don't have rights. You're lucky you even get to walk the streets. You and every other carrier." He's panting, each word like a bullet fired. A semi roars past us, shaking the van. I dig my fingers into the upholstery. "As far as I'm concerned, you all should be wiped from the face of the earth."

I flinch. This is me he's talking about. My life. And this guy with hate glowing in his eyes is my caseworker. He decides my fate.

He slams the door and gets in the front again. Webber pulls off the side of the road, showering gravel into the air.

I blink burning eyes and stare out the window. *What will Mom think when she gets my message?* As the hill country rushes past, I start to wonder if I should have messaged my father. Mitchell. Anyone else. Mom clearly hasn't been able to stop any of this from happening to me so far. What could she do now?

As we drive along, I notice a trio of vultures circling high above a hilltop. They're tiny and black in the distance, but I stare at their fluttering and dipping shapes in the sky.

It dawns on me that no one can do anything. No one can help me. Just like Sean said.

I'm as alone and lost as whatever prey lies dead below those vultures.

The building is nondescript. Pale rock. Single story with an aluminum roof. The double doors gleam darkly with the letters PIF etched on the glass. There are more words beneath the abbreviation, but I don't have time to read them before Webber ushers me inside, one hand firmly gripping my arm.

"So I guess you're the muscle," I mutter. "You like roughing up girls? What about you? Have you been tested for HTS?" I don't know where the attitude comes from. Anger . . . *fear.*

He smiles. "You bet. And I'm clean."

I snort. "Yeah. That makes sense." He's clean. This guy with his hard hands that squeeze like a gorilla's fists.

A receptionist wearing floral scrubs smiles from behind a counter. "Ah. Mr. Pollock. We haven't seen you in a few weeks."

"Miss me, Brenda?"

"Always." She hands him a clipboard. "But no worry. We've been busy just the same."

"Good to hear." He quickly fills out the form, his pen scratching the surface. He hands her back the clipboard and then reaches inside his jacket, pulling out a small packet of papers.

Brenda's gaze finds me, widening a little as she takes the paperwork from him. "Oh. A girl. We don't see too many of them."

"Don't let her gender fool you into thinking she's not dangerous."

Brenda blinks. "Of course. We will take all the usual precautions." She quickly looks over the information on the clipboard and then moves on to the additional paperwork, skimming each page. "Okay. This looks in order." Rising, she motions to the door. "Follow me, please."

We follow her through the door and into a brightly lit hall, passing two doors before we reach another room. It reminds me of a dentist's office. There is a long, lounge-type chair with straps and buckles hanging from the sides. Behind it lie several pieces of unidentifiable equipment.

Instantly, I understand. And really, the suspicions have been there all along, nipping at the edge of my awareness, begging to be acknowledged.

A strange calm comes over me. "What did I do?"

Because I did something. Unwittingly. I must have for them to bring me here.

Pollock flips open a file and reads: "On Friday evening, March twenty-second, several witnesses signed statements alleging that you assaulted a young man."

I stare, unblinking, uncomprehending.

"Who did I assault?"

He glances down again. "A Zachary Clemens."

I suck in a breath. *Zac . . . my friends . . . They reported me?*

My gaze swings back to the straps and buckles dangling off the side of the lounger. The equipment suddenly looks especially menacing.

I whirl around and step as close to Brenda as possible with Webber still holding my arm. "Please, help me. I'm here against my will. I didn't hurt anyone! This is a mistake!"

"Shut up." Webber forces me toward the lounger. I dig in my heels, but he's too strong.

Brenda laughs. "Against my will," she echoes, shaking her head. "That's a good one."

"Please. Do I look dangerous to you?" I struggle wildly against Webber, trying to break loose as he presses me back onto the leather upholstery, his hands crushing my shoulders.

The leather squeaks beneath my wild movements. He grunts as he wiggles one hand free to buckle a restraint around my wrist. "Hold still. You're just going to make it harder on yourself. This is going to happen. Might as well stop fighting."

"Oh, honey," Brenda answers me, "you never can tell these days. My grandmother was assaulted a month ago by two boys that couldn't have been a day over ten." She clicks her tongue and nods with freakish cheerfulness at Pollock and Webber. "These men are doing God's work. This is a dangerous world we live in, and they're making it safer."

"So are you, Brenda, so are you," Pollock intones from where he sinks into a single chair. "We all do our part."

"Kind of you to say, Mr. Pollock." She smiles broadly as she moves to the door. "Richard will be with you in a moment. He's just finishing up in another room."

"Thank you." As the door clicks shut, Pollock slides his phone out of his pocket and begins studying it. Typing occasionally.

Webber finishes the second strap on my wrist and moves on to my ankle. Sean flashes across my mind. Did Webber restrain him like this? Or had Pollock brought more *helpers* for Sean? It's hard to imagine Webber alone overpowering Sean.

I kick with my leg, thrashing. Even though my wrists are pinned at my sides, I don't give up. At this point, getting one good kick at this gorilla would at least make me feel better.

He slams one ham-sized hand down over my knee, forcing

my leg flat so he can tighten the strap around my ankle. I cry out, arching off the lounger against the pain.

Pollock murmurs without looking up from his phone, "I'd advise you not to resist. You don't want him to break your leg."

"You can't do this . . . to me," I pant, my head falling back on the cushioned headrest.

He shakes his head. "Apparently, we can." He looks up from his phone, his expression annoyed. "Haven't you followed the news lately? The Wainwright Agency is about to go federal. We'll be in every state and not merely to identify and monitor. We're going to be bigger than the CIA. The police will be under us, following our command. Mark my words, there will be carrier prisons in every state."

I sag against my seat. "I haven't done anything," I grit between my teeth.

"No? You viciously assaulted a young man. I have eyewitness testimonies. I would say that behavior has all the markings of a carrier lacking control. I'm not going to have you walk into school with a gun one day. Not on my watch—"

"I wouldn't do that!"

"The Indianapolis Shooter had HTS. Looked as normal as can be. Played the cello, I believe."

The door opens and a man in blue scrubs steps inside. His arms are decorated in various tattoos. His neck, however, is unmarred, the skin tan and smooth, pristine. Bare of ink.

"Gentlemen," he greets with a nod. He gives me the barest glance before moving to the sink and quickly washing his hands, his movements brisk and efficient. Without looking at me, he comments, "I don't get too many females in here."

As though I'm not even human. Just a female. An animal before him.

"Trust me, she's a carrier."

He turns, wiping his hands with a paper towel. "Oh, I have no doubt. Just commenting on the rarity. She doesn't look very dangerous."

"I'm not! Please," I beg. "Don't do this."

He frowns, his reddish eyebrows pulling close as he finally looks at me.

"She attacked a boy. Unprovoked—"

I hold his gaze as I appeal to him. "No . . . it wasn't like that. . . ."

Pollock sighs and stands, slipping his phone back into his pocket. "Is this going to be a problem, Andersen? You're not the only outfit around. We can—"

"No problem," he quickly replies, snapping his gaze away from mine.

Pollock smiles and sits back down.

Andersen lowers onto a stool. I crane my neck, watching him as he soaks a piece of gauze with some kind of strong-smelling fluid . . . an antiseptic, I guess. I flinch as he wipes down my neck. If there was ever a doubt, it leaves me now. I know what's coming.

"Please," I whimper.

He lifts my head and wipes the back of my neck, fanning my hair out of the way.

"The less you resist, the less it will hurt," he instructs, not meeting my eyes as he maneuvers a white circular device over me. He cracks it open at a joint with a sharp snap and it comes at me like a great set of jaws. "Don't move."

And I don't. I'm frozen in fear. Shock. Both. I'm not sure. Emotions I've never felt before wash through me, take over everything, become everything. All that I am.

He locks it around my neck with a click. It's tight and uncomfortable and I immediately surge against it, gasping, claustrophobic, my airway constricted. Panic drowns me.

The collar bites into my windpipe and I gag. I'm pinned everywhere. Wrists, ankles, and now my throat. I can't move. Not without pain.

Andersen places a hand on my forehead and lowers his face until it's just inches from mine. He talks in a low, soothing voice. "Breathe. I know it's tight, but you can breathe just fine. See? There you go." His bright blue eyes lock on mine intently. Even though he's the one doing this to me, I stare into those eyes, sink into the blue, grab at the hint of kindness greedily.

"Good?" he asks.

*No! Not good . . .*

"I'm going to begin now and if you struggle there will only be more pain. Do you understand?"

I start to nod and then wince at the movement. Tiny pin-pricks of pain radiate all over my throat. The sensation is so severe that the discomfort spreads across my shoulders, down my chest, and up into my face.

A hot tear rolls down my cheek and into my hairline. "Please," I whisper. "Don't."

His hand smoothes my forehead. “Shh. I know you’re frightened, but this will go easier if you just calm down. Relax. Don’t fight it. Think of someplace else. . . .”

I take a moment and try to steady my heart rate with deep breaths through my nose. I take his suggestion and try to think of something else, search for the music that’s usually in my head, but I can only think about what’s happening to me.

Andersen flips a few switches and a low humming starts to drone on the air. He applies some goggles to his face and then slides a pair on me.

He fiddles with my collar, making sure it’s positioned to his liking. He brushes back a few errant strands of hair off my neck. “Now this will hurt. I’m not going to lie, but don’t move no matter what. You don’t want a smeared or smudged imprint.”

*I don’t want it at all.*

I’m not sure it matters whether it’s neat and tidy or smeared. Still, I hold stiffly and stare straight ahead, my gaze flying blindly over the tiles in the ceiling, blurring with tears.

“Easy now. Relax,” he continues to murmur.

There’s a faint clicking sound and then pain. Red-hot.

It slices into my neck and feels like someone is garroting me. For a moment, I think my head is being severed from my shoulders.

The low droning buzz grows louder, thicker. Like a drill. The instant injection of tiny, vibrating ink-filled needles arches my torso up from the chair.

A shrill movie scream spins through the air, and I realize

it's me. The sound is nearly as startling as the sudden pain. I never knew such a sound could exist inside me.

My body forgets his instructions to relax as the ink bleeds into me. Spasms ripple through me as currents of ink are injected from countless tiny needles deep into my flesh.

"Almost done," Andersen croons. "Just a few more moments."

His hand on my head bears me down, holds me still as the imprinting is happening, and I go from a girl who can walk the streets like a normal person to a monster recognized by all.

Agency Interview

**AGENT POLLOCK:** So you're saying she struck you, son?

**ZACHARY CLEMENS:** Yes, but she was angry. . . . I hurt her . . . said things—

**VICTORIA CHESTERFIELD:** She was totally out of control. I—I was afraid she was going to turn on me next. You should have seen the look in her eyes.

**AGENT POLLOCK:** And you, Zachary? Did you fear for your safety, too?

**ZACHARY CLEMENS:** I wouldn't say that—

**VICTORIA CHESTERFIELD:** Well, he's a guy. He's bigger. I was very afraid. I thought she was going to hit me, too. I'm still afraid of her and what she might do.

**ZACHARY CLEMENS:** Tori—

**VICTORIA CHESTERFIELD:** What, Zac? You want me to lie? You may not want to say how it really went down, but I can't pretend. You still want to protect her out of some misplaced sense of loyalty, but I'm trying to protect the world from her.

**AGENT POLLOCK:** Thank you for your concern, Victoria. I know coming forward can't be easy.

**VICTORIA CHESTERFIELD:** You have no idea. She was my best friend. It's like she died. She was here one moment and now she's gone. Only I wish she had died. At least others wouldn't be in danger then.

**AGENT POLLOCK:** We'll make sure that doesn't happen. Davina Hamilton won't hurt anyone else.

# FOURTEEN

I HARDLY REMEMBER AFTERWARD. IT'S ALL A BLUR. Movements and words I can't process.

The collar clicks free. Andersen rubs some kind of ointment on my neck and wraps it with clear plastic and then covers it with gauze. I lose sight of the ceiling as he helps me sit up and gives me two aspirin.

I don't want to sit up. I just want to sink back down with my eyes closed and never get up. Never open my eyes again.

I watch Andersen's lips move, catching only a word or two. A phrase. Enough to know that he's giving me aftercare instructions, but I just can't process. I just don't care.

Webber takes my arm and I'm moving, walking, my feet barely skimming the ground.

Soon I'm back in the van.

I don't bother with the buckle. I slouch to the side and lie on the seat, staring sightlessly at the back of the driver's side seat, my body limp, my limbs merely appendages that don't even feel like they belong to me . . . and I dimly wonder if that was aspirin he gave me or something else.

I lift a shaking hand to my throat, touching the soft gauze there. Tears well in my eyes, blurring everything around me, washing my world in water.

I sniff, refusing to cry. At least not until I'm alone in my room. No witnesses. I won't break down in front of Pollock. It's strange that I can still cling to pride now. Imprinting should have stripped me of that. I jam my eyes closed and hold them that way for a long while, not opening them again until we've stopped in front of my house.

We're not even to the front door before it opens and Mom charges out. "What happened?" She wraps an arm around me just as my knees give out. She struggles to keep me from falling.

Pollock hands Mom a piece of paper. "Aftercare instructions to avoid infection."

Mom glances from the paper to me, the whites of her eyes red as she gazes at my neck. "You had no right. . . . You'll be hearing from my attorney—"

Pollock angles his head sharply, looking up at my mother, who's got at least three inches on him. "Go ahead, Mrs. Hamilton. Waste your time and money. Get your fancy lawyers.

They'll tell you that we had every right under the Wainwright Act. Your 'angel' committed assault. The agency is well within its authority to have her imprinted."

"Mom," I croak, my throat muscles crying out at the effort. It hurts to even speak. "I want to go to my room." I look at her, compelling her to listen, to drop it, to take me away from these men. It doesn't really matter anymore. It's done.

Her wild eyes scan me, and I know she's trying to decide the best thing to do. As calm and accepting as she's been . . . *this* happening to me has pushed her over her limit.

If I wasn't so weary, so beaten, I'd lash out at her. Why is she angry now? What happened to the afternoon Pollock first showed up with the headmaster? Why didn't she get angry then and do something? Take me away, run off with me to some remote cabin in the mountains where I would have been safe from the world?

Now it's too late for me.

Mom must read some of this on my face. My knees wobble and she tightens her arm around my waist. "C'mon. Let's get you inside."

We're on the porch when Pollock calls back, "She can stay home tomorrow, but I'll expect her back in school the day after. And I expect no more incidents from her in the future."

Mom stiffens beside me. I hear her inhale and she starts to turn. I know she's about to respond.

"Don't," I hiss, understanding how this game needs to be played. Maybe I didn't understand before, but I do now. Fighting back—*openly* fighting back—isn't the way.

I urge Mom ahead into the house. When the door shuts behind us, I want to weep with relief. I feel safe inside these walls. Finally able to drop my guard. However false the perception, my body turns to lead, almost taking Mom and me both down.

She cries out my name, wrapping her arms around me and heaving me up. "Davy! Davy!" A feat. She doesn't weigh much more than me.

She manages to slow my descent. The floor rises up to meet me, the tile cool and slick under my cheek. I sigh and press my palms to the tiles, welcoming the chill into my body. My neck burns like fire.

Mom's voice is frantic above me.

"Just want to lie here . . . for a bit. . . ."

She tugs at my arm. "Let's get you into bed."

"Mom! What's wrong?" I turn my face at the sound of Mitchell's voice. He clears the foyer and hurries toward us. "Davy? What happened?" His fingers gently brush the gauze covering my neck.

"Mitchell," I breathe, a slow smile curving my lips. "How are you?"

"Is she high?"

"They must have given her something. Let's get her to her room."

Mitchell picks me up and carries me up the stairs and into my room. Mom pulls back the covers. He sets me down and stares at me, his gaze riveted to my neck as Mom slips off my shoes.

"They imprinted her," he spits the words out. Not a question. A statement. His hands open and shut at his sides like he wants to punch something.

Mom nods, not saying a word.

"Why?"

"I don't know. . . ."

I find my voice. "I slapped Zac . . . at a party. . . ."

"You slapped Zac?" Mom sounds appalled.

"He was being . . . jerk." I giggle at this.

"This is because of Zac?" Mitchell growls. "I'm going to kill him."

Now I laugh harder. "That would be funny. You ending up . . . killer . . ."

"Mom . . . how could you let them do this?" There are tears in his eyes, and this sobers me. I can't remember my brother crying. Nothing ever gets to him. Not the fighting with our parents, not getting in trouble at school—not getting kicked out of school. Not flunking out of college and moving into the guesthouse.

It's not that he was indifferent to all that happening. I know he cared. I know he hated being the "disappointment." But he never cried. Not like now. Not like he's crying for me.

"I didn't have a choice. They just took her. I didn't know until it was done."

"You should have stopped them!" He whirls from my bed and faces Mom. "They can't do this to our Dav!"

"I know!" she explodes, waving her arms through the air at her sides. "But she's not our Davy anymore!"

This hangs on the air.

Mitchell doesn't react, and I'm past reacting. I stare at his back. He's rigid, his spine ramrod-straight—gone is the chronic slouch that is so very him.

Right now, I just want to pull a pillow over my head and hide in my room forever. Even though I can't. The Agency won't let me. And I have to finish high school. Not just for them but for me.

And yet there's some comfort in this bed I've slept in all my life, my head resting on my familiar pillow with my stuffed duck staring at me. Dot is faded to a dull yellow now, the polka dots beneath its wings no longer identifiable.

I blink burning eyes. The days of my youth when this duck had been bright and shiny—when *I* had been bright and shiny—are like a dream. A dream growing dimmer and dimmer with each day. The bed sucks me in deeper and I never want to leave it.

A door slams downstairs.

"Caitlyn!"

Mom inhales at the sound of her name and squares her shoulders like she's bracing for battle. "Up here, in Davy's room!"

Footsteps pound the stairs. Then Dad's in the doorway, panting like he's run a mile. His hair is wild around his head, like he dragged his hands through the strands. The tie around his neck droops, mangled and twisted, the knot loosened around mid-chest. His suit jacket is missing.

"I came as soon as I got your message. What happened—"

His voice dies the instant he sees me.

My eyes well with tears as his gaze lands on me . . . on my neck.

All the life, the last of his energy, bleeds out from him in that one look. Suddenly, he appears smaller, shrunken. A shell of my dad. Empty and dead-eyed.

Just like Mom said: I'm not *their* Davy anymore.

I'm something else. Not a daughter they can guide through life. They have no control over what happens to me. The Wainwright Agency decides my fate.

I'm relieved when Mom and Dad leave. Mitchell lingers, sinking down beside me on the bed. He touches my back and I flinch.

"Please. Just go."

I hear his breath, ragged and sharp beside me, and I can't even summon enough emotion to care that I might have hurt his feelings with my dismissal. The bed lifts back up as he stands.

The door clicks shut after him and I curl into the tightest ball possible, dragging Dot against my chest. Closing my eyes, I stop resisting the fog rolling into my mind. Latching onto a random tune, I wrap myself in it and slide into sleep, where I don't have to think about anything anymore.

The first time I wake, Mom's there, trying to force soup on me. Like I have a cold or the flu. Like it's just a sick day and I'm home from school.

She holds the spoon to me like I'm a baby—or an invalid—in need of feeding. I motion it away with a moan.

"C'mon. You have to eat, Davy."

"Not hungry," I mumble, and roll onto my side, facing the window, my head pounding. After a while, I feel her weight lift from the bed.

"I'll just leave the soup here."

I don't bother telling her to take it. I don't want to eat. I just want to sleep and wake up in the morning like none of this ever happened. Like everything has been a bad dream and I'm the girl I used to be.

The following morning, Mitchell wakes me, shaking my shoulder gently. "C'mon, Davy. We need to remove your gauze."

My eyes fly open with a gasp. The burning throb in my neck instantly reminds me of everything that's happened. His fingers brush the edge of the gauze and I give a little yelp and shoot up, pressing as far back as I can into the headboard.

Mitchell holds his hands up wide in the air like I'm pointing a gun at him. "Hey, Mom showed me the aftercare instruction paper. We should have removed it already. You don't want to get an infection. We need to clean it." He holds out his palm. A fat white pill sits there. "And I brought you one of Mom's pain pills left over from her knee surgery."

I shake my head and clasp both hands around my neck. "I—I . . . No. Don't touch me." I don't want anyone to touch me.

"Davy—"

"I don't want to see it."

He dips his head as though understanding that. "Okay. You don't have to look at it. Let me take care of it then."

"No. You don't understand. I don't want anyone to see it. Especially you."

He blinks. "Why not me?"

I punch the mattress beside me. "Because you're my brother. I don't want you to see this thing on me!" I motion furiously to my neck.

"Davy, it's not going to change how I see you."

"It changes everything!" I hear my words, recognize how shrill my voice sounds, but I don't care. "Out!" I point to the door.

Mitchell's lips compress, making him resemble Dad a lot, but he doesn't say anything else. He just rises and turns for the door. I watch him walk away, my heart in my throat, my fingers still clasped around my neck, like he might turn back and try to pry my hands away and see the imprint for himself.

Once the door clicks shut, I slide back down on the bed, my fingers loosely clinging to my throat, still holding my neck as if I can somehow hide what's there. Cover it up so that no one can ever see it. Even me.

Article 13B of the Wainwright Act:

Imprinting falls under the purview of the State. No civilians or local police agencies may impede a representative operating at the behest of the Wainwright Agency. . . .

# FIFTEEN

I DOZE IN AND OUT ALL DAY. THE GAUZE AT MY NECK begins to itch and chafe terribly. It stings with a heat that seems to come from beneath the skin, but I still can't bring myself to remove it. The fear of infection serves as no motivator.

I just can't look at it. And neither can anyone else.

I stare at the fan blades whirring above me. The spinning slats hypnotize me, matching the rhythm of the song humming softly from my mouth. Lyrics escape my chapped lips, practically soundless on the air. Even with the pulsing warmth in my neck, I'm cold. Goose bumps break out over my arms, but I can't will myself to move. Even to cover up. The blanket I kicked off in my sleep is wadded up at the foot of the bed. I shiver, letting the song in my head and the whirring fan lull me.

A knock sounds at my door.

I don't say anything, waiting for them to go away. Mom checked on me when she got home an hour ago. Like Mitchell, she tried to talk me into removing the bandage. She finally left when it became clear I wasn't in a talking mood. Nor was I inclined to remove the gauze from my throat.

Idly, I wonder if I'll ever be in a talking mood again. The prospect of staying here in this bed forever seems alluring.

My head falls to the side, and my gaze sharpens on the photo on my nightstand. It's a close-up of me and Zac. My fair hair is swept up off my shoulders. The sweetheart neckline of my pink homecoming dress is just barely visible. I thought I had looked so sophisticated that night. I never felt like I was particularly pretty. My eyebrows are a little too thick, my chin a little too sharp, my eyes too big. Like some kind of elf creature. But Zac had called me beautiful. And the way his eyes widened when he first saw me, I believed him. In the photo, Zac's hand covers my shoulder so completely, almost possessively, like he feared I might slip away if he didn't hold me. Obviously, he doesn't feel that way anymore. I guess I can understand his ability to let go of me now. But not the betrayal. My hand drifts to the bandage. Not this.

Staring at our photograph, I remember the way his hand felt on me, the sensation of it on my shoulder . . . everywhere, really. Like he couldn't keep himself from touching me. An ache starts at the center of my chest and I curl myself tighter. Reaching out, I put the photograph facedown.

The knock comes again.

"Go away!"

"Davy, you have a . . . guest."

For a moment, hope zings through me that it's one of my old friends. Then reality sinks in. No one wants to see me. And there's no one I want to see. No one who can take this away . . . who can make me feel better, whole again.

"I don't want to see anyone," I call out.

Mom's voice is coaxing through the door. "Davy . . . please . . ."

Guilt seeps inside me at what this is doing to her. What *I* have done. But then the emptiness in my heart finds that, too. Kills it so I'm numb again.

"No," I say loudly, sharply, in a tone I never use with my mother. I've never needed to. I was the respectful daughter who made all the right choices, and only good things ever happened to me.

Her footsteps fade away and I fix my gaze on the fan again, letting the whirring blades mesmerize me.

I start at another knock on my door. It's different. Solid. Two raps in swift succession. I scowl and glance from the fan to my bedroom door before looking back at the fan again, intent on ignoring the person on the other side.

"Go away!"

I glimpse the swing of the door peripherally, from the corner of my eye. Annoyance flares in me that someone ignored me and invaded my solitude. Irate words burn on my tongue.

And then I turn and my annoyance pivots into a combination of shame and bewilderment.

Sean's gaze arrows directly on me. He doesn't give the rest of the room even a cursory glance. He stares only at me.

"What are *you* doing here?" I watch him warily.

"I heard that they came for you yesterday."

"Yeah. So?" I sit up and swing my legs over the side of my bed, feeling less vulnerable that way. The sudden movement makes me dizzy and I close my eyes for a long moment, breathing through my nose. Dipping my head, I wait for the dizziness to pass. My hair falls forward, the blonde strands covering much of the white gauze wrapped around my neck, but not all. Not enough. It will never be enough.

"I thought I would check on you."

I open my eyes and glare at him. "Doesn't that go against your philosophy? Never get involved. . . . Be strong and tough and all that . . . an island unto himself."

He crosses his arms but otherwise gives my taunt no reaction.

I notice Mom then. She hovers behind Sean, looking wide-eyed and uncertain, her hands locked together in a death grip, her knuckles white. Her mouth parts and I know she's on the verge of asking if it's okay for this boy to be here—an imprinted carrier. My lips curl in a smirk. A little late for that. She already let him up. I guess that just indicates how at a loss she is . . . how desperate.

Of course, I could tell her it's *not* okay. That he's just as dangerous as the imprint on his neck declares. My gaze fixes on the wide band around his neck, seeing it in a new light. Now, more than ever, I want to know what he did to deserve it . . . if he did anything at all.

"It's fine, Mom," I say before she can find her voice. Rising, I stride across the room. Sending her a reassuring nod, I close the door, giving me privacy with Sean. Normally, my parents don't let me close the door with a boy in my room. But nothing is normal anymore.

I move back a few steps into the room, still a careful distance from him, waiting for him to say something.

"You need to remove that gauze."

I wait a beat and cross my arms over my chest, mirroring him. "So I've been told. You didn't need to come here to tell me that."

"So, what? You just don't care? You want to get an infection?" He shakes his head almost like he's disgusted with me. And that irks.

He moves into my adjoining bathroom. I watch his back as he stands at the sink and turns the water to warm. A bottle of antiseptic still sits on the counter where Mom left it, along with some little nail scissors.

He pulls out the bench in front of my vanity chair and motions me into the bathroom.

I don't move.

He sighs, sounding tired. "Get in here."

"What?" I snap. "Are we friends because we're alike now? Is that it?"

His gaze meets mine in the mirror. "First of all, just 'cause we share the same tattoo hardly makes us alike. I still have an identity. So do you. There are plenty of imprinted carriers out there. Don't mistake us as all the same. Some of them, probably most of them, are just as dangerous as the Agency says."

*And what is he? Is he truly dangerous?*

"And secondly . . ." His voice fades and I wait, expecting him to add that we *are* friends now. With a start, I realize I want to hear him say that. I want a friend. I need a friend. Now more than ever.

"And secondly?" I prompt, feeling stupidly hopeful.

"Secondly, stop asking so many questions . . . hurry up and get over here. I'm already late for work."

I drop my arms to my sides and move, lifting one leg after another. Grudgingly, I sink onto the cushioned bench and stare at myself in the mirror, seeing what he sees.

My hair is a mess, the light strands lank and tangled—in need of a good wash. The gauze around my neck is no longer a pristine white. Rusty streaks stain the bandage. I would never have been caught dead looking like this before. *Before.* "Before" doesn't exist anymore.

Before, I looked like someone who had it all together. In control. I inhale. I couldn't be that girl anymore, but I could take back some of that control. I could stop simply allowing everything to happen to me.

It's time I decide what happens next.

Gazing at Sean's profile, I get the impression, wrong or right, that nothing *happens* to him without his consent. Even with the imprint on his neck, he's somehow in control.

I inhale a deep breath and face myself, confront the me in the mirror that I've been avoiding for the last twenty-four hours. I nod at him.

He squats next to me, examining my neck. His voice cuts through me so no-nonsense that I blink. "It's not the end of the world."

"How come you haven't run away?" I hear myself ask, my voice small and faraway sounding.

I tremble as Sean slides the hair back off my shoulder, clearing it away from my neck. He shrugs as he concentrates on me. "Thought about it. But it's not like I can run to anything better. We're in the national registry. We can't get into a college or get a decent job. They screen for everything. You can't hide from this. Why? You thinking of running?"

I shrug. Maybe. After today, running away has its temptations.

He glances around my room again. "You won't find anything better out there than what you have here. Off the grid . . . or in the cities." He shakes his head. "That's a brutal existence."

His touch is gentle, at great odds with his words and tone of voice. He peels back the edge of the gauze, flicking enough material away from my neck so that he can snip at it with the scissors.

I hiss as he peels it back.

He pauses. "Sorry. It's sticking."

And he doesn't say it, but I hear the mild accusation in his voice. I know it's my fault. Because I left the wrapping on too long.

"Just rip it off." I clench my fingers around the bench as I say this.

He gives me a look. His lips twitch and he breaks into an almost smile. The closest I've seen from him, and my stomach does an odd little tremble. "It's not like a Band-Aid, tough guy. I need to ease it off, okay?"

"Oh," I murmur, and steel myself for the slow tug and pull of the gauze on my raw skin.

"There," he announces, dropping the soiled fabric on my counter. "Now I'll just clean it up for you."

I stare at myself in the mirror—at my neck. There's a lot more ink than I expected even though I've seen it before. On others. On Sean. It's one thing to know, and another thing to *know*. To see it on yourself.

I know what an imprint looks like, but the band looks so thick, the H so large and stark against my neck. Tiny flecks of crusted blood mar the tattoo. The skin around the collar of black is an angry red.

"It looks bigger than yours." Turning my neck from side to side, I scrutinize it almost clinically. It's hard to connect the girl in the mirror with an imprint around her neck as me. It's like I'm watching someone on television. Or looking at someone else from a distance, across the street. A stranger with greasy hair and wild eyes. An inked collar with an obscene circled H stamped on her neck.

"Your neck is just smaller. It's the same as mine."

"That makes sense." I nod once and marvel that I can talk so calmly—appear so normal about this.

"Let me clean it up." He wets a washcloth and gently wipes at the tender flesh. I wince but don't utter a complaint. "You'll get used to it."

"Will I?" I say this curiously. In a voice that doesn't even sound like me. And maybe it's not me. Maybe the real Davina Hamilton is dead, left back there in that room. Replaced by the girl in the mirror. A shadow of myself. A new creature without lip gloss or tidy, brushed hair . . . with an ugly tattoo on her neck.

He flicks me a glance as he wraps a hand around my hair and lifts it from my neck to dab at my nape. "You can't let this define you . . . beat you." Dropping my hair, he trickles antiseptic onto a fresh washcloth. My gaze catches on his bicep, on the tattoo there, the one he wanted to have. I watch as it moves over his skin with his actions, the pattern crawling and alive. Then I watch his face again. He studies my neck intently, eyebrows drawing close over his deeply set eyes. Leaning in, he lightly presses the cloth against my neck, not even glancing at me as he treats the skin.

*Don't let it define me?*

Isn't that the purpose of it? The point? To define me for everyone who crosses my path?

"You need to keep going," he continues, saying more than he's ever said before. For once, I'm the quiet one, and he's the one with all the words. "Go to school . . . do whatever else it is you do."

"I don't have anything else," I say through numb lips. No friends to hang out with. No job. All my extracurricular activities at school . . . voice, orchestra, student council . . . that's gone. Ripped from me like everything else. "Just school. The Cage." I laugh bitterly. "My friends . . . my boyfriend. They're the ones who did this to me. So. Yeah. My social calendar is pretty open."

"What do you mean?" His eyes lock on my face.

I lift one shoulder in an awkward shrug and then wince at the sudden sting in my neck. "I had a fight with my boyfriend. . . . *Ex*," I amend.

"How are he and your other friends responsible for this?"

"I mentioned the fight with my boyfriend, yes? Well, I slapped him. There were plenty of witnesses. Pollock knew all about it. That's why he came for me. I'm obviously violent," I mock, air quoting the word with my fingers.

"Why did you slap him?"

I stare at him for a moment. "You're the first person to even ask me that." *To even care why.*

"Why?"

I sigh and look away. "He was being a jerk."

He places a single finger under my chin and forces me to look at him again. "Why?" he repeats evenly.

A single word, but it hangs between us, demanding the truth. Painful as the memory is, the words tumble heavy and hard from my lips, like marbles falling to the ground. "Since I turned out to be a carrier, he thought I should fall gratefully into bed with him."

Sean says nothing as we stare at each other. The sensation of his fingertip on my chin makes me hyperalert of him, of our nearness. "I guess you probably think I'm silly to get offended over something like that."

"No. I don't." He drops his finger and returns his attention to my neck. "Well, don't even think about not showing up tomorrow. They'll be watching for that. They'll give you a break for one day, but they'll come down hard on you if you don't turn up tomorrow."

Part of me wants to know what coming down *hard* means exactly. After getting imprinted, what's left? What's worse? Unlike a few other states, Texas hasn't started implementing internment camps, virtual prisons from all reports.

I watch him in the mirror as he tends to my neck with efficient movements. Still, there's a warmth to his touch. A gentleness I did not expect. "Did you have someone do this for you? Look after you when you were imprinted . . . ?"

"No. I did it myself . . . with a bunch of my foster brothers giving me a hard time through the bathroom door."

"They made fun of you?" I frown. "That's . . . not nice."

He shrugs. "Just bringing some levity to it, I guess. Two of them were already imprinted. I was the third. I'm sure it's just a matter of time before the other two are."

"You're *all* carriers?"

"Martha—" His gaze flicks to mine. "That's my foster mother. She gets paid more for fostering kids who are carriers. And she's not afraid of us. Her brother's a carrier. He's in prison."

"I see."

"No. You don't." He shrugs like that's no big deal. "You can't even wrap your head around any of it." He glances at my bedroom. "How could you when you come from this?"

And he's right. Naturally. Even though I'm a carrier—an imprinted one at that—nothing about his life makes sense to me. For starters, I can't see how anyone would open her home to multiple imprinted carriers.

I moisten my lips. "Isn't your foster mother frightened of letting you all into her house? I mean even with her brother . . . anyone would be."

"True. Martha isn't anyone though. She doesn't scare easily. Besides, since she took us in, no one has broken into her house. She says we're the best security system around." There's that hint of a smile again.

He sets the washcloth down and stares at me. The proximity, our closeness, makes me nervous, but I don't move.

"Why did you come here?" I finally ask. "Why are you doing any of this for me?"

He doesn't answer for a while, just looks at me in that intense way, like I'm a bug under a microscope. "Because I know this is hard for you. Harder than it ever was for me."

I frown. I don't like thinking of myself as worse off than *him*—if that's what he even means. It makes me feel all the more alone.

"How so?"

"You have more to lose than me." He shrugs one shoulder. "I was a kid when I learned I was a carrier. I was already parentless. Poor. No future. Hard to hit bottom when you're already there." His mouth flattens into a grim line. "I was used to being nothing."

A *nothing* who showed up here today when I needed someone the most.

A *nothing* who marched into the bathroom after me when Brockman cornered me.

A *nothing* who picked me up when I was stranded and out past curfew.

A myriad of responses rush to my lips. "You're not nothing." *You're here.*

For a reason I still don't understand, he came when no one else did. Discounting my own family, and they kind of have to be there for me when I live in the same house as them. He's the only one who went out of his way to see me. Not only are my friends not here . . . they are the ones who made sure I got imprinted.

He turns away and gathers up the scraps of gauze. "I didn't say that for your pity."

"I'm not saying it because I pity you—"

He snorts and rises to his feet. "No? Ever since we first met, you've looked at me with either fear or pity."

"Okay. Maybe that's true." I speak hurriedly as he heads for the door, aware that he's about to leave and I'm going to be alone again, and suddenly I don't want to be alone. "But you're not *nothing*. If you're saying you're nothing, then . . . what does that make me?"

He stops. I stare at his back. I hold my breath, waiting for him to keep on walking right out of my room. To leave me without fully explaining why he came here in the first place.

Then he turns. With just a few strides, he's in front of me. My heart thumps hard and fast as he reaches for my face, cups it with one hand. And then he answers me with one word. Just a breath. A whisper.

My heart seizes in my chest.

I lean forward, savoring against my better judgment the sensation of his hand on my face.

Dropping his arm, he turns and leaves my room. Only the echo of his voice stays behind, lingers on the air, in my head.

*Perfect.*

---

To Ms. Davina Hamilton:

We have been alerted of your recent HTS status and must, unfortunately, revoke our offer of admission. As you know, entrance into Juilliard is extremely competitive. Every year the most talented, most promising students vie for a place at the School, and it is the Office of Admissions' responsibility to see that only the most deserving gain entry. Clearly, you no longer possess the necessary qualifications to be included among those ranks. . . .

*—Letter from the admissions office of Juilliard*

# SIXTEEN

I DRAG MYSELF DOWNSTAIRS THE FOLLOWING morning. Dad's not there but Mom is, sipping from her oversized coffee mug, looking once again her usual put-together self in a pantsuit. Pearl drops dangle from her ears. She hardly looks the mother of someone like me. This strikes me almost at once. How easy it's become for me to alter my perception of myself. It makes me wonder if I ever really knew me.

I dressed in jeans and a dark T-shirt that Mitchell outgrew—some band I never heard of emblazoned across the front. I finally washed my hair. Still wet, it looks dark brown in the twin braids that hang low across my shoulders.

My imprint is there for the world to see. I don't try to hide it with my hair or a high collar. When I got ready for school this morning, I kept thinking of Sean. How proud he appears. Unapologetic. And I want to be like that. I don't want to look cowed or ashamed. I may not want to be *this*, but I don't want to be *that* girl, either. I don't want to be afraid.

"You're going to school?"

"Yeah. I kind of have to."

Mom nods. "Yes. Of course. I'm glad to see you up and moving around." She fixes her gaze on my face, her eyes strangely wide and unblinking. Like it's taking everything inside her not to look down. Not to gawk at my neck. At what I've become.

She sets down her coffee cup and picks up some papers from the table. Sliding them into her brief bag, she murmurs casually, "You sure you want to wear your hair like that?"

"What's wrong with my hair?"

She shrugs. "It's just a little . . . young for you."

This almost makes me laugh. She doesn't care how young it makes me look. She cares about how much it exposes my neck. "I can't hide it from the world. Figure I better get it over with and let everyone see it today."

Her cheeks pink up and I know it's because I saw through her words. She opens her mouth as if to deny this, but then presses her lips shut. Instead, she nods. Picking up her bag with one hand and her coffee with the other, she nods at the door. "You ready now? Your car is still at school. I can give you a lift."

"Sure." Grabbing my backpack, I follow her out.

We're a little early arriving to school. There are still a lot of kids mingling in the parking lot, gradually making their way to the double front doors. She pulls up to the curb, and I hesitate in my seat.

Mom waits a moment, glancing at the clock on her dash. "Sorry," she finally murmurs. "I have a meeting."

"Just take me to my car. I'll wait inside until the bell rings," I snap, clearly annoyed. She knows the rules. I'm not supposed to arrive until twenty minutes after the first bell. What does she expect me to do?

Mom doesn't comment, which only aggravates me further. I don't say good-bye, just open the door and start to climb out, pausing when she calls out, "I won't be home for dinner. You can order pizza."

"All right." With a grunt, I slam the door shut and punch the UNLOCK button to my car. I'm already sliding behind the wheel as she drives off.

No one really notices me, sitting alone in my car, watching the swarm of students. I start the car and listen to the radio. One guy races across the parking lot, his letterman jacket a blur as he grabs a cheerleader off her feet. He twirls her, sending her little yellow-and-blue-pleated skirt flying around her tan legs. She swats his back, laughing, loving the attention.

Several of her friends look on enviously. I stare with a hollowness in my heart. I used to be that girl with the envious friends, the coveted boyfriend, a bright future. It had all been an illusion. None of it real. Just as I hadn't been real. If my life had been *real*, if it amounted to anything, it would have survived a DNA test that declared me potentially dangerous. I'd still have that boyfriend, those friends, the life that was going somewhere. I have to make my own way now, figure out a new future.

The students thin out. I tap my fingers against the steering wheel and keep an eye on the clock. When it's finally time, I turn off the car and get out. Coco and I enter the building almost simultaneously. She forgoes her usual pattern of ignoring me and stares openly.

When I meet her gaze, she gives me a slight nod and falls into step beside me. "It's a good look on you."

Unbelievable as it seems, I smile.

I realize I forgot to pack a lunch when Brockman announces that everyone can eat. I continue working on my assignment, not lifting my head. Not even when I hear the metallic clang of the door.

"Did you hear me, Hamilton?" He nudges my shoulder, and I pull away sharply in the opposite direction. He never touches me when Sean's around. I wince at the realization, wishing there's something I could do to earn the same results. Sean can't be around all the time. "Time for lunch. I'm not going to let you eat later. This is your one chance. Don't think that mark on your neck changes anything. It doesn't impress me—"

"I don't have a lunch," I interject, hoping to end his diatribe. Did he really think I thought this mark on my neck would earn me *better* treatment?

He grunts and mutters something. I can't understand him. I'm just glad when he walks away.

A few moments pass and Gil slides into the desk in front of me. Facing me, he hands me half a peanut butter and jelly sandwich.

I look from the half sandwich to his earnest face, hesitating before saying, "I'm not hungry."

"Yes, you are. Take it."

"I don't need your pity. I'm not starving. I just forgot to pack my lunch today."

"It's not pity. It's food. Take it."

Feeling a little silly for being so unfriendly to one of the only nice people I've met since this all started, I take the sandwich and bite into it. Instantly, the sweetness of the jelly floods my taste buds, and the peanut butter sticks to the roof of my mouth.

"I don't think I've eaten peanut butter since I was ten," I get out around a gooey mouthful.

He pats his almost concave stomach. "Lines your belly."

I point. "What belly?

"Oh, this belly can put away more food than you probably eat in a month. It's an endless pit."

"And that's just tragically unfair."

He starts digging around in his brown paper sack. "I've got cheese puffs in here, pickles, fruit snacks, a couple of Snickers, and three pudding cups."

I gawk at the load he starts spreading out on my desk.

He motions before him. "Help yourself."

After a moment, I pick up one of the fruit snacks and tear the wrapper. "Your parents must have one hell of a grocery bill."

"It's just my mom. And she's actually the manager at the convenience store where I work."

"I didn't realize she works there."

He leans in conspiratorially. "Don't tell anyone, but she sneaks me the candy bars." He points to his drink. "Sometimes she even scores Gatorade."

I nod with mock seriousness. "Perks of the trade."

"Precisely."

He sobers. "Soon, I'll be able to reap the benefits, too. She's almost convinced the owner to promote me from stock boy to cashier when I graduate."

He looks genuinely pleased. I bend the corner of the spiral notebook on my desk, looking at him quizzically. "Is that what you want to do when you get out of here?"

He gives me a funny look. "C'mon, Davy. You know it has nothing to do with what any of us want. Did you want *that* on your neck?"

I resist the urge to touch my neck, as if I can feel the thing he sees, like a serpent wrapping around my throat. It's easy to forget it's there during the course of the day. Until someone reminds you.

"You're going to have to think beyond this room and what comes after. There are limitations."

*What comes after . . .*

I nod slowly. Of course, he's right. I need to start planning.

Before, my whole life had a plan. Ever since I was three I knew my destiny. And now that plan is dead, gone. If Gil is to be believed, I can't aspire to any type of high-level position. A bitter taste fills my mouth. Maybe I can live at home forever. Or in the pool house when Mitchell finally gets his act together and moves out. The very possibility makes me feel slightly ill. It's so far from the dreams I had for myself.

The door clangs. Sean steps inside. I don't look away. Not like before. Not anymore. After yesterday, I don't need to look away anymore. If not friends exactly, we're at least friendly. This conviction grows as I meet his gaze head-on.

"Hey, Sean." Gil gives a small wave.

I stare, smile a little. As much as I can manage. "Hello." It's the first time I've even greeted him.

He stares back, his pale eyes missing nothing. Not the hair scraped neatly back from my face. He sees all of me. He hesitates, not taking his usual seat. I feel Gil watching us. Finally, Sean moves forward and takes the seat behind me.

I turn so that my legs stick out in the aisle. This way I can see both boys.

"Hey," he greets. To both of us, I guess, but he's looking at me.

Gil's voice pipes up from my right. "So, you two are friends now?"

I feel my face heat.

"Makes sense, of course," he adds, motioning to both our necks with a flick of his hand. "You've got matching ink and all."

I could strangle him. My mouth works, at a loss for words, and I'm sure I look like a fish.

Sean laughs low. "Yeah. 'Cause we picked them out and everything, Gil. Like matching T-shirts. Next, it will be wedding bands." He's obviously joking, but that doesn't stop the heat from spreading to my ears.

"Well, you know." Gil shrugs. "You have something in common now."

"Yeah," I murmur, meeting Sean's eyes. "I guess we do."

---

**Group MMS**

To: Mika, Billy, Miguel
From: Kevin

Kevin:
2:30! Don't b late! We gotta do this right

Mika:
Which mall again?

Kevin:
Srsly? Northchase!
And ur not doing mall
ur going 2 stadium
I'm picking u up at 1:30, remember?

Mika:
Y—got it

Miguel:
We've only gone over 100x!

Mika:
K—gonna roc!!

Billy:

Glad ur babysitting, dumbass. U know how 2 shoot, right?

Mika:

Screw u!

Kevin:

Cut the crap—stay focused

treat us like animals

we'll show them animals

Mika:

Hear that!

Miguel:

Payback a bitch!

Mika:

Can't wait! Gonna blow some shiz up!

# SEVENTEEN

MR. TUCCI APPEARS MID-AFTERNOON WITH TWO uniformed campus security officers. I'm slammed with the same sick feeling I got the last time he showed up, but this time there is no Pollock. That makes me breathe a bit easier.

Gil leans sideways in his desk and hisses, "What did you do?"

I'm not sure who he's whispering to—Sean or me. My pulse jackknifes against my throat as I strain to listen to whatever Tucci whispers at the front of the Cage. It feels like forever before he enters and addresses the group. Everyone swings around in their seats.

"All right, everyone. Listen up. We have a bit of a situation." He waves his hands in the air like he's mollifying an unruly mob. "We're dismissing you all early today. Gather up your things. Security is here to escort you to the doors."

Nathan and Brian whoop loudly.

Tucci sends them a stern look and waits a moment before continuing. "You'll all learn soon enough. There's been an incident." He clears his throat. "A terrible tragedy."

"What happened?" This from Gil.

Tension tightens across my shoulders as we all wait for Tucci to answer. He looks to the side, blinking rapidly with obvious emotion, and I know it's going to be bad. When he does finally speak it feels like all the air is sucked out of the room.

"A mass shooting. At a mall and stadium in Houston."

A hush falls over the room. No one says anything, but we all look at one another. And I know we're all thinking the same thing, wondering why we have to leave school early. Escorted by security guards.

Tucci sighs. "The body count is high. Over fifty so far. They have multiple suspects in custody. They're carriers. All of them. It's been confirmed. It's all over the news."

And it all clicks together. The bottom drops out of my world. This is bad. Very bad. For all of us.

Tucci continues, "We need to hurry. It's twenty minutes until the next bell." And, presumably, news of the catastrophe has infiltrated the student population. There's no way news this big isn't on everyone's radar.

For a long moment, no one moves as this sinks in, and then there's a sudden flurry of activity. I fly into action, grabbing my backpack.

"Do we have to show up to school tomorrow?" Nathan asks as we file out from the Cage.

Tucci looks over his shoulder as he strolls ahead of us down the hallway. "I need to consult with the Agency. I'm unsure what protocol is in place. Your caseworkers will be in touch with each of you."

*No school tomorrow? What about next week? Will we still graduate? Does that even matter anymore?*

Nathan leads the pack, his strides hurried, eager to exit campus. Sean walks ahead of me. I watch his back, studying the play of his shoulder blades beneath the cotton of his T-shirt . . . wondering if he's as knotted up with tension as I am. Has *this* affected him? Does anything?

Tucci leads the way with one security guard at the back of our little group and another flanking us. The guard keeps pace to my left. Several times he sends sidelong glances at me, eyeing my neck, one of his hands drifting to the baton attached to his belt. He's probably worried that I'll go berserk like one of the carriers who just massacred innocent people in Houston.

"Pick up the pace," Coco mutters, passing me. The rear guard moves up, stepping beside me on my right. Unlike his colleague, he doesn't seem that interested in me or my ink.

We're almost to the front of the building. The front office looms ahead. The afternoon sun winks off the glass of the main double doors.

Suddenly, pain bursts in the back of my skull and I'm falling. My hands barely have time to rise up and break my descent.

"Carrier scum!"

There's a commotion. Voices. Loud grunts. A flurry of feet pounding around me, stomping down on one of my braids. I cry out, unsure what's going on. I curl my hands around the back of my head, trying to make myself as small as possible.

"Davy! C'mon! Can you stand?" Gil's face comes into focus. He tugs on my arm.

I nod and he helps me to my feet. I look around, taking in the mad scene. Fear lances through me as I spot Sean wrestling with a boy on the floor as the security guards try to wedge them apart, using their batons. Oh God! He's already been imprinted. What will they do to him for this?

Nathan and Brian dance around the writhing bodies, shouting encouragement, landing kicks when they can to the boy attacking Sean.

Tucci's voice lifts over the din, directing the rest of us down the hall. "Outside! The rest of you! Now!" Soles squeal on the tile. Coco's the first to escape through the doors. Nathan and Brian tear themselves away much more reluctantly.

Gil pulls me along. I only manage a few feet, watching, mesmerized as Sean climbs atop the boy and unleashes his fists in a powerful fury. This is him, I realize . . . the savage he's purported to be. The wild animal the mark on his neck proclaims.

I lightly rub at the back of my head where a knot is already forming. The boy hit me either with his fist or some object.

Even after everything, even after I'd been bound and branded like an animal, the idea that I would be attacked still rattles me.

One of the security guards locks his baton around Sean's neck and drags him off the boy. Sean's face purples as he struggles for breath.

I lunge forward, ready to help him, but Gil's hand tightens on my arm. "You want to get in more trouble?"

"We have to help him!" I pant. "They're killing him!"

"No, they're not! Don't worry! Sean can handle himself."

As Gil pulls me through the front doors, I watch the guards drag Sean down the hall like he's the one who did something wrong.

Outside, it's like stepping into a hothouse. The morning's rain has passed and the air immediately sticks to my skin.

Tucci motions us away from the front door to where he stands near the flagpole. He drags both hands through his hair, clearly shaken. "Look. You all need to leave before the bell rings and the students see you. Or we'll have more of that." He points to the building where we left Sean. My stomach twists. "Given the present climate . . ." He shakes his head as if the possibilities are unspeakable.

"I don't need to be told twice." Nathan and Brian head into the parking lot, a bounce to their strides, and I'm convinced they see this as nothing more than a holiday and not the end of something. An end to carrier tolerance and the beginning of something else. A new era . . . where carriers are more than simply reviled. Where we're less than animals. Where we're more than identified. More than monitored.

Coco follows them, her pace swift, humming with urgency. There's none of Nathan's or Brian's levity to her. She understands what it takes to survive. And to a certain degree, I admire her for that. She'll always land on her feet.

I linger with Gil, looking toward the front door, reluctant to leave Sean still in there—especially after he got himself into trouble for helping me. I didn't expect that. He's helped me before but never at risk to himself.

"Go on, get out of here." Tucci waves at us before turning back and disappearing inside the school. The final bell rings inside the building, the echo discordant, vibrating on the air. Still, I stand there, my feet rooted to the sidewalk, staring at the doors, willing Sean to appear.

"Davy, we gotta go. They're going to pour out of those doors and we can't be here when they do."

"What about—"

"He's with campus security. We're not. He's safer than we are standing out here. Let's go."

I nod jerkily and move, my head still ringing from the earlier blow. I cup the back of my neck as if that will help. Gil walks close to my side, one hand wavering between us as if he's prepared to support me if I should trip or fall.

"You mind if I get a ride again? My apartment's not far. I usually walk, but today . . ." His voice fades, but I can hear his apprehension, see it in the way his eyes scan the parking lot, pausing on the doors in the distance where the first students start to exit. I'm reminded that he's been a student here before he was ever declared a carrier. These were once his fellow classmates and they know him on sight. He doesn't need an imprint on his neck to identify him. Walking home, any student driving past will know who he is . . . *what* he is.

And as Tucci pointed out, with the current events, anything could happen to him.

"Sure," I respond, punching the UNLOCK button. He dives into the passenger seat.

The parking lot is already crowded by the time I back out, cars in the front impeding our exit from campus. As I inch behind vehicles, I glance to the doors and the exodus of students, scanning for one taller than the most. An ink collar on his neck. But he never appears.

## FBI Interrogation

**AGENT CALLEN:** Why did you do it?

**KEVIN HOYT:** What are you talking about?

**AGENT CALLEN:** C'mon, man. We've confiscated your computer. Your phone. I've talked to the other three. They didn't pull off the largest mass shooting in this country's history on their own. We know you're the brains behind this.

**KEVIN HOYT:** That's kind of you to say.

**AGENT CALLEN:** So. Why?

**KEVIN HOYT:** Why not?

**AGENT CALLEN:** You don't even care? You feel no remorse? One hundred and twenty dead. Over fifty injured . . .

**KEVIN HOYT:** Pretty good. We were aiming for two hundred but, like you said. Over fifty injured. We might get there yet.

**AGENT CALLEN:** You're a monster.

**KEVIN HOYT:** That's what everyone keeps saying. . . . It's good to know they were right. Isn't it?

# EIGHTEEN

IT DOESN'T TAKE TOO MUCH INVESTIGATING TO FIND out where Sean lives. I still have my notes from his interview, including the name of his foster mother. A quick online search uncovered only one Martha Delaney in the area. I plug the address into my phone and head downstairs, finished with sitting at home with nothing to do. Four days of no school. No friends. No leaving the house. Mom says it's too dangerous for me to go out. It isn't safe for imprinted carriers to walk the streets. All over the country we're targets for vigilante justice.

She's right, of course. I should just stay home, but there's only so much television a person can watch.

Snatching my keys off the hall table, I abandon the empty house. I haven't seen Dad since the day I was imprinted. Mom says work keeps him away, but I know it's not that. It's me.

Mom faces me every day, her smile in place, but even she has taken to avoiding me, increasing her hours at the office. Mitchell's Jeep sits out front and I'm sure he's sleeping late. I heard him back out of the driveway last night while I was in bed.

With one eye on my phone's map, I drive, leaving my safe neighborhood behind and getting on the highway that takes me closer to town. I pass the exit to Keller High School and keep going. I pass the next exit that would take me to Gil's apartment.

I never would have visited anyone this close to the city before. Not only would my parents have forbidden it, I would have been too afraid. Bad things happen within the city limits. Even on the outskirts, where I'm headed. Like an infection, crime is spreading, spilling into what once used to be safe suburbs.

The hills get smaller. More houses and buildings appear as I head south. Buildings that look like they've seen better days. Graffiti is everywhere. I exit the highway and take a right at the first stoplight. The buildings aren't rock here like where I live. They're mostly a mud-colored HardiePlank that reminds me of cardboard. I weave to avoid hitting a stray cat that looks more like a skeleton. Patches of fur broken by raw flesh cover the poor beast.

The road narrows and I have to ease off the gas so that

I can maneuver around cars parked in the street. The apartments get shabbier, interrupted by houses with cracked concrete porches and yards overrun with weeds and miscellaneous junk.

A siren shrieks in the distance. A moment later, it soars through the cross street in front of me. I watch it for a moment and find myself wondering where they're going, who they're after. A carrier? Like the ones splattered all over the news. Shaking my head, I glance down at the address again.

I mutter under my breath, searching for house numbers that aren't visible on most of the homes. At a corner sits a rusted Dumpster. A hand peeks out from its depths throwing something that might be a rotting watermelon into the arms of a waiting youth.

I slam on my brakes as a body bolts across the street in front of my car. A split second later another person flies after the first. He tackles him on the sidewalk with a bone-jarring crack I hear through the windows of my car. The two tussle, arms swinging, fists slamming.

I blink and gawk, unsure whether I'm witnessing an assault or high-spirited horseplay. Given where I am, it's pure optimism to think I'm watching a couple of boys wrestling good-naturedly.

I step on the gas and drive on, almost missing Sean's house, the numbers mostly hidden behind an overgrown bush.

I consider his home for a moment as I idle in the street. It's a little better than the neighboring houses. The yard is mowed and there's a pot of flowers in the window. I park directly behind his truck and step outside, taking my time to shut the door, assessing my surroundings.

From somewhere inside the house, music blares. I stand motionless for a moment in the driveway before walking up the uneven sidewalk and stopping on a threadbare doormat. I lift the chipped brass-plated knocker and let it fall twice.

The door opens and the music hits me harder. It's a fast beat, heavy on the electric guitar. The vocalist is more screaming than singing and I wince.

The guy in front of me is shirtless, wearing only gym shorts, and I almost don't notice the imprint around his neck because I'm so distracted by the tattoos covering every spare inch of him. He's grotesquely muscled. Not an ounce of body fat.

"Who are you?" he asks, his voice lifting over the music.

My gaze jerks off the tattoo of a dragon on his chest to the dark eyes watching me curiously.

He quirks an eyebrow. "Have yourself a good look?"

I shake my head, tossing my hair. A few strands stick to my lips. Lip gloss. Why the hell had I worn lip gloss? Was I hoping to impress Sean? I just wanted to make sure he was okay. To thank him for the other day.

I swipe the strands away from my mouth. "Davy," I answer, letting my name hang, shifting my weight between my feet as he studies me. I hadn't really thought about coming face-to-face with the others. His foster brothers. Carriers. I should have guessed when I heard the loud music that he wouldn't be the only one home. Sean doesn't seem the type to listen to music at eardrum-shattering levels.

"Davy." He stretches my name into something three or four syllables long. He props one hand on the door frame and leans forward a little. "You seem a little nervous, so I'll make this easy, sweetheart. Who are you here to see?"

"Sean. Sean," I answer quickly.

He leans back again. "Of course. Sean!" he shouts loudly, still looking me over. "You got company."

I think I hear a thud from inside, but it's hard to tell with the blast of music.

His head bobs as he speaks. "Haven't seen you before. I'd remember." His mouth curls. "Not too many girl carriers. Especially imprinted ones. You don't exactly look the type."

I can't help myself. "No? What type do I look like?"

He gives a short laugh. "Not Sean's type, that's for sure."

I suck in a breath, stupidly stung. *Sean has a type? And I'm not it?*

His gaze flicks over me again. "You look like you're headed to choir practice or something."

I glance down at my khaki shorts, bright blue tank top, and tennis shoes. I thought I looked fairly ordinary. It's not like I dressed in a cotillion gown. What does he see when he looks at me?

He waves at my necklace. It's a simple silver chain with a cute ladybug charm. "That's sweet. Gift from Daddy?"

My cheeks burn at the accuracy of his guess. Dad got it for me on my thirteenth birthday. He always called me his "ladybug." I cover the charm with my hand, oddly more self-conscious of that than the disfiguring tattoo circling my neck.

"You go to school with Sean." It's more statement than question.

I nod.

He smiles. "I'm done. Graduated last year."

I want to say, *But you still live here . . . with your foster family.* Martha Delaney can't still be collecting money for keeping him. And yet he's here. There's a lot I don't know about Sean and his life in this house with these people.

I press my mouth into a hard line. Just because I'm curious, just because I brought myself to his door, doesn't mean I have a right to pry.

My stomach turns. When had I become curious? When had he stopped being something strange and frightening?

"I'm Simon, by the way."

"Hello, Simon."

Sean appears behind his foster brother. For a brief moment, his expression cracks and his surprise seeps through. He blinks and then it's gone. The hard-chiseled mask back in place.

"Davy. What are you doing here?"

Simon stands to the side. "Man, don't be rude. Invite your friend in." He emphasizes the word *friend.* Heat fills my face.

Sean stares hard at his foster brother and something passes between them. Something I can't read, but the words are there. I look from Sean to Simon and back again, trying to decipher their silent exchange.

"Sure. Come in, Davy." He looks at Simon warningly

and holds out his hand for me.

I stare down at that hand for a moment, the long tapering fingers, the wide, broad palm. We've never held hands before. This thought enters my head dumbly. Along with the knowledge that maybe I *want* him to hold my hand. Maybe I want someone to touch me. *Him.* As I am. Like this. And not just some jerk who thinks it's okay to put his hands on me because I'm a carrier. Like Brockman. Or even Zac.

My chest suddenly grows tight and I'm not at all sure about entering this house, but I remind myself that I did this. I brought myself here to see him. And despite everything, despite my discomfort in this moment, I'm not afraid of him. Not anymore. Not in the way I first was. Now, if there's any fear, it's a different kind. Fear for the unknown. For the breathless way I feel around him.

I place my hand inside his and try not to think about how it feels to hold the hand of someone other than Zac.

Sean pulls me after him. The inside is clean enough, filled with worn and faded furniture. He cuts through the living room. We skirt the bench press where Simon had presumably been working out when I knocked on the door.

The hallway is narrow and dim. A few photos line the walls, the faces shadowy blurs. I try to glance at them, to see if any are of a younger Sean, but we're moving too quickly. From somewhere in the house, the music stops abruptly.

As soon as I step inside his bedroom, he drops my hand. Chafing my palms on my thighs, I stop in the middle of the room and look around. There are two beds, both unmade.

The room is otherwise tidy. One desk. Two dressers.

"You share the room with Simon?"

"With Adam."

I nod like he's told me all about Adam. Like he's told me about anything.

"What are you doing here, Davy?"

"I wanted to make sure you were okay."

"I'm fine."

"Pollock didn't come after you for what happened?"

"The Agency's got its hands full right now trying to decide the fate of all carriers. Not just one. Me by myself . . . I'm not that important."

"Do you think we'll be back in school soon?"

"Doubtful."

I moisten my lips, uncomfortable beneath his glittering gaze. Crossing my arms, I sink onto the edge of one of the beds. "Why do you sound angry?" My voice comes out a whisper.

"Because I am," he bites back, dragging one hand through his hair and pacing the middle of the small room.

"I came here because I wanted to thank you for what happened at school when that boy hit me and you're treating me—"

"You shouldn't have come here at all. It's not safe."

At this, I give a little laugh and wave at my neck. "Where will I ever be safe now? Am I supposed to never step outside again?"

He stops and stares at me in a way that makes me feel like

I've said something really wrong. "Carriers are being attacked just for walking outside their front door. It's not safe for us. But *you* decided to get in your car and come here of all places? You're just asking for it." His lip curls up at this last bit and succeeds in making me feel officially stupid.

I rise in one motion, flustered, embarrassed . . . angry. "Sorry. I'll leave you to hide in your house then."

I start for the door, but he stops me, grabs me with both hands. His breath crashes with mine, lips so close I can almost taste them. "You're just begging for trouble—"

I jerk free and look around at his sparse room. "What's worse than this?"

"Oh, c'mon. You really don't know? Where's your imagination?"

He advances on me and I inch back until I bump into the mattress. Sinking down, I gasp when he follows and straddles me, his knees on each side of my hips.

"W-what are you doing?" I press a palm against his chest.

"Painting a picture of what's worse than this. Wasn't that your question?"

I nod, at a loss for words.

"You have no rights. You're a sublevel human. That means anything can happen to you and no one will care." His face dips closer. His cheek rests against mine as he hisses close to my ear, "Anyone can *do* anything to you. There is no protection. No place in this whole country where you should feel safe now." His fingers flex on my shoulders. "Understand?"

After a moment, I nod again.

He lifts his face back up. "And it's only going to get worse for us. It's been getting worse every year, but after this shooting, the Agency is only going to get more powerful. . . ."

The gust of those words so close to my lips does everything he intends—they frighten and intimidate me.

All of me shivers, quakes inside.

Something in his eyes shifts, darkens. His gaze sweeps over me and then, as though realizing just how close we are, he pulls back. "Sorry," he mutters, the word a rough rasp. He drags a hand over his face. "You just need to be more careful. There won't be someone around to protect you all the time."

I nod again. I could push him off me. He wouldn't stop me. I inhale, breathing in the smell of him, soap and spearmint, and realize I don't want to shove him away. Butterflies start to flutter in my stomach. I don't say a word. It's impossible. I couldn't get a word past the lump in my throat. My fingers move, burrow against his shirt, testing the texture, the firmness of his flesh beneath the thin barrier.

"Don't look at me that way," he says, his voice almost gruff.

"What way?"

His hand covers mine, stilling the movement of my hand against his chest, and I detect the fast thud of his heart through flesh and bone. Feeling his heart, it occurs to me that it beats just like everyone else's. Like mine. A month ago, I would have crossed the street to avoid him. Now I seek him out, go to places I would never have dared.

"You're going to end up dead." His gaze scans my face with hot-eyed intensity. "You need to stay inside the walls of your house . . . with your family. Your chances are better there."

"And what about you? Shouldn't you follow your own advice? You attacked that boy in school. Not too smart."

"You don't need to worry about me. I come from this." He nods at his surroundings and I know he doesn't just mean his room but the streets outside. "I've had to fight my entire life." He shakes his head. "You can't understand that. You're different. You're not violent, not a killer."

"And you are? Is that what you're saying?" Without thinking, I slide my hand against his throat, grazing my thumb over the H. "This is you then? You deserve this?"

For a moment, he says nothing. He holds himself still above me, but I get the sense he's about to spring. Like something tightly coiled, ready to break loose. A muscle feathers the flesh of his jaw, and his eyes burn charred-gray.

My thumb continues to caress his neck.

"Don't," he rasps. The sound is oddly satisfying. I'm getting to him. Penetrating his armor.

My fingers move, exploring, brushing his hammering pulse. Fascinated, my gaze slides over his face, stopping on his mouth. I want to kiss him with a fierceness I've never felt, heightened by my loneliness. The constant fear. The earth that won't stay firm beneath me.

I lift my head off the bed and lean up for his lips. He jerks away with a gasp of dismay and scrambles off me. "Get out of here. Go home, Davy."

I stand, feeling like the most repulsive girl alive. Rejected in action and words.

And why shouldn't I feel that way? Suddenly, I see the girls he talked to in the hall at school. Maybe he prefers his girls normal. Normal and unmarked.

He turns his back on me. I stare at him, the stretch of his shoulders beneath his shirt, the dark gold strands falling against his neck. "You think I'm safer there than here?" I demand hoarsely.

The nerves in my neck tingle. It's almost as though I feel the imprint there, a living thing awake and crawling. My hand goes there, presses against the too-warm skin.

He turns sideways, looks back at me like he wishes I was gone already. A stupid ache fills my chest.

"I'll go, but it's no longer my home. Home is safety and I don't have that any more than you do."

Before he can answer—if he even intends to—I leave the room. Simon looks up from the kitchen table, hunkered over a bowl of cereal. Milk dribbles from his chin.

He calls out a good-bye, but I don't stop. I can't. I can't keep doing this. Everyone I had is gone. Everyone has turned from me and I can't even find solace with another carrier.

CNN interview with Harlan McAlister, former classmate of alleged Texas gunman Kevin Hoyt:

**REPORTER:** Mr. McAlister, you attended high school with Kevin Hoyt, did you not?

**HARLAN McALISTER:** Yes . . . we played football together. He was captain of the JV team before we all found out he was a carrier. It's all just such a shock. A real shame . . . he was a good football player. Could have gone pro.

**REPORTER:** Can you tell us a little bit about Kevin Hoyt? What was he like?

**HARLAN McALISTER:** Everyone liked him. He was a real leader. I mean, before, you know . . . not after.

**REPORTER:** Are you surprised that he did something so brutal and horrendous?

**HARLAN McALISTER:** Yes . . . well, no. I mean . . . he was a carrier. Once that came to light, we all knew there was nothing he wasn't capable of . . . right?

# NINETEEN

MOM ORDERS PIZZA THAT NIGHT EVEN THOUGH it's Mitchell's twenty-first birthday and we always go out for sushi at his favorite restaurant on his birthday. Mom and Dad usually wink at the waiter and order mai tais for me and Mitchell. This year, Mitchell could have ordered his drink himself.

"Pizza?" I look at Mitchell from the kitchen table where I browse through a magazine. It's strange having so much time on my hands. I've taken to reading Mom's décor magazines. "You don't want your favorite spider roll?"

"Pizza is good. Let's get pineapple and ham." Mitchell

shoots a quick look to Mom and smiles in a way that tells me they discussed this in advance.

"You just don't want to take me out," I say. "In public. Afraid Mrs. Doyle is going to be standing in her yard? Giving us the evil eye?"

"Davina, that's not true," Mama chides, but her eyes dart to my brother, clearly looking for help.

He sighs and props his hip against the counter. "After last week . . ." He motions to the small television above the kitchen counter that's still replaying the tragedy. There hasn't been much new information, but they keep flashing the faces of the four carriers. They look about my age. One or two of them might be in their twenties. Three of the four are imprinted, and the ink collars look so large on their necks . . . bigger and darker in their mug shots. "The Agency hasn't even let you go back to school yet. It just seems like a good idea to stay inside."

I nod and cross my arms. "I understand. You're right. It makes sense. I should just stay a hermit in my home."

"Davy." My brother doesn't look at me in the careful way Mom does. He's too sincere for that. Too honest. Like the time he told Señora Ramirez the only Spanish he needed to know was *cerveza*, *el baño*, and *quiero sexo*. Yeah. He was *that* high school boy. "Don't be a drama queen about it."

I start to leave the kitchen. "Call me when the pizza is here."

"Davy, wait."

I turn, watching as Mom grabs a remote and increases the volume on the television set. The president stands there in the

House chamber before members of the House and Senate, waiting for applause to settle. A reporter drones on in whispered tones about this being the second time the president has addressed the nation since last week. I watch numbly, half listening, certain he will wax on about loss and tragedy and prayers for the victims and families. Which is why I don't fully comprehend his words at first. Not until he mentions "HTS" and "carrier" several times do I begin to process.

". . . for the protection of this great nation, the time has arrived to give full attention to the HTS threat so that we do not have a repeat of last week's tragedy." There is a pregnant pause as the president stares out at the room. "Detention of all carriers has become of utmost necessity. . . ."

"Mom," I whisper, still staring at the screen, hearing nothing else. "What does he mean?" I understand his words, but none of it seems real. She waves a hand for me to quiet, her gaze riveted to the TV.

"The Wainwright Agency in conjunction with the Department of Justice, Homeland Security, and FEMA are mobilizing as I speak to amass all registered carriers throughout the country and transfer them into suitable locations. No small undertaking, but one that shall help us achieve the ideals upon which this great nation was founded . . . life, liberty, and the pursuit of happiness. . . ."

Mitchell grabs the television and wrestles it from the wall above the counter. Mom screams his name, but he ignores her, howling with rage. I watch, stunned as my brother wrenches it free and sends it crashing to the floor.

I look up from the sparking TV to my brother, his face flushed with rage, chest heaving with exertion.

"I'll help you," he pants. "We can run away, Dav."

"And go where?" I ask, a strange calm coming over me. I'm listed in the national database and I'm wearing an imprint on my neck. There's nowhere to go. No border I could cross. No plane I could board. Nowhere to hide.

"They can't do this to you." Mitchell looks from me to Mom, his eyes pleading with her, seeking support. She stares ahead, her features pale and drawn.

I touch my brother's arm, sliding my hand down to his. "No running, Mitchell. I've got to stay."

He steps back until he collides with the wall. His face scrunches up and a choked cry breaks loose, rattles from his chest. He slides down the wall until he hits the floor. I watch as he buries his face into his hands. I feel every one of his jagged sobs like a claw-swipe to my heart.

# PART TWO

# MOUNT HAVEN

The situation of overcrowding must be attended. Please stop sending carriers to this location. Our present population demands relief. I can reach no solution against the rising tide of disease that has befallen this camp. We lost six carriers this month alone, and even a guard died, infected with the same illness that has plagued the camp since we opened. . . .

*—Correspondence from director of Camp 19 to Dr. Wainwright*

# TWENTY

WITHIN TWO MINUTES OF THE PRESIDENT'S address, we receive an automated phone message informing us that we will be contacted soon with information regarding my assignment and that I'm not to leave my residence for any reason under threat of arrest. Funny, that doesn't even strike a chord of fear in me. Not when I'm about to be forced into some kind of camp for carriers.

Days pass. Mom flinches every time the phone rings on the counter. If Mitchell's around, he goes still, his eyes fixing on her as she answers. Dad, if he's even home, quickly flees to another room. The days roll into a week. I move about in a fog. I know they haven't forgotten me. It's only a matter of time before they come for me.

The media shows around-the-clock coverage of carriers being rounded up and forced onto buses. Well, maybe not forced. Most go along with it.

There are a few instances of runners that make it on to the news. One car chase outside Detroit replays every thirty minutes. A carrier tried to escape with his family. He used to be a high school art teacher until he was identified as a carrier and dismissed from his job. I shouldn't watch. It's just a blatant ploy to sensationalize what's happening, but I'm helplessly captivated, watching as the Mini Cooper drives off a bridge and crashes into a gravel pit, killing the entire family instantly. A wife and two small children. They show footage of the burning car. For a split second, you can even see the dark writhing shadows within the vehicle.

All that night, I dream of dying in a car explosion, flames licking at my flesh, devouring me as I fight to get out. The weird part is my family stands outside the vehicle, watching me trapped inside the car, doing nothing to reach me or put out the fire. Mom, Dad . . . they make no move to help me. Even Mitchell. He weeps and pulls at his hair, but can do nothing.

I can't deny that I feel a bit like that in reality. That my family is doing nothing, merely standing on the sidelines as I go up in flames. They're passively watching everything happen to me. There's nothing they can do. I know this. I said as much to Mitchell when he suggested we run away. Still, I can't help feeling abandoned.

Walking into the kitchen, I find Mitchell watching TV. All evidence of the one he broke is gone. Someone moved a television from a guest room into the kitchen. It's smaller and sits on the counter. Mitchell balances his weight on a bar stool in front of it.

"Hey." He looks up, his spoon freezing from scraping the last of his yogurt from the container.

"Hi." My gaze drifts to the screen and the protestors congregating in front of the White House. An anti-Agency group waves posters and shouts at the anti-carrier group. The anti-carrier group outnumbers the anti-Agency group. Police patrol on horseback, trying to prevent rioting in the clogged streets.

I grab a soda from the fridge. "Isn't there anything else on television?"

He flips the channel to a local station. Instead of its regular television show, a reporter stands outside Oak Run, a faith-based summer camp in Kerrville where kids learn the Bible alongside how to rock climb. A few of my friends went there. I never did. Mom always sent me to music camps and voice programs throughout the summer instead.

The reporter explains how the government has requisitioned the camp for carriers. With housing for six hundred campers, staff not included, it's an ideal setup for all carriers in South and Central Texas. I assume it's where I'll be going whenever they get around to collecting me.

I lean on the counter and study the fortified fences with

winding ropes of barbed wire at the top. Guards with guns man the front gate and roam the fence line. Several red-colored buildings dot the background, nestled in the hills among thick trees.

It's just one of many new internment camps popping up across the country overnight, rushing to meet the demand. Staring at the screen, I feel my throat closing up.

Mom strolls into the kitchen. "What do ya'll want for dinner tonight?" She looks at me. "Davy, you could make your delicious French toast?"

I blink at her, hating how she's acting as though everything is fine. Normal. When it's so . . . not. "I don't feel like cooking."

"Oh." She looks down at her hands, and I feel wretched. I don't know how much time I have here. I'd rather spend what's left getting along. I walk over and kiss her on the cheek.

"Let's order Chinese," I suggest, wrapping an arm around her. She relaxes, softening against me.

Her lips curve in a smile that doesn't quite reach her eyes. "That sounds good." I scan her face, trying to memorize it, realizing I don't know when I'll see her again—after they take me. The gray is starting to appear at her temples and I realize she's behind on coloring her hair. She's usually so on top of stuff like that.

"It will be okay, Mom."

She nods, and I realize this is as much as we'll ever talk about it—about me. Her daughter with HTS.

And that's okay.

I don't expect her to save me. I don't expect anyone to do that. I'm alone in this. Just like Sean said. Whatever happens, I don't have anyone. I have to learn to live with that.

The knock at the door finally arrives.

Only it's not Pollock. It's a woman. Dressed in a sleek pant-suit, her dark hair pulled back into an equally sleek ponytail, she looks like what I imagine a government agent would look like.

With a flash of identification and murmured words I can't hear from where I lurk in the living room, Mom ushers her inside.

"Davy, this is Ms. Stiles."

"Agent Stiles," the woman corrects.

Mitchell enters the room and his entire demeanor changes. He pulls back his shoulders as though bracing for a punch. I notice the way his eyes follow the agent.

She smiles at me. "And you must be Davina."

"Davy."

Her smile stays in place. "Davy. Yes. I've heard a lot about you. Or read, rather."

"Really? What have you read?"

"Oh, this and that. You're an accomplished young lady." *Young lady? Not carrier? Not killer?* "Your college essay was particularly good. You have a way with words. I even saw your recording for Juilliard." She nods in approval. "Very impressive."

She had access to my college essay? My audition tape? What else did she know about me?

"Can I offer you a drink, Agent Stiles?" My mother, ever polite.

"No, thank you, Mrs. Hamilton. I have several more houses to visit in the area today. I'll be quick."

*Other carriers?* My pulse quickens, wondering if she's going to call on anyone I know. Any of the carriers from Keller. Gil. *Sean.*

She opens her satchel and pulls out a few sheets of paper. "This is a contract for Davy to attend a government-managed training school."

She hesitates, looks at me, then Mom. Like she wants this to sink in before she continues.

"You mean Davy doesn't have to go to one of those detention camps on TV?" Mitchell gets to the point.

Mom's face creases in bewilderment. "I don't understand. . . . How is it different?"

"In lieu of entering into a detention camp, Davy can receive specialized training. Only a select number of carriers are receiving invitations to this program."

Mom takes the papers, hope starting to wash away her confusion. "What kind of special training?"

"For how long?" Mitchell cuts in.

"Instructors will train Davy and other carriers between the ages of eleven and eighteen to better . . . channel their destructive tendencies. They'll be given the tools to not only function in society but to serve their communities . . . their countries."

I can only stare. My heart races. It's too good to be true. I could be part of the world again. I could belong . . . and serve a purpose. Be more than a dishwasher. More than someone it is okay to abuse.

Mom skims the papers. It's doubtful she's even reading them the way her hands tremble. Like me, she probably only hears what the agent is offering me. She clutches the papers like someone might dare to wrest them away from her and steal this future from me.

Mitchell cocks his head. "Why Davy?"

Stiles studies him a moment before answering, "Your sister was an exceptional student. A talented musician and singer. We're looking for carriers like her that showed promise in their past lives. . . ."

*Past lives?* Like I've died and am now reborn into something else, something less, something bleak and undesirable. A blight.

She continues, "Young carriers who possess special qualities and skills we can optimize." Her gaze falls on me, and she smiles vacantly. "It is our belief that you can be taught . . . your violent urges redirected into something more positive."

*You can be taught.* Something about those words makes me feel like a dog being sent to obedience school. I dismiss the feeling though. She's offering salvation, an escape from a detention camp.

"How long is this . . . training?" Mom asks, and I hear what she's really asking. *When will I come home? Will I ever?*

"However long necessary for her to reach a level where she can be assigned a duty and perform with adequate success."

I shake my head. *Isn't that bureaucratic smoke-blowing at its finest?* "Perform with adequate success." What did that even mean?

"What if I can't?" I hear myself ask.

She looks at me, her expression mildly annoyed. "If we decide you're untrainable, then you'll be moved to a detention camp. Where you were headed before you were flagged for special ops training. It's not a fate I would choose, were I you." Again, the empty smile is back, and this time it feels vaguely threatening. "So don't fail."

I nod mechanically.

Agent Stiles adjusts her grip on her satchel and glances at her watch. Her gaze drifts toward the front door before looking back at me. "You need to decide now. It's your call. Training or detention camp?"

There's really no choice. As she stares at me, I see she knows this, too.

I nod at Mom. "Sign it."

She moves to the desk. I follow closely, watching as she signs her name and then hands me the pen to sign.

"Excellent," Stiles announces, taking the papers from me. "A van will be collecting you tomorrow morning between seven and eight. Be ready." She takes a satisfied breath, squaring herself in front of me. "You're one of a chosen few. You should consider yourself very honored."

*Honored?* I want to point to my throat. Did she miss that?

She continues, "We've been granted permission for roughly fifty carriers. We conducted a nationwide search. It was difficult to choose. Harder to find quality females."

She makes me sound like livestock. Not a person. Not human.

Then that other thing she said sinks in. Fifty carriers nationwide. That's not many at all. But she mentioned needing to visit other houses in the area today. Could Sean be one of them?

I have to know. Even if our last encounter left a bad taste in my mouth, I have to know he's not going to be behind that barbed fence being guarded by all those men with guns. I can't wait until I'm on some van headed God knows where to learn he's not headed there, too—to discover that he's been shipped off to a detention camp with all the rest of the carriers and that I will never see him again. I'll never know what happened to him. Or Coco. An image of her fills my head. All she put up with . . . the Cage, Brockman. For nothing, it seems.

"Who else?" I blurt. "Who else are you taking?"

Out of the corner of my eye, I notice Mitchell studying me curiously, and I know I'm giving myself away. At least to him. He knows me well enough to read me, to see that I care a lot about Agent Stiles's answer. *That I care about someone.*

"I beg your pardon?" She slides the papers into her satchel efficiently, already finished here and eager to move on.

"You said you had other houses to visit nearby. Other carriers. Did any of them go to Keller with me?"

She angles her head, considering me. "I believe so. Gilbert Ruiz scored perfect on his ACT. And his computer knowledge is nothing short of astonishing. He can write code and hack into the world's most complicated programs."

Anxiety trips through me. Just Gil? Not Sean. I see the buses in my mind, the people being shoved onto them. Their wide eyes, their faces stark and haunted. My stomach twists sickly, hoping that Sean possesses some skill, some talent that can get him away from that.

"Oh, I almost forgot." She fumbles for another sheet and hands it to my mother while I wait breathlessly, hoping for her to say another name.

"Here's a list of what to bring. Only the essentials. It's not a summer camp."

"No one else from Keller?" I press.

She turns for the door. "You'll see for yourself tomorrow."

"Please." I can't stop the whisper from slipping free.

She looks back at me, her expression shifting, awake with curiosity. "Who do you want to be there, Davina?"

Heat swamps my face. I feel Mom and Mitchell staring at me, sensing their surprise. They wouldn't have expected me to grow so attached to another carrier.

"Come. Out with it. There must be something special about him to have you in such a state."

My face burns hotter. If I give her Sean's name would it truly help? Or is she asking to make sure he isn't included? I can't fathom Agency rationale.

She considers me thoughtfully. "Interesting. Actually, I've had to cross one carrier off my list . . . turns out he preferred suicide." She says this like it's nothing. "I suppose a carrier charismatic enough to charm you could be evaluated. Who knows? He might be an asset . . . especially if his presence there makes you more at ease. Maybe he could fill the vacancy. What's his name?"

"Sean," I respond, unsure if she's messing with me or not. "Sean O'Rourke."

She nods. "We'll look into him."

And I don't know whether to believe her or not, but the tightness in my chest eases. He might not be headed to a detention camp. I cling to that hope. He might be going with me—to a place where we can both find a future.

---

Phone call from President Pitt to Dr. Louis Wainwright

"I'll give you your damned training camp, Wainwright. You just better be right about this. . . ."

# TWENTY-ONE

I'M WAITING WHEN THE VAN PULLS UP THE driveway. Three figures sit in the back, two people in the front, one of whom opens the door and steps down. Agent Stiles. The sun hits her sleek hair, firing it almost blue.

I let the curtain fall back into place. Sucking in a deep breath, I turn and locate my bag.

I only packed what was on the list Agent Stiles gave my mother. Underwear, toothbrush. My favorite shower gel. A few changes of clothes and an extra set of shoes. The bag hangs lightly in my hands.

My parents come down the stairs at the sound of the

doorbell. Even Dad stayed home to see me off. He pulls me into his arms and hugs me so hard I can hardly breathe. "You'll do great," he murmurs against my hair. "They know you're special. That's why they chose you. You're not like the others—"

I pull away, cutting him off. "I'll miss you, too, Dad." I can't hear him say that I'm not like the others . . . that I'm better than all the rest of them. Not when I don't know if it's true.

To know that, I have to know that what's inside them isn't inside me. And I can't know that for sure. I don't know anything except that I'm going to absorb everything they teach me. I'm going to learn and make something of myself. I'll find new goals and new dreams.

Mom opens the door to Agent Stiles. The woman nods at us and then turns, marching to the van, expecting me to follow.

"We'll see you soon," Mom says, even though we know no such thing. I let her say it. It seems the thing for people to say when parting ways.

I nod, hugging her.

I turn to my brother and a lump forms in my throat. He pulls me into his arms, clutching me with wide-splayed fingers. "I've got your back."

"I know."

His voice lowers so that only I can hear. "You come home if it doesn't work out. I'll help you. . . . There are places you can go, hide. . . ."

The van honks.

"I gotta go." I step free and squeeze Mitchell's arm, trying to convey to him that I'm going to be okay. He looks at me intently.

"I hear you," I assure him. Lifting my bag, I'm out the door, moving swiftly down the front walk, not looking back on the only home I've known.

The side door to the van yawns open for me. Gil sits in the bench seat behind the driver, waving merrily and motioning for me to take the space beside him. Like we're heading to some kind of fun summer camp. I hop inside, nodding at Agent Stiles as she slams the door shut.

I glance behind me to the shapes sitting there. Sean and a boy I've never seen before.

Sean looks at me but he doesn't speak. His expression is stoic, impossible to read. His fuller top lip presses into an unsmiling line. I wonder if he knows that I had something to do with his being here. I wonder if he cares.

I hold his gaze for a moment and then face forward again.

We're moving now, leaving my house behind.

They're taking us to a place called Mount Haven. This much I glean during the van ride and plane trip. Our group grows as we travel. By the time we land in New Mexico, there are nineteen of us. Agent Stiles and five others escort us. We get plenty of stares as we're led through the airport and ushered through security. At least ten of us bear the imprints, and people actually press to far walls and clutch their children close as we pass. We are monsters in their eyes. Real live bogeymen in the flesh.

Although Sean speaks very little, he stays close to me and Gil, his eyes constantly moving, assessing everyone. Everything. I guess there's comfort in the familiar—and that happens to be me and Gil. Or maybe he just feels protective of us. Again. Like in the Cage.

With Gil, there is no risk of awkward silence. He keeps the conversation flowing as we munch on the sack meal they provide, driving deep into the mountain wilderness, leaving civilization behind. Not that it's very civilized anymore.

It's dark when we arrive at Mount Haven, passing through a gate set amid a tall stucco wall. As soon as we emerge from the van, they divide us. Boys to the right, girls to the left. A reed-thin, military-looking man introduces himself as Commander Harris. His head is cue-ball smooth. Light gleams off his shiny scalp. We stand beneath the bright glare of spotlights as he looks out at all of us, weighing us with hawk-like intensity for a long moment before directing the guards to take us to our quarters.

Blinking, I look after Sean and Gil, my chest growing tight with anxiety at leaving them. Gil grins and gives me a thumbs-up. I know him well enough by now to know he's trying to be encouraging. I nod, still wishing I could have gone with him and Sean. Sean's gaze holds mine, communicating something. What, I don't know.

I watch Gil and Sean for as long as I can, until I'm afraid I might run into the girl in front of me. Facing forward, I mind my steps while scanning the building and grounds. There are only seven girls. A woman leads us. She's dressed gender neutral in a khaki shirt and slacks. I haven't seen Agent Stiles since the airport. Somehow I don't think I'll see her again. Or if I do, it won't be good.

I heard one boy on the way from the airport tell another boy in the back row of the van that Mount Haven used to be a mental institution. I don't know how he knew this, but with bars on the windows, I can believe it. Still, it's not a gloomy place. Not like an asylum from a horror movie or anything. Nothing that grim. The whitewashed walls stand out against the star-studded night. The building is shaped like a V, two wings stretching out on either side of a rotunda in the middle. At three stories, it could house well over fifty-odd students.

"I wonder if we'll get our own rooms," a girl murmurs, looking back at me hopefully. She's so thin, her limp blouse falls against pointy-sharp shoulder blades. I doubt she's had a meal to herself, much less a room. I can't help but wonder what her special skill is. Did she score perfectly on her ACT like Gil? Or is it simply that she's a girl? Stiles mentioned the dearth of female carriers. Did my test scores really matter? Or was it just that I was female and had a pulse? But no, Coco isn't here, so there must be something to my selection.

The line stops suddenly, and the skinny girl in front of me, too busy staring up at the building, collides with the girl in front of her. I hardly draw a breath before they're tangled together, screaming and thrashing and tearing at each other on the ground. It happens so quickly, I struggle to process it.

The remaining girls immediately break ranks and close around the writhing figures, watching, shouting indecipherable words. Only my lips don't move. I shake my head and look to the guard, certain she will break up the fight.

She lazily reaches for the radio on her belt. "Hey, Jensen, we got a situation with the girls."

The reply comes back scratchy. "Stand by."

I look back down, watching in horror as the other girl climbs atop the skinny one. She outweighs her by at least forty pounds. The skinny one arches her slim body, struggling to buck her off. It's useless. She can't do anything. The bigger girl grabs a fistful of Skinny's long hair and holds her steady as she pounds her in the face with her free fist.

Still, the guard does nothing.

When I look down again, I gasp. My stomach churns sickly. I can't even recognize Skinny's face anymore. There's so much blood now.

I add my voice to the din: "No. *No. Stop!*"

I dash at hot tears with my hands, blinking rapidly. I can't look anymore.

"Help!" I shout at the guard.

She arches an eyebrow and nods at something behind me. I turn. Three guards approach. A baton swings in the hand of one of the men, and I quickly learn it's not a simple baton. He reaches down and jabs the bigger girl. She shrieks and rolls off her victim. But he doesn't stop. He presses down with his stick, sending volts of electricity into her thickset body. The girl jerks madly, flopping like a fish. She starts to bleed from the mouth and I'm convinced she's bitten her tongue.

He leans down to address her, his voice loud enough to

carry over her cries and grunts. "You will not jump another carrier again unless it's part of a training exercise, understand?" He eases up for a moment to hold her gaze. "Understand? Another attack and there will be more of this." He digs the prod into her side again for emphasis.

Unable to watch, I turn away. My gaze narrows in on the other guards, their faces smug, satisfied.

And suddenly I know. I haven't escaped anything. I've walked right into it.

We're led to the second floor of the building's east wing. The elevator opens to reveal a wide lounge. A few tables help fill the space. A couch and loveseat are positioned in front of a television. I smile bitterly, imagining the seven of us watching reruns of *Glee* together. Unlikely.

"Welcome." Another individual waits for us, standing in the center of the room. She's dressed in civilian clothes and hugs a clipboard and several file folders to her chest, rocking on her heels. She smiles at us as we drift forward. Her face is so tanned and sun-weathered it's hard to estimate her age. A pair of guards flank her. They don't smile. It's as if she's the only one allowed to.

"Take a seat." She motions to the tables. "We have a few things to go over before we give out room assignments. Count yourselves lucky. With so few girls on the floor, you can each have your own room."

I sit at the same table as the skinny girl. Maybe because I feel sorry for her. Or maybe I simply feel safer with her. She's hardly a threat with her broken face and slight body tucked in on itself. I can smell the coppery scent of her blood. It's a hard reminder of where I am and what can happen if I drop my guard. Of what can happen even if I don't.

Another girl joins us at the round table. She moves with an inherent grace, holding her elegant, well-shaped limbs close to her body. Her dark hair gleams blue-black. The only thing darker is her gaze. Her black eyes watch me warily, eyeing my neck.

The four remaining girls sit at a neighboring table. The one who beat up Skinny crosses sinewy arms over her chest and assesses all of us with supreme confidence. Blood stains the front of her shirt, and it looks somehow right on her. Her face is horribly broken out with acne and pitted with old blemish scars. She bears no imprint. As though aware of this—and it's some manner of shortcoming that marks her as soft—her stare passes between me and the other imprinted girl at her table, a redhead who busies herself by chewing on her thumbnail.

The redhead's green eyes glitter in an unnerving manner, reminding me of an animal that's ready to bite the first person who tries to touch her. I cross my arms, my hands chafing over my skin.

"The seven of you will sleep on this floor. The boys are quartered in the west wing. Every night, your doors will automatically lock, and every morning they will unlock."

I glance at my hands, thinking locked doors aren't a bad thing among this bunch. I might actually get some sleep.

"Let's begin with introductions, shall we?" The woman opens her first file. "Zoe Parker. Florida State Soccer Champion two years in a row. Midfielder." She nods and glances at the redhead approvingly. The girl drops her thumb from her lips and lifts that wild green gaze to the guard. "That takes stamina. Impressive."

She moves on to the next file. "Amira Bustros." The girl with the ink-dark eyes beside me stiffens and slides her gaze to the woman fearfully. "You're first-generation American. Your parents are from Lebanon. You speak fluent Arabic." She continues nodding. "Useful."

She flips open another folder and nods to the most petite member of the group. "Moving on. Marilee Davison. You're a gymnast. Been training since age three."

That would explain her tiny stature. She must be older, but she looks like a twelve-year-old.

"I *was* a gymnast." Marilee juts her chin out defiantly. Her squeaky, girl-like voice makes me wonder if maybe she isn't closer to eight.

"Yes, well, we'll see about that," the woman answers vaguely. "Your background will come in handy."

"Davina Hamilton." Her eyes scan my file. I wait, every muscle inside me pulling tight. "Piano, violin, guitar, and voice. Accepted into Juilliard. Very nice."

I don't waste my breath reminding her that that's all in the past. Accepted and then rejected. But she knows as much. I'm here, after all.

The girl who beat up Skinny snorts and mutters beneath

her breath, "A freakin' Mary Poppins. Maybe she'll sing for us."

I shoot her a look. She holds my gaze, her thick forearms tightening across her chest. The woman continues down the list and I return my attention to her. Skinny's name is Sabine Stoger. She moved here as an infant from Austria and speaks both German and French. Sofia Valdez is from Texas and speaks Spanish. Clearly being proficient in a language is an asset to them here.

The last name on the list is the stocky girl who attacked Sabine. Addy Hawkins, a track-and-field star. She preens as her qualifications are read, staring at each of us in a way that declares she is the strongest. In case pounding Sabine hadn't illustrated that.

Apparently, she jumps a mean high bar and throws the javelin. She qualified for the US Olympic team in both events before she was detected as a carrier. I shiver, imagining her throwing that spear. Only I don't see her throwing it into the ground. I see her impaling someone with it.

"My name is Dusty," the woman announces as she closes the last file.

"Dusty?" Addy snorts.

Dusty stares at her coolly before continuing. "I'm in charge of you seven while you're all here. You've been selected because you possess special talents. You'll be expected to cultivate these strengths and add other skills to your repertoire. If you're not already bilingual, you will be expected to learn an additional language. If you're in poor physical condition, consider that temporary. You will become a perfect specimen by the end of your stay here. If you can't fight with any finesse, you will." Her gaze sweeps over each of us, letting these words sink in. "Your DNA already tells us you can kill, but to succeed here you must become controlled, you must master your baser impulses and serve a purpose that is higher than yourself. We've assembled a staff to help you reach this goal."

No one breathes. I stare at this woman. She's more than a guard, I recognize that at once. Suddenly, I see her as some kind of Yoda figure, offering hope.

She removes several sheets of paper from her clipboard and hands them to us. "These are your schedules. Memorize them. There is no excuse for tardiness. We expect total obedience or you will be ejected from Mount Haven."

I sense Amira tense beside me. It's a fate I don't want to face, either.

"You'll send us to the camps if we don't make it in here," Addy states more than asks. It seems she's the only one bold enough to say anything.

"If you're lucky, you'll be transferred to a detention camp." Dusty's expression turns grim. "You want to make it here. Trust me on that."

Transference to a detention camp would be *lucky*? What would be the *unlucky* alternative?

Unthinkingly, I hear myself answer, "Agent Stiles told my mother if this didn't work out I would go to a detention camp."

Dusty looks at me then, her gaze hard as steel in her

sun-browned face. My earlier hope that she'd be a benevolent mentor withers under her stare. "Agent Stiles is no longer here. I am."

With schedules in hand, we're led from the lounge area. The doors to our rooms are a pristine white just like everything else. A small, thick-glassed window is positioned at the top of each door—a reminder that we'll never have total privacy here.

Sabine is in the room next to mine. Her wispy-thin form darts inside, clearly eager to escape everyone. Zoe, the imprinted redhead, is on the other side of me. She moves at a slower pace, looking at me eerily with those wild, green eyes of hers before disappearing inside her room. I shiver a little, knowing that I should have anticipated this. Even though the carriers here have all been screened, they're positive for HTS. Some of them have to be dangerous . . . maybe even a little unhinged.

Dusty stops me before I get inside my room. "Hamilton, we expect great things from you."

"Really?" I swallow uncomfortably. I didn't want them to expect great things from me. I just want not to fail.

"You have the breeding the other girls lack. Gentility, if you will . . . it's important that you don't lose that here. We're going to train you to be tough . . . a skilled fighter, but don't . . ." Her voice fades as though she's searching for the right words. "You still need to maintain some sophistication. It will serve you well when you're on assignment in the field." She reaches up and taps a finger against my throat. "Shame about this. Perform to our expectations and we'll see about getting that removed. It's a painstaking process . . . delicate, but it can be done."

*They could remove my imprint? I could walk freely in the world with no one marking me on sight as a carrier?*

My chest swells at the promise of this. I never dreamed of such a possibility.

I nod eagerly. "I'll do my best."

"Excellent." She motions to my room, indicating I should go inside. "Have a good night."

Once I'm in, the door clangs shut. As I sink onto the single bed, a bolt falls into place on the other side, the sound heavy, jarring.

At least we get our own rooms. Clearly, they don't trust us alone with each other. No telling what would happen in the middle of the night. I might wake with someone's hands around my throat.

Sitting there, I think of Sean and Gil, somewhere on the other side of this building with forty-odd boys. Did they get the same type of introduction? Were they, too, expected to cultivate their talents? Gil's a computer genius, but what about Sean? What did they expect from him?

A soft sound starts up on the other side of my wall. Sabine is crying.

I move from the bed and tap the wall, pressing my face close to the plaster. "Hey, you okay?"

Her words come out muffled. "I'm never going to make it."

"You'll do great," I say. "They want us to succeed. They'll train us."

She doesn't say anything else. After a while, I sigh and step away from the wall. I change into a fresh T-shirt and shorts and lie down on the bed. Grasping the collar, I inhale the soft fabric of my favorite T-shirt. It smells like home.

I notice a pair of training pants and a black T-shirt folded neatly on the chair. For tomorrow, I assume. Probably standard issue.

Sinking back on the bed, I study my schedule and try to block out the sound of Sabine crying next door.

Mount Haven Camp Schedule

**ATHLETICS 6:00–6:45 A.M.**

**BREAKFAST 7:00–7:45 A.M.**

**ATHLETICS 8:00–9:30 A.M.**

**INDEPENDENT STUDY 9:45–11:45 A.M.**

**LUNCH 12:00–12:45 P.M.**

**CONDITIONING 1:00–2:30 P.M.**

**GROUP DRILLS 2:45–4:15 P.M.**

**INDEPENDENT STUDY 4:30–6:00 P.M.**

**DINNER 6:15–7:00 P.M.**

**COMMUNAL TIME 7:00–8:00 P.M.**

**LIGHTS-OUT 8:15 P.M.**

# TWENTY-TWO

IN LESS THAN TWENTY-FOUR HOURS, I DISCOVER just how out of shape I am. It's a painful lesson. After seventy-two hours, I'm not sure I'll survive one more day.

Every morning, the doors unbolt at six a.m. We have only a few minutes to dress before heading outside for a pre-breakfast run. The Mount Haven staff greets us with shouts and whistles and a clanging bell that makes me think I'm in a boot camp. The hard-core kind you see in movies. The type where cadets are driven to suicide. Only this isn't a movie. And none of us are here to die. By the time we get to breakfast, we fall on our food, ravenous. Sean and Gil sit at the same table as me, but we're so busy eating we barely speak.

This is my new life. We eat, work, sleep. Nothing more. Even Sabine has shaken off the effects of her thrashing. I haven't heard her cry again since that first night. She even beats me downstairs most mornings.

We run a second time after breakfast. The grounds are vast, winding through thick trees, the mountains a great hulking shape in the horizon. The run lasts over an hour and they shout at us the entire time. I try to block them out, letting music fill my head as I lift one leg after another. Somehow, I'm not the last in the pack, which I like to think is saying something. Especially since we run as one group. Boys and girls.

"You'll run together, sweat together, bleed together," the guards yell from the back of ATVs. "Out there, your gender doesn't matter! It's not going to matter in here."

Even though I'm not the slowest, I'm the slowest girl. Four boys trail me. One sounds like he's ready to cough up a lung, so that is rather lowering. And worrisome. Especially when during one of my first runs, I see a guard with a stopwatch frown and jot down my time on a clipboard.

I have to be better. Each day this is my sole thought as my feet pound over the ground. Except I'm convinced my legs will give out any moment and I'll fall flat on my face to be trampled by the boys behind me.

I push past pain. Past the stitches pinching my side.

Saliva floods my mouth one morning as I catch myself from falling. Staggering, I keep on and suddenly notice I'm not running alone anymore. Someone keeps an even pace next to me.

"C'mon. Speed up."

Gasping, lungs burning, I turn my head. Sean runs beside me, his arms swinging lightly, his strides smooth and easy like we haven't been running for an eternity. Of course this would be easy for him.

I huff at the sweaty hair falling in my face. "Just let me die."

He gives a short laugh. "You're not going to die."

"Yes. I. Am." I pant each word, marveling at how he can talk like he's strolling in the park and not fighting for every breath. It infuriates me and gives me the strength to push my legs harder.

"Not today." There's something in his voice that draws my attention. A grimness that carries over the sound of my pants and the pound of feet around us. A quick glance at his face reveals Sean focused straight ahead, his stare fixed on Sabine. Her delicate face is still bruised and swollen, her lip scabbed up. His gaze slides to Addy. The stocky girl hasn't hurt anyone else. No one has. There haven't been any altercations . . . not since the guards used that electric prod on Addy. Word got around about that.

His gaze flicks to me and he speaks in a low voice. "You need to watch your back in here. The guards can't keep us all in line. Not all the time. Some of these kids . . ." His voice fades, but I understand.

I look ahead, scanning the few dozen backs running ahead

of me. All of them carriers. Some of them must be violent at their core. The threat of electric prods and the promise of a future won't be enough to stop any true killer.

I start running harder, pushing past the burn, ignoring the tremble in my legs, the lungs that ache, determined not to be weak. To become faster, stronger. No one's victim.

I don't look to see if Sean keeps up behind me, but I sense him there. As I move ahead, I feel multiple sets of eyes on me, calculating, sizing me up. I don't back down, don't slow my pace, too aware that if I do they'll remember that I can't perform.

The only thing I need for them to remember is that I'm not weak. Not a target.

The following morning we're led into the refectory after our first run. We fall on our breakfast like wolves. As usual. We're always famished. It's a constant state of being. My stomach rolls at the generous fare spread before us. Eggs and bacon. Toast, muffins, biscuits, waffles the size of encyclopedias. Clearly, they don't intend to starve us.

I hardly chew before swallowing a mouthful. Still, I'm cautious not to overeat. I don't want to be too stuffed. We have another run and more grueling activity ahead. You eat too much and then you're left puking up your guts.

A tray loaded with food slams down in front of me. A massive, thick-necked boy sinks down across from me. His plastic chair creaks in protest. Sabine tenses beside me. She doesn't talk much, but she's always there, a shadow beside me. She especially doesn't talk with Gil and Sean, eyeing them with distrust, but her presence has become reassuring. One of the few things I can count on.

"That all you're gonna eat?" The guy nods at my plate of eggs and toast.

I take another bite of toast and shrug. Sabine has even less food on her plate, but he doesn't comment on that.

"Saw you running. My name is Tully." He fixes his gaze on me alone even though Gil and Sabine sit on either side of me. I haven't seen Sean since our run. He's probably still in line getting food.

Gil takes a loud sip from his coffee mug, his way of insinuating himself. I slide him a quick look before answering. "I'm Davy. This is Gil and Sabine."

He looks Gil and Sabine over quickly. Dismissing them, he looks back at me. "Where you from, Davy?"

"Texas."

He nods as he folds a slice of bacon into his mouth. "I'm from Oklahoma."

I've noticed Tully before, but this is the first time he's approached me. He's one of the bigger boys here. From his size, I would guess he's a jock, but I know better than to assume anything about anyone. I wonder what special skill landed him in here and not a detention camp.

"Good food," Tully remarks as he chomps on another slice of bacon. "I lived with my grandmother before this. She couldn't even boil water. Most of my food came out of a vending machine. When they expelled me from school, I was stuck out in the country with her. Nearly starved."

I eye his immense body, thinking there is little evidence to support that.

Tully suddenly waves his fork in the air. "Hey, Jackson! Over here!" He motions another boy to our table. My heart rate picks up at the arrival of the second boy. I can't help myself. I should be used to the idea that carriers surround me at every side. I'm a carrier, too.

Still, I scan the room for Sean. That first glimpse of him intimidated me. Hopefully, he has the same effect on others.

"Hey." Jackson lowers himself into the seat next to Tully. When his gaze lands on me, a wide smile stretches his lips. He's handsome in a slick kind of way. Nothing about him screams *killer* except the imprint on his neck. "Trust old Tully here to make friends with two of the girls." His gaze narrows on me. "One of the prettiest, too."

I can't stop myself from rolling my eyes. Do I look like someone to be sucked in by empty compliments?

He didn't miss the eye-rolling. His smile slips. "Nice collar. Ink looks fresh. I've had mine three years. What'd you do to get that?" A hardness enters his voice and it's like he opened a window for me to glimpse inside him and see what really lurks there.

"Nothing."

Which is true. But I know he won't believe me. He would never believe me guiltless of doing something violent and ugly. Because that's what he is . . . what he *does*. I know it. See it in the dead eyes. He's everything the world fears and rightly so.

"I'm sure," he says.

"What would I do?" I shrug and force a teasing grin. "I'm just a girl."

"That's right." Tully grins idiotically. "You're here for us."

My grin evaporates.

"That's not true," Gil cuts in.

Tully frowns at him. "You don't think the girls are expected to be trained to be anything special. . . ."

I start to get annoyed. "Why not?"

"Dude," Tully laughs. "We're going to be superspies and assassins . . . like James Bond and crap. You girls are just here to keep us entertained." He waggles his eyebrows at me and I want to slap him.

"You're wrong," I say quietly. "Each one of us was selected . . . although why you got picked is beyond me. You're clearly not here for your IQ."

Sabine inhales sharply.

Tully's face flushes. "Aren't you a lippy bitch?"

Gil tenses beside me, and it's like we're back in the Cage again with Nathan giving me a hard time. Gil's going to get himself hit again if he doesn't tread carefully. I place a hand on his arm under the table, cautioning him.

Jackson very deliberately clears his throat, drawing my attention. His fingers touch his neck. "Want to know what I did?"

"No."

He smiles and continues anyway. "There was a little girl who lived on my street—"

"Stop," I say, sensing where this story was going, but he keeps talking anyway.

"She was maybe nine, ten . . . she had this tabby cat. She loved that cat. It would actually let her push it around in this stupid doll stroller."

Sabine starts scraping the inside of her yogurt cup faster like she's desperate to do something with her hands—or just cover the sound of his voice.

"I caught that cat." Jackson's eyes hold mine. They're dead, emotionless. His fingers toy with his fork, rotating it where it rests on his tray. "I cut it open." His head cocks to the side. "Just to see what it looks like inside. I still wonder about the blood, the organs . . . how they compare to human blood."

*How they compare.* As though it's a certainty he will find this out for himself.

Jackson laughs then, low and deep, his gaze scanning the three of us. "Oh, you should see your faces."

"Is that a joke?" I ask, suddenly not sure.

He stops laughing, but the amusement still lingers in his light-colored eyes. "I'm going to enjoy you."

A chill skates my spine. Tully's announcement that girls are only here for entertainment echoes through me. I won't be entertainment for anyone here.

Gil clears his throat and, even though I warned him not to, I know he's going to speak up, stick up for me like he did in the Cage. I can't let him do that. This cage is bigger . . . with more predators in it.

"I doubt that," I say before Gil finds his voice. I stare at

Jackson, returning his snake-oil smile with one of my own. "I'm really not very likable."

"No argument there." Tully folds another slice of bacon into his mouth, evidently still smarting over my insult.

"But I like you so far." Jackson sips from his glass of orange juice. "I think we're going to be friends. It's just a feeling." His gaze skips to Sabine. "Maybe your quiet little friend here, too."

Sabine lowers her yogurt cup to her tray, and I can't help noticing how much her slender hand shakes. I hope Jackson doesn't catch it. A guy like him will pounce on the first sign of weakness.

"What's your name?" he asks her mildly. "Bet you're pretty when your face isn't so banged up."

"Sabine," she answers softly, ducking her head. Her hair falls in a brown curtain, shadowing her face. I look from her to him, concern for the smaller girl surging inside me. He glances at me, a disturbing smile curving his lips, and I know he knows. He reads me easily, knows that I feel protective toward her.

I once saw a show on a nature channel about portia spiders. They're one of the world's top predators. Spiders generally are, but this spider . . . this particular one is the most dangerous of all because it actually targets other spiders, cleverly tricking them. It identifies each individual spider's weakness and then implements the best method to attack the prey it hunts. Yeah, it's that smart and diabolical. It's him. Jackson. I know it instinctively. Hopefully, that makes me decidedly unlike the spiders that get tricked and devoured.

He refocuses on Sabine and clucks his tongue. "That lip looks like it hurts," he murmurs in a deceptively sympathetic voice.

Sabine touches the deep crack in her lip self-consciously.

"Aren't you Captain Obvious?" I snap, deliberately drawing his attention back to me.

He studies me, that smile still there. "We should all be friends. Hang out tonight during communal time. I bet I could make you both like me," he adds with a wink.

It's his choice of words—the "make you" part—that leaves me slightly queasy.

"I don't think so."

A tray drops on the table so abruptly that I jump in my seat. And I hate that I jump. That I come across so . . . affected and on edge here when I most need to appear calm. Natural amid predators. A predator myself.

Because acting the opposite would mean that I'm the prey.

"What's up?" Sean's voice rings out.

I look hard at Sean, just so glad he's here. Something flutters inside me as he tosses the sun-streaked hair back from his face and sweeps his gaze over everyone, his eyes inscrutable but no less penetrating.

He acts like everything is ordinary. Like Mount Haven is nothing new. He pops the top on a can of peach juice and takes a long swig. I watch, mesmerized at the play of muscles in his throat.

"Friend of yours?" Jackson asks, and there's something in his voice, a guardedness that wasn't there before.

"Yes," I say.

Sean sets his can down and levels his gaze on Jackson and Tully. He looks imposing, his shoulders pushing against the fabric of his T-shirt. I scan him, admiring the cut of his biceps. The intricate tattoo pattern spiraling over sinew and muscle. He's no Gil. They can't dismiss him. There's nothing soft about him. Dead eyes. Flat, cold. He's the boy I first saw in Pollock's office. This glimpse of him now brings that all back. He scared me then.

The silence lengthens. Jackson and Tully stare back at Sean, unblinking. Tension lines their shoulders and thickens in the air.

Gil speaks up. "We all came here together."

"Nice," Jackson murmurs. "To come here with friends." His gaze shifts, lingering on me. "Comforting."

"Yeah." Reaching for my plate, Sean lifts a slice of bacon off it. The action is familiar. Deliberate. It says we're together. Friends. *Maybe more than that.* Untrue, of course. He made that clear when I visited him at his house and he sent me home. That rejection still stings when I think of it. We'll never be more.

Leaning back in his chair, he tears a bite with his strong teeth. "It is nice."

No one says anything else for the remainder of the meal. I force down food and cast surreptitious glances at my table-mates. Jackson does the same, taking turns looking at me, Sabine, Sean, and Gil.

"Five minutes, people!" one of the instructors shouts.

Relief ripples through me.

Jackson and Tully shovel in several more bites and hastily rise, taking their trays with them.

Sean follows their retreat with narrowed eyes before sliding me a look. Emotion sparks in his eyes. I'm reassured to see his dead stare gone. "You need to keep a low profile."

"Like that's possible. I'm one of seven girls here."

"You were a bit antagonistic," Gil points out.

I glare at him. "What am I supposed to do? Just roll over for him?"

"You saw him." Gil jerks his head in the direction Jackson left. "He got his rocks off every time you mouthed off to him."

Heat scalds my face because he's right.

Sean looks at me intently. "I can't be here every minute."

Meaning he can't be here every minute for me. And *that* infuriates me. "I don't need you to be." I start flinging trash onto my tray.

"Davy." His hand snatches hold of mine. I feel the hard imprint of each finger on my flesh. "We need each other."

"Do we?" It sounds as though he thinks I just need him. Pain tightens my chest as I realize just how much I want *him* to need *me*.

"It doesn't matter," Sabine whispers. "Nothing can protect us in here."

I pull my hand from Sean and gently squeeze Sabine's shoulder, so slight and delicate beneath my hand. "Hey. We're getting trained in here. They don't want us to hurt each other. We'll make it through this," I vow.

Standing, I deliberately avoid looking at Sean. Sabine rises beside me, her hands tight around the edges of her tray.

Turning, I move to the line where everyone waits to dump their trash. Sean and Gil follow. I can feel their presence behind me, hear the low murmur of their voices.

I feel eyes on me. And it's not just Sean and Gil looking at me. It's everyone watching everyone, sizing each other up, probably wondering who's going to be the first to crack in this place and let their killer out.

Quarantined Zones:

**ATLANTA, GEORGIA**

**BALTIMORE, MARYLAND**

**FLINT, MICHIGAN**

**ST. LOUIS, MISSOURI**

**OAKLAND, CALIFORNIA**

**DALLAS, TEXAS**

**PHILADELPHIA, PENNSYLVANIA**

**MIAMI, FLORIDA**

**DETROIT, MICHIGAN**

**LITTLE ROCK, ARKANSAS**

**CLEVELAND, OHIO**

**PHOENIX, ARIZONA**

# TWENTY-THREE

AFTER AN HOUR AND A HALF OF SPEED AND AGILITY drills, we're released. It's Independent Study, so this is our time to work on areas where we need particular improvement. For me, the list feels endless. I could go to the firing range and practice shooting. I could work in the lab with Gil. We all need above-average programming and tech knowledge. There's also a room with musical instruments for me to practice. They don't want me to get rusty. Although that's the area I'm least worried about.

Or I could just work out. That's probably where I need the most help . . . building my strength. Not being so weak.

Releasing a great gust of breath, I drag a hand through my hair, tugging my ponytail, and collapse on the bed. It's tempting to not get up. Only I must. I don't want to fall behind. I can't. The threat of being sent to a detention camp—or worse—is there, hanging over me like a dark cloud.

With a moan, I pull myself up off the bed, drop to the floor, and start doing push-ups. Even though my muscles are shot and my limbs feel like pudding, I lower myself to the ground, making sure my nose brushes the floor. I have a flash of Zac doing this in my bedroom. A lifetime ago. Trying to impress me, I'm sure, and it worked, every time. I remember how awed I'd been that he could make it look easy even after he completed fifty.

With a pained grunt, I push myself. Up and down, up and down. Again and again, until my body trembles with exertion. I pass fifty.

And keep going. Because I won't be a target. I won't be the puny one who needs Sean and Gil looking out for me. If I'm that person, I'll never make it in this program. I'll never be the person I'm meant to be.

I'll be the mindless monster the DNA test says I am.

And that can't be right. I'm not that.

I'm not.

"Tell me about yourself, Davy."

My attention snaps to the therapist. She sits several seats to my left, about halfway down in the middle of our circle. Gil is to my right and Sean to my immediate left. His hand holds his ankle across his knee.

I'd been staring at that broad hand ever since we sat down. The light spattering of gold hairs on the back. The veins beneath the tanned flesh. It's strong and capable, tempting me to put my trust in him. Except I have to be strong in my own right, too. Allies are well and good, but I can't be weak.

The counselor looks at me, waiting.

I'm the first person in Conditioning she's addressed and this catches me off guard since there are twelve of us in the circle. I guess I thought I'd get to hear others talk first. They call this Conditioning, but it's just group therapy.

The session is part of our training, and I don't know what to do. I haven't figured out what it is they want to hear. I want to give them what they want so I can get their seal of approval and start leading a normal life again. Or close to normal anyway.

Moistening my lips, I study her carefully. The serene expression. The flawless skin. It looks like she's never stepped in the sun.

I need to say the right thing. I worry my bottom lip with my teeth. She stares at me patiently.

Worse than her stare are the eleven others, all watching, waiting. I slide my gaze to Sean and Gil, relieved that we managed to go to Conditioning together—and then feel annoyed at myself. My overwhelming relief doesn't say much for my independence. I know everyone thinks of us as friends—a clique. Sabine, too. My shadow. Except right now. She got stuck in another Conditioning session.

I've felt the eyes on us, measuring, sorting us into whatever category they think it is we belong in. Other cliques have started to form. Only a random few keep to themselves.

I say dumbly, "I'm from Texas."

The therapist looks at me with disappointment. She expects more.

Zoe yawns and stretches her arms above her head. Her T-shirt stretches taut over small, bra-free breasts, revealing a sliver of flat belly.

Several of the boys watch the redhead, varying expressions on their faces. Hunger. Contempt. She drops her arms, a cat-like smile on her makeup-free face. She wiggles in her chair as if settling in and trying to get even more comfortable. The action is inherently satisfied. She curls a finger around a bright red strand, pleased at the attention she's getting.

It's in her, too, I think. The kill gene. A part of her is capable of terrible things even though she looks like a regular girl. I glance around the circle. There's nothing about any of us that screams *danger*. No sign. No warning. A whisper slithers inside me. *Except the few of us with imprints on our necks. Except me.*

The counselor's pen scratches something in her notes, and my heart stutters nervously. "What kind of things do you want to know?" I ask, vowing to be more accommodating.

The counselor's eyes squint at me through the lenses of her glasses. "Well. For starters, what did you do to get imprinted?" She motions to my neck with her pen.

I'm sure she knows—that it's in that file sitting on her

lap. She just wants to hear me say it. I struggle not to fidget beneath her stare.

"I might have hit a guy."

This gets me a few chuckles. Not Sean though. His expression doesn't crack.

"Tell us about that." The counselor angles her head, the tip of her pen coming to rest on her chin.

Again, I'm at a loss for words, wondering what it is she truly wants to hear from me. What the right thing is to say.

"How did you feel when you hit this boy?" she prods.

Furious. Hurt. "Shocked . . . that I did that," I respond. Not a lie. It was mortifying to lose control like that in front of the kids I've known all my life.

She scrawls on her pad. "No fear for consequences then? Were you worried about that?"

"Yes," I lie because it seems like what she wants to hear.

"But remorse? For the boy? That wasn't present?"

I see Zac's face. Feel his hands roaming me, urging me to have sex with him . . . hear his words ruining the love I thought we shared.

She asks again. "Did you regret striking that boy?"

I snort. I can't help the sound escaping. Or the words: "No. He deserved it."

"And do you often feel like expressing yourself physically? With violence?"

I stare, thinking I've said too much already. This isn't going well.

She sighs, her voice slightly louder as she asks, "Did it feel good? Hitting that boy?"

My mouth works. Everything inside me urges denial. An ordinary person would never admit to such a thing. It would horrify people. But I'm not here because I'm ordinary. They don't want ordinary from me. But before I figure out what it is they do want and respond, someone else does.

"Hell. Doesn't it always feel good to ram your fist in some asshole's face?" A boy with hair like straw—the color, the texture, that way it juts all around his head—interjects. He stares at me. "Let me guess. It was some 'normal' kid, too. Right? Getting all up in your shit? Acting so superior. Like they're allowed to do whatever they want to us."

"And that justifies you lashing out?" The therapist glances down at her clipboard and flips a page. "Dylan, is it?"

"Hell, yeah, it justifies it." Dylan nods. "I want to stomp all over them."

She nods, and there's no judgment in her gaze. Quite possibly, I detect a little gleam of approval.

"I see you have an imprint, too. How did you come by it, Dylan?"

Relieved that she's moved on to someone else, I lean back in my chair.

"Last year, I was hanging out at an arcade with a friend, and the manager made us leave. Said we were too loud. I could tell he thought we were a couple punks."

She waves her pen in a small circle. "And you hit him?"

He smiles. "You could say that."

No one speaks for a moment, watching Dylan. His hand clenches in a fist on his lap and you can tell he's battling his memories.

"What happened?" the therapist prompts.

"We waited for him that night in the parking lot. Cracked his ribs. Dislocated his jaw." He chuckles. "Asshole was begging us to stop at the end." His smile turns into something twisted. It chills my blood. "I had to serve six months in juvie, but it was worth it for the look on his face before we messed it up."

I realize I'm holding my breath. I release it slowly, trying to look normal, unaffected by the story. Everyone sits quietly, scrutinizing Dylan. I wonder how many of them think what he just described is wrong.

The therapist's voice scratches the thick silence. "Do you think you have a problem taking instructions, Dylan?"

He shrugs. "I never liked doing what my caseworker told me to do."

She taps the paper. "Yes, you have a history of insubordination. But I see you were on your school's football team at one time. You must have taken commands from your coaches."

"Well. Yeah. But I liked playing ball."

"So you did what they said because you wanted to play."

"Right."

"Hm. Interesting. And now you *like* stomping all over people."

"I guess. I mean . . . you got to stick up for yourself."

"What if . . ." She searches faces before pointing at Gil. "He insults you . . . calls you a name?"

Dylan looks Gil over, clearly unimpressed. "Wouldn't take much for me to teach him a lesson."

"What if you were teamed up together and he's your partner on an assignment . . . would you still teach him a *lesson* then?"

Clearly, his answer should be no. Dylan's smart enough to catch on to that. He grins and drags two hands through his straw hair. "Oh, no. If we were working together, I'd control myself. Sure."

"But what about your anger? Your aggression? What do you *do* with those feelings?"

"Guess I'd work out, go for a run . . . and focus my energy on completing whatever job you people give me."

She stares at him contemplatively, saying nothing for several moments. Then she lowers her pen to paper. Everyone watches her as she writes on her clipboard, nodding. "Very good," she murmurs.

I resist the urge to roll my eyes. Clearly, he's passed her test . . . this borderline sociopath. It all comes together for me then. She seems to approve of admissions of violence. As long as we can claim we can be controlled. As long as we follow instructions.

Suddenly, I don't feel quite so lost. I know what she wants to hear. What they want to see in us while we're here.

My gaze flicks to Dylan. I think about what he did to get imprinted. What he did and I did just doesn't even compare, and yet we're both imprinted. We both, presumably, possess an aptitude for violence. I have it in me. At least according to my DNA. It just hasn't surfaced yet. God willing, it never will.

And yet I have to believe I'm what they're looking for. I need to make sure they see that. I cross my arms.

Looking up from her clipboard, she asks cheerfully, "Anyone else want to share?"

The question makes me think of all those first days of school when we would share our names and adventures from the summer. Trips to Vail, Costa Rica, Disney World. I don't expect to hear any of that today. No. Here, I'm more likely to get confessions that make my blood run cold.

Maybe the day will come when I get used to this. My face starts to prickle with awareness and I turn sideways to catch Sean staring at me, his blue-gray eyes all smoke and shadows. Unfathomable.

Every time I've asked him how he got his imprint, he stays ominously silent. Would it horrify me? Apparently, it didn't land him in jail. Would it be like in the beginning when I was afraid of him again?

I inhale, suddenly certain that I won't ask again.

---

**Transcript of interview with one of the first confirmed HTS carriers.**

**DR WAINWRIGHT:** . . . and do you remember the moment you took the knife from the drawer? When you cornered Monica Drexler and her daughter in the kitchen?

**RYAN YATES:** Yeah.

**DR. WAINWRIGHT:** When you approached Mrs. Drexler and her daughter . . . did she say anything to you?

**RYAN YATES:** Yeah. She begged me not to hurt them . . . not to hurt Amy.

**DR. WAINWRIGHT:** And then what happened?

**RYAN YATES:** I stabbed Mrs. Drexler first. In the chest—

**DR. WAINWRIGHT:** You stabbed her seven times. . . .

**RYAN YATES:** Yeah. I guess. I had to stop when Amy ran out of the room. She was fast. She almost made it to the door, but I caught her. . . .

**DR. WAINWRIGHT:** And then . . .

**RYAN YATES:** I told her she should have gone out with me. That she should have liked me. And I cut her throat.

**DR. WAINWRIGHT:** How did you feel then, Ryan?

**RYAN YATES:** . . . Better . . .

# TWENTY-FOUR

THE AIR SWIRLS WITH THE ODOR OF HEAT AND sweat. Tully bounces anxiously like he's some sort of prize-fighter. I can actually hear the thud of his bare feet smacking the red mat as he jogs in place, his face quickly growing red—whether from exertion or his eagerness to pummel me, I'm not sure.

Tully has one silver tooth that seems to wink in the light as he grins widely at me. He thinks this is going to be easy.

Even if I hadn't met him already, I would know his name by now. I've made it a point to learn all the carriers' names. The same way I've made it a point to mark the truly dangerous ones. Probably a useless task. It's not always the ones who look dangerous you have to watch out for. Sometimes it's the quiet ones. The ones with downcast eyes and fidgety hands. Just the other day, one kid jumped another one during a run and stabbed him with a fork for no reason I could determine. They were both taken away. One to the infirmary. Who knows where the other one went? I haven't seen him since.

Tully slaps one gloved fist into his other hand. I roll my eyes. It's like he's acting out some fantasy movie. I wonder if it dawns on him that fighting a girl who weighs a buck twenty hardly makes him a hero.

I glance at the tae kwon do master who has been instructing us and raise an eyebrow. He stares back mildly without saying a word—doubtlessly waiting to see if I'm going to complain about being paired up with Tully. Apparently, matching me with this Goliath makes sense to him.

I bite back any objections and square my shoulders. Complaining won't get me anywhere. Except maybe sent away. Of that I'm convinced. If I've learned nothing else since arriving at Mount Haven, it's that my place here is far from guaranteed.

I've been giving everything of myself to make sure I can hold my own. That I can hang with the boys. And not just the scrawny ones. All of them. The best of them. Bruises of varying shades decorate my body as testament to that.

Going into our third week, we're down from fifty-two to forty-eight. The kid attacked during the run is still in the infirmary. At least I think he's still there. He could have been sent away. Or died. The boy who attacked him is, of course, gone. Another boy, a twelve-year-old who cried all the time, left on the fifth day. I noticed him missing in the morning at roll call.

The fourth kid missing is a boy who slipped in the shower. His injuries were too serious for the infirmary and he had to go to the hospital. That's the explanation given anyway. In this environment, I suspect something else happened. There are other ways to get a cracked head. Other more *probable* ways when living among sociopaths.

The instructor ties off my gloves and then tests their fit with several hard tugs. "Good?"

I nod.

He looks over his shoulder at the guy who outweighs me by at least a hundred pounds. "Good luck."

Before he steps off the mat, I scan the gym. We've all been broken into various groups. Other couples spar on mats like me with Tully. A few take personal instruction with trainers. Others run, circling the track.

I've lost sight of Sean and Gil. They're here somewhere, but I don't have the time to locate them. Not with Tully getting ready to pounce. I focus all my attention on him. Squaring off, I balance on the balls of my feet. In my mind, I replay all the tricks the trainer showed me. Specifically, the ones to use when I'm seriously outmatched. Which will be most of the time when it comes to me facing off with a guy.

Tully charges me. Fortunately, he's slow. I pivot on my feet and he barrels right past me. He staggers and almost loses his balance. Arms flailing, he rights himself.

Whirling around, he scowls at me. "You can't run forever."

Maybe not, but that's basically what the trainers taught me to do. Evade. Tire out my opponent. All their advice runs through my head: *You're always going to be smaller than the average opponent. So be quicker. Dodge them. Don't let them get their hands on you.*

He charges again and I cut sideways, managing to stick out my foot and swipe his leg out from under him as he passes.

I hear a bark of laughter and someone claps in approval. The trainer? Another carrier? I'm not sure, and I don't dare take the time to look around and see.

Apparently, Tully hears, too. And he doesn't much care for anyone laughing at him. He roars and lunges for me again, swinging his arms widely as though he's going to sweep me up in one of those thick tree trunks.

He clips my shoulder, which makes my heart pump harder that he's even that close to me. *Don't let him get his hands on you.*

I skip away faster, leading him on a merry chase. We do this for a while. Me just barely avoiding him. Him getting red-faced and angry. It's working. He's gasping. Getting tired. Frustrated. If I didn't have to stay on this mat, I'd be long gone by now. But I do. Just like in real life—I can't always run. Sometimes I have to stay and fight.

Instructors are watching and I want them to be if not impressed, then satisfied with my performance. I need them to scrawl down on their clipboards that Davina Hamilton needs to stay here longer . . . for the duration of the program.

Suddenly, Tully grabs my ponytail. The unexpected move catches me off guard. I scream as he uses my hair as a handhold and slams me back on the mat. My head bounces and I can't help thinking that the mat isn't nearly as soft as it looks.

The air escapes me in a pained whoosh. He straddles me and forces any remaining bubble of air from my lungs.

I try to buck him off, but there's no moving the ox. My hands scrabble, punching, scratching until he traps them at my sides with his knees. I fall still, panting beneath him. No whistle blows, no shouts to stop the match. Grimly, I wonder how long they're going to let this play out. In a sane world, in my old world, someone would put a stop to this now. Before the boy hurts the girl.

But I'm not in that world anymore. There's only this.

I can feel dozens of eyes on us. Carriers and instructors alike, watching us like two specimen under the glass.

Feverishly, my mind works, trying to recall the practice moves I learned over the last week and if any of them can help me out of this situation.

He leans close and that silver tooth catches the light, winking down at me. "Think you're so good now?" His gloved fist floats inches from my face, ready to connect. I fight the need to flinch that shakes through me.

I swallow my fear in a bitter wash of saliva. "Made you work for it though, didn't I?" It's all bravado. For him. For anyone watching. But I say it . . . spit the words out.

His face burns ever redder. A drop of sweat rolls off his nose and splats onto my cheek. "Yeah. So this is going to be even sweeter."

He spares my face.

A gloved fist connects with my side. Pain explodes in my ribs. I gasp, choke for air through the blur of agony. I haven't recovered before he does it again.

The world darkens for a moment. And then flashes of light spin and twirl above me until my vision eventually clears. It's him again. Tully in my face. Filling my world.

"So tough with your imprint? But you know what I think of all you guys walking around here with imprints?" He leans his face close to my ear. "You're a bunch of tools to ever get caught doing anything in the first place. Me? I've done lots of things. Especially to girls like you. There was one girl that rode my bus. She had a big mouth. It was so easy to pin her to the backseat . . . break her finger. Like snapping a twig. Her mouth wasn't so big after that. And I made sure she knew it would be worse if she told on me." This he says with particular relish, his eyes getting an almost glazed look . . . like he's remembering the pain he's inflicted. "And I ain't never been caught."

He lets this sink in. Doubtlessly to feel and appreciate my chill of horror. I school my features, struggling to let nothing bleed through.

He continues, "If I hadn't been tested, nobody would ever have known about me."

The irony is that he's probably right. Wainwright did

something good getting this guy off the streets.

I struggle to free my arms. No luck there, I scan his fleshy, perspiring face. His nose, like the rest of him, is larger than average. Bulbous almost, veins popping along the outsides of his flaring nostrils. Before I chicken out, I lift my neck and crash my forehead into his nose. I hit him as hard as I can—overlooking the pain in my skull, knowing it's only a fraction of the agony he's feeling.

He howls and pulls back, slapping his hands over his nose.

It does nothing to block the gush of blood. I ignore it, shoving back my disgust at the dark red spray splattering my shirt.

Taking advantage of the moment, I jump to my feet. While he's still down, I kick him in the stomach. Once. Twice.

He turns, angling his body into a protective ball, one hand still clutching his nose. I deliver a few more kicks, seizing my opportunity, knowing he could recover at any second and be on his feet. I simply act, not thinking about what I'm doing . . . about how it feels . . . heady and euphoric. He starts to push up, and I press my gloves together and bring them down on his head. He collapses back down from the blow.

My chest rises and falls with heavy pants. My arms hang at my sides. Incredulous, I hesitate, gawking at him . . . marveling that *I* beat him. All by myself. Grinning, I look around.

And that's my fatal mistake.

He rushes me, shouldering my legs at the knees. I hit the ground like a limp doll. I fall harder than last time. My head collides into the mat so hard I think it rattles my brain. Jars my teeth and whips my neck.

He shows no mercy. This time his fist connects with my head in a vicious crack. The force stuns me. Every nerve in my face screams out. And when he brings his glove down a second time, I feel the skin split in my cheek.

My vision blurs, but I can make out his mangled face, the mashed nose dripping blood. His gloved fist is pulled back for another blow, and something tells me this time, when he hits me, I won't stay conscious. It will knock me out. No way can I stay awake for more of this.

Then he's gone.

I'm free. My aching lungs swell with air, but even that movement makes the pain in my face worse. Unbearable.

I force myself up, but my movements feel slow . . . like I'm underwater. My side screams and I clutch my ribs.

I hear them before I see them, before my gaze focuses, locating the pair on the mat. Sean wrestles with Tully, their bodies writhing and straining against each other.

Sean is fierce and wild, his body moving with a fluidity and ease that almost seems at odds with the power behind the violent blows he's delivering every chance he gets. He's getting more punches in than Tully. Pounding him in the face, the side of the head, the shoulders, the torso . . . anywhere he can reach. Finally, Tully's not lifting his arms up to defend himself at all anymore. He just takes every blow, lies there like a sponge.

Dimly, I realize a crowd has gathered to watch. Several call out words of advice and encouragement. To Tully or Sean, I'm not sure.

Sitting on the mat, seeing what everyone else sees—Sean rescuing me, pummeling my opponent because I failed . . . because *I* had dropped my guard—disgust washes over me.

I stand, swaying a little. Another weakness. I blink, fight through the dizziness. Luckily, no one pays attention to me; all eyes are focused on Sean trouncing an insensible boy. I step forward to stop him and drop, falling to my knees. I don't reach him before an instructor is there, tugging Sean away.

"C'mon, O'Rourke. He's finished."

*He's finished*. Meaning Sean finished him. *Not me*. Disappointed in myself, I watch Sean as he climbs off Tully.

His gaze scans the crowd, searching. For me, I realize. As though he needs to see me and satisfy himself that I'm okay. His gaze lands on me, and his shoulders seem to relax, the rigidity slipping away ever so slightly, water through a sieve.

For a moment, something unfurls inside me and lightens. A loosening in my chest. A flutter in my stomach. And then I remember myself and what I am. What I'm supposed to be. . . .

Not some girl who swoons when a boy flexes his muscles. Not someone who should be letting her heart *feel* anything. In this place, feelings, sentiment, will only bring me down.

"O'Rourke?" The instructor faces him, his expression annoyed. "Why did you abandon your assigned activity?"

Sean says nothing. The instructor follows Sean's gaze, glancing back at me, and I resist the urge to cover my face. I can feel the warm blood trickling down from the gash in my cheek. He surveys me from head to toe with a quick sweep of his eyes. His lips quirk, amused. The instructor nods as if he understands perfectly. And I'm sure he does. Everyone does. Sean fought my battle because I made a mistake and dropped my guard.

The instructor sighs and shakes his head. "It's critical for your training that you prove you can follow directions." That said, he pats Sean on the shoulder, glancing down once at Tully on the mat. He snorts at the pitiable sight of him.

Sean might have broken away from what he was supposed to be doing and interfered in my training, but he demonstrated his strength. Apparently, that scored him some points today.

Just what I was trying to do.

Sean's gaze locks on me. He's slightly winded, but as far as I can see there's not a scratch anywhere on him. His eyes are bright, alive, and alert in a way they never are when he's his usual stoic self. Which makes me wonder if this isn't the real him. More beast than man, reveling in breaking someone else down.

The instructor is at my side now. Something in his voice heightens my sense of failure. "C'mon, Hamilton. Let's get you to the infirmary so they can clean up your face."

The infirmary. Where no one has managed to come back from yet.

"I don't need to go—"

"Your face is bleeding. C'mon." He grasps my arm. There's no refusing him.

I look away from Sean's searching gaze. As I'm marched

out of the gym, I keep my eyes straight ahead, determined to meet no one's gaze. To give no one the slightest clue of what's going on inside me. That I'm not screaming inside, panicked that I'm not strong enough for this place, that I'm stuck with this imprint on my neck forever. That I just put myself one step closer to a detention camp.

Dear Davy,

They said we could write to you. I don't know if you can write back, if you have the time, but I'll keep sending you letters. It's enough to know that you're getting them and you know that we're thinking about you. We're so very proud of you. They've quarantined San Antonio like so many other cities now. Things are bad. Since the mandatory testing, more and more carriers are being identified and they're running. Not that there's anywhere to run. They're trying to get to Mexico, but anyone caught crossing the border is shot on sight by patrols. They might not be screening and testing over there yet, but they don't want our carriers, either. I can't tell you how relieved I am that you're safe, that you've been spared. You're going to be great at whatever it is they're training you to be. . . . You have to be. . . .

*—Letter sent from Mitchell Hamilton*
*Never opened*
*Destroyed upon receipt at Mount Haven*

# TWENTY-FIVE

AFTER AN HOUR IN THE INFIRMARY, ONE OF THE nurses releases me. My heart pounds with elation as I hurry down the building's steps. I walk quickly, as if I'm escaping . . . as if they might change their minds and pull me back and throw me into a vehicle and drag me out of here to the detention camp I saw on TV.

I leave Tully behind in the infirmary, too. I heard him several curtains down from me, moaning as they treated him. One of the senior instructors entered, walked right past me where I sat on a cot, and whispered for several moments with the nurse, their voices too low for me to understand. Maybe

Sean hurt Tully badly enough that he needed a hospital. Even if Sean beat him, I can't imagine they would kick a guy like Tully out of here. And thanks to Sean, he'll probably keep his distance.

I know Sean was trying to help me, but this isn't a game where I get a second chance. I have to prove myself. Nobody can doubt that I belong here for even one second.

I pass the dining hall. Through the glass windows, I can see dark shapes moving around. Dinner must have started.

I keep going, deciding I'd rather skip a meal than walk in there with a bandage on my face advertising my weakness. I can imagine the smirks. They probably all think I'm a wimp who can't cut it on my own without Sean.

A golf cart approaches, its engine a low, bug-like buzz. The cart slows. The driver squints at me in the fading daylight.

"Just coming from the infirmary." I motion behind me. "The nurse told me to rest." I risk the lie.

He nods. I watch as the guard drives off to continue his surveillance. Aside from the perimeter wall and guarded gate, his patrol is the extent of security and only heightens my need to stay here, where I have a semblance of independence. I don't kid myself that I'm totally free, but if I left here I'd be trading that in for barbed wire and guards with guns herding us around the clock, ready to shoot. Here, I have the hope of a future.

The building is tomb quiet as I enter. Once dinner is over, the halls will fill with footsteps and voices. The pipes will creak in the walls as the showers start running.

I take the stairs instead of an elevator, ignoring the way my body aches like it just got stomped all over. My face throbs, and I start to fantasize about a warm shower with none of the other girls in the bathroom watching, sizing me up. Always watching. Judging.

I gather my things from my room and enter the girls' showers. As soon as the water meets my body, I close my eyes and use the cucumber shower gel I brought from home. For a moment, I can pretend I'm still in my shower. That when I step out it will be onto a rug so plush I actually sink an inch. And when I look up it's going to be my bathroom with its familiar gilded mirror.

Shutting off the shower, I wring out my hair and wrap myself in my towel waiting on the hook. Stepping out onto the tiled floor, my plastic flip-flops squelch under me. I wipe the fog off the glass and proceed to brush out my hair, examining my reflection.

I want to look away but can't. The left side of my face is swollen so much my eye is slightly squinty. Two butterfly bandages cover where the skin is torn open in an ugly, crescent-shaped cut.

For a moment, I can only stare. Take in the face. The straggly dark blonde hair. The notably darker eyes, a tawny brown with faint smudges of blue underneath. Twin bruises. And then there's the ink band circling my neck.

*Who is this girl?* The well-bred girl who sang opera and carefully styled her hair every morning so that it looked artfully messy is gone. As good as dead. Strangely enough, she has to be if I want to survive.

Shaking off morbid thoughts, I quickly braid my hair into one long rope, not even bothering to tie the end. I let it hang down my back as I change into shorts and a cotton T-shirt.

Sabine enters the bathroom. "Hey," she murmurs, propping a narrow hip against the bathroom sink. "You missed dinner."

"Yeah. Not that hungry."

"You okay?" Her gaze travels my face. "Saw what happened during drills."

"Looks worse than it is. They gave me a couple Tylenol. I should be fine tomorrow."

Her nostrils flare. "You smell nice. Is that the soap they gave us?"

"Uh, no." I fumble for my bath gel. "It's this. Want to use it?"

She takes the bottle, looking it over as if it's vastly interesting. "Thanks." She looks up at me, her gaze probing, hopeful. "It's pretty nice here. I mean, we have it good. Right?" Despite her words she sounds uncertain.

"It's better than the alternative."

"Is that the only alternative then? A detention camp?" She toys with the cap, glancing up at me and then looking back down. "We could run away . . . maybe go to Mexico. I hear that's where lots of carriers are heading. They don't screen over there."

*We?* I'm not sure if she's speaking in the hypothetical or not, but I feel the need to squash the notion of "us." At least when referring to the possibility of running away. I look around nervously, as though we might be overheard by some invisible person.

"How? How would we get there? We have no transportation. No money." I point to my neck. "I wouldn't make it into the next town."

She nods, her wan expression all the more stark with the yellowish bruises on her narrow face. "I know. I heard security at the border is really tough. My father looked into it. He might have risked it, ran with me . . . but he was worried about the rest of the family." She shrugs as if it's okay that her father chose the welfare of his other children over her.

"Our best shot is sticking it out here."

She waves at me. "That might be easier for you than me."

"Hey. Have you seen me run? And what are you talking about? You speak three languages. They want to keep you around, too."

She nods again, still looking miserable. "I just miss my family."

"I know, but we'll probably see them again after we finish here."

"You think so?"

I smile encouragingly, unable to bring myself to say an outright yes. I don't want to make her that promise. I couldn't.

"You're lucky you have those guys. Sean and Gil. I wish I came here with someone."

My smile falters. "Yeah." Suddenly, I feel wrong for being so angry with Sean. What am I going to do? Ask him not to care? To ignore me and not lift a finger if I get into trouble?

That's not him. Ever since I met him in the Cage, he's proven himself to be the type who helps others. Gil. Me. He tried to help Coco, only she didn't want it. Well, I'm not Coco. I need people. Friends. Sean.

Snapping my attention back to Sabine, I squeeze her arm. "You have me now."

Smiling, she ducks her head and studies the bottle of shower gel again. "I think I'm going to try this now. I'll bring it back when I'm done."

"Take your time." Turning, I leave the bathroom.

I'm alone during Independent Study, practicing guitar in a room on the second floor. It's a beautiful instrument. Solid, flamed maple wood. Triple-bound body inlaid with intricate rosettes. My fingers move over the strings, strumming, testing the sweet, pure sound.

In the distance, I can hear pops from the firing range. Occasionally, voices drift from the corridor outside, other carriers or the guard talking on his radio to someone. Next door, an instructor teaches Spanish to a handful of students. Her muffled words carry through the wall.

I already spent an hour on the piano. Several other instruments occupy the room. A violin and bass. An electric guitar with the requisite amp. It's my very own music room. I guess it makes me feel better . . . knowing they went to so much trouble for me alone. They must really want me to succeed. But that's not the only reason it makes me feel better. Losing myself in music is a familiar comfort, a reminder of what I was.

Still, being in here, indulging like this makes me feel guilty. I should be running or working out in the weight room during this time. Especially after yesterday. I haven't forgotten how to play or sing. It's imbedded in my DNA. Among other things. A year-long break from the piano, and I would still be able to play it. That's what they don't get about me. No one taught me when I was three how to play. I just knew.

I don't have a choice though. Dusty said I had to spend Independent Study in here.

My fingers move, falling into their own rhythm. A song buried somewhere in my subconscious stirs within me. Without deliberation, the smooth, smoky chords of an old Johnny Cash song come to me. I slide into it, humming the lyrics of "Hurt" lightly. Closing my eyes, I lose myself in the song, letting the words sweep through me and flow from my lips. "If I could start again, a million miles away, I would keep myself, I would find a way. . . ."

My fingers graze the strings, letting the final chord reverberate through the room long after the last words die on my lips.

I flatten my fingers against the strings, killing that final, haunting echo. I'm aware of the warm slide of tears on my cheeks. I lift my face, letting the air dry them.

"Davy."

My eyes fly open and I spin on my stool, the back of my hand wiping furiously at my face.

Sean stands just inside the room, his back to the closed door.

I push to my feet, my fingers squeezing tightly about the guitar's neck. "Sean? What are you doing here?" His shirt clings damply to his chest. He must have come from working out.

"That was beautiful."

My face heats. "How long were you standing there?"

He pushes off the door. "I had no idea you could sing like that . . . and play the guitar. . . ." He shakes his head as though marveling. All my life people have reacted this way. Awed. Impressed. But it's different coming from him. Somehow, it feels special. For the first time in a long time, in his eyes, I feel important. I feel like I'm someone again.

"No wonder you're here. You're amazing."

The heat in my cheeks intensifies. My ears burn. I inhale deeply, fighting back the emotion swelling inside me. "What are you doing here?" I repeat.

"I needed to see you."

"You saw me at breakfast," I remind him. "You'll see me at lunch."

"But we can't really talk. We're never alone."

I nod. "We never are." We're always with other carriers, guards, and instructors watching our every move. "You shouldn't be here. Where are you supposed to be? The guard outside—"

"I'm supposed to be in Spanish, but don't worry. The guard stepped out."

"But he'll be back." Anxiety rides my voice.

"Yesterday—"

"You have to go." I set my guitar on its stand. I don't want to talk about yesterday. About how Tully got the best of me. How Sean stepped in to rescue me. My feelings about that are all a-jumble. Relief. Humiliation. Fear. How am I ever going to make it in here? Or even out there?

He moves across the room and grasps my shoulders in both hands, forcing my gaze back up. I flinch at his touch, his nearness. I haven't been touched . . . or touched anyone since arriving here. Discounting getting my ribs punched, of course. It's amazing how, in so short a time, it could become such an alien thing for me. How I want to melt into his hands.

He raises an arm, and I jerk reflexively. I guess I've learned that here . . . how to be on guard. He frowns but doesn't back off. Instead, his hand lifts to my face. I tense, forcing myself to stand still, resisting the urge to bolt as his fingers lightly land on my cheek. He gently brushes the bandage there. I know from my reflection this morning that a bruise discolors the flesh beneath my eye. He winces as if it hurts him.

"Why are you here? Are you going to tell me I need to watch my back again? That's kind of hard to do when I'm sparring with someone, you know?" I laugh hoarsely.

His fingers slide around my neck until he's cupping the back of my skull in his hand, and any hint of laughter flees. "I just want you to be safe."

"Look where we are . . . this world. How can that ever happen?"

He drops his forehead to mine. Our noses almost touching, he whispers, "You just need to make it out of here, okay?"

*Me.* He makes no mention of himself. It's almost like he doesn't care what happens to him and this saddens me. He should care. Someone should care. He deserves that.

His smoky eyes mesmerize me, pull me in. "What about you?"

"Me? I'll be fine."

And I realize, of course, he has someone who cares. *I care.*

I step back. His fingers drop from my face and I can breathe a bit easier again. "You need to go. We'll both be in trouble if you're caught in here."

He nods slowly and moves for the door. "I'll see you at lunch."

I nod and bite my lip to stop from asking him to stay. As if he could. As if there's a choice in the matter. Every once in a while the girl I used to be rouses and wants all those things she had before. Friends. Freedom. A boy who looks at her and touches her with lingering hands.

It's a hard battle. The life I had is a dim dream that haunts me still. Somehow, Sean makes me forget. And remember.

A dangerous combination when I'm only supposed to be looking ahead to the future.

Carriers are like a cancer to this once great nation. And like any disease, sometimes the only way to battle it is with poison. . . .

*—Dr. Wainwright in a hearing before Congress*

# TWENTY-SIX

THE FOLLOWING EVENING, A SIREN PEALS OUT across the air an hour before lights-out. We all step into the dusk wearing similar expressions of confusion. We never deviate from the schedule. Several kids are wet from the showers. A few stragglers join us, looking sweaty and red faced. Evidently, they were getting in an extra workout. Sabine materializes by my side, her long brown hair damp from a recent shower.

We converge as a herd on the center of the grounds in front of the main building, where we meet up for our morning run. Several instructors wait there beside a table loaded with small black packs. Colored stripes mark each one. Guards on ATVs surround the table, watching us with their ever-wary stares.

Harris calls out, "We have an exercise planned for you tonight."

I glance to the sky, wondering how long this exercise will take. It will be dark soon.

"We are dividing you into seven groups, to be identified by color. When your name is called come forward with the rest of your team."

Sabine inches a step closer. "What's happening?"

"I'm sure it's just a team exercise. Probably for morale."

She nods, but her hazel eyes still look nervous.

Harris holds up a clipboard and shouts: "Blue team! Jones, Henke, O'Rourke, Morales, Stone, Bustros, and Ruiz."

I jerk at the sound of Gil's and Sean's names and then quickly try to cover my reaction. Stare straight ahead, pretending that I'm unaffected to learn that I'll be on a team with six or seven other carriers who aren't Sean. Aren't Gil. Not even Sabine, I realize, as names for the red team are announced. With a glance full of regret, Sabine moves to join her group.

It soon becomes apparent there is only one girl for every team.

"Green team: Hong, Miller, Lionetti, Hamilton, Ramiro, Knolls, and Hauser. Step up."

My legs walk a steady line to join my group. Tully's on my team, his face gruesomely bruised and swollen from yesterday. That can't feel good. He avoids looking at me. I haven't had any dealings with my other teammates, and I'll take that as a positive. We wait until the last team is announced. The packs sitting on the table are handed to us according to colored stripes.

"You will have however long it takes to capture and return the target." Harris waves an arm and suddenly there is a new arrival in our midst. A guard leads a man forward. He's nondescript, wearing workout clothes similar to our own. Only I've never seen him before. This guy is in his late twenties, his fierce, alert eyes at odds with his bland expression.

"Our volunteer here served in the Marines not too long ago. He should prove quite the challenge for you."

The volunteer scans us all, and I get the impression that he's memorizing and categorizing us in that one glance.

Harris claps him on the shoulder amiably. "Go ahead. You've already been briefed on the local geography. We'll give you a five-minute lead."

The volunteer takes off, practically a blur as he vanishes in the trees, and I know we shouldn't underestimate him.

Dusty continues, "There is a GPS inside your pack along with a few other essentials. Your team may attempt to track the target however you see fit. I don't need to remind you that your performance is being evaluated. Should your team successfully return the target, you shall be rewarded. You have five minutes to discuss and devise your plan, starting now."

I turn to face the six other members of my team.

"We should split up," a caramel-skinned boy announces. I think his name is Ty. He's fast—usually runs at the front of the pack in the mornings.

"And go after him individually? That defeats the purpose

of a team exercise," Felix remarks. I've seen him walking with Gil into the computer lab for Independent Study and I'm pretty sure he's another tech whiz. Whatever the case, he can't be that bad if Gil voluntarily talks to him.

"No, not individually," Ty says. "But we should split into pairs . . . increase our odds of finding him. I'll go with Tully here."

Nodding, the remaining four boys pair up. I shift uncomfortably on my feet, waiting to be noticed. They're too busy rifling through their packs now, assessing supplies.

"Flashlight, pocketknife, some rope. Oh, look. A GPS. The school and perimeter walls are already plugged in. This is good." Felix starts punching buttons on the device. "We'll divide the area into three sections—one for each of us."

Still, no one has claimed me as part of their pair. I'm not included in the plan. Annoyed, I start to speak up, but the words fade at the sound of several shouts and excited whoops.

We all look up as two teams take off into the woods like kids released from recess. They tear off like hounds on a trail. Only they look scattered and unorganized. A few of the kids run at a sprint, their expressions feral, wild. They haven't even thoroughly investigated their packs yet. A few are even left on the ground, forgotten.

"Idiots," Felix mutters before looking back at us. Nodding, he announces confidently, "We got this."

"What about her?" Ty asks, nodding at me. Finally. They remember my existence.

The six of them stare at me like they don't know quite

what to do with me. In their eyes, I'm just a useless girl. My performance with Tully yesterday probably didn't help in that regard, either.

"Leave her," the jerk himself grumbles.

"She can come with me and Richard." Felix's gaze steadies on me. "Just keep up. And do what I say."

My lips compress. I grab my pack and sling it over my shoulder. Nothing I can say will prove that I'm an asset. I'll just have to show them. "Let's go."

We set out at a steady pace. Before I dive into the trees, I pause and look out across the quad, searching for the blue team. My gaze lands on them. They're heading in the opposite direction. Sean follows at the rear, his face turned in my direction, and I know he's kept a bead on me this whole time.

I drag a breath deep into my lungs, wishing I could close the distance between us. Wishing we were on the same team. Stupid, I know, that I can still wish for anything in a world, a life, I've ceased to hold any control over. I should know better than to wish for anything anymore.

He nods at me once, his gaze sharp, the smoky blue bright and penetrating with a message I've heard from him time and again: *Watch your back.*

Turning, he disappears with the rest of his team, leaving me with mine.

Thankfully, Felix and Richard don't break into a sprint and I'm able to keep up with them. Or maybe I'm just faster than I was a week ago. I can only have gotten better, faster, stronger.

At least I tell myself this, determined to keep up and prove myself. If it kills me, I will. I'll show them I'm not someone to be overlooked.

Felix moves with one eye on the GPS. We hear shouting in the distance, other carriers acting like morons, crashing around like a herd of elephants in the deepening night. With all that racket, the target will easily evade them. I motion for us to move away from the worst of the noise. Felix nods, agreeing. When Richard starts to speak, Felix punches him in the arm and motions for him to shut up. Apparently, we're on the same page regarding the need for stealth. The quieter we are, the better our chances.

Leaves rustle nearby and we still.

Richard brandishes his pocketknife, twirling it in his fingers. He's one of the youngest of us here. Maybe thirteen or fourteen, but he holds the knife with such ease, like it's an extension of his arm.

The blade glints in the moonlight and I wonder why the weapons were even put in our packs to begin with. A bunch of armed carriers doesn't strike me as such a great idea.

Initially, I assumed it was a tool, like the flashlight and rope... something we might need to use out here in the woods. Now I don't know. Are we expected to use it on the target?

On each other?

A knot of unease settles into the pit of my stomach as I walk one pace behind the two boys, scanning the press of foliage around us. Knowing we're not alone out here, the sudden hush is eerie. My skin prickles. Moving as quietly as possible, I slide my pack around and remove my knife, palming the slight weight of it.

Something snaps to our left, and branches rustle again. This time louder. We form a wall and face the direction of the sound.

Three bodies burst through the undergrowth. My stomach lurches at finding myself face-to-face with Zoe and two other boys from her team. In the moonlight, her green eyes are as wild as ever. Of course, they're armed with their knives. At the sight of me, she lifts hers in a menacing manner.

Felix holds up his hands. "Hey." His voice is calm, placating. "Easy, there."

"This is our area," Zoe hisses, lifting her chin and shaking back her bright red hair as though she wants to make sure he sees her imprint. "Move on."

Richard snorts. "I didn't see a sign."

Zoe's eyes flash. "Keep moving, runt." She motions an arm behind them, to the area they already covered.

"How generous," I mutter, moving past them, Felix and Richard following.

We continue to walk, stepping stealthily, but we're still too loud. Our boots crack over leaves and twigs. The whoops are few and distant now. Maybe the others have finally figured they have to try for stealth to capture the target.

Richard steps on a branch and it cracks loudly on the air. Blowing out a frustrated breath, I place a hand on his arm, stopping him. Felix turns, silent question in his eyes.

Bending, I unlace my boots and slip them off, leaving my

feet clad only in socks. Soundlessly, I tuck my shoes inside my backpack. Felix's eyes gleam in approval and he and Richard follow suit. On the move again, our steps tread silently. Everything around us is quiet. Too quiet, and I wonder at that. The crickets aren't even talking anymore.

Somehow, I end up leading the way. Wincing at a sharp rock beneath my foot, I step behind a small copse. Squatting, I motion the boys down low to the ground with me, figuring we have better odds lying in wait and seeing who makes an appearance.

For several minutes, nothing happens. Clouds drift over the moon, plunging us into heavy gloom. We wait, draped in darkness, silence pulsing all around us.

The clouds part suddenly and the moon breaks cover. Once again, a dim glow suffuses the forest. I spot movement ahead. A shadowy shape drops low into some shrubbery, obviously trying to stay clear of the moonlight. I nudge Felix. He nods, seeing the figure, too.

I don't breathe, waiting for him to make a move again . . . for his sense of security to return. For him to think that he's safe. That no one watches him.

Just as I begin to doubt whether he's even still there, he rises. My chest lifts high on an excited breath. My pulse hammers fiercely against my throat.

Our target hunkers low, inching toward the west. A quick glance at the GPS in Felix's hand reveals that the perimeter wall is closest in that direction. He's headed that way, of course. If he gets over the wall, he's free. He wins.

Richard starts to move, but I stall him with a hand on his arm. Shaking my head, I try to convey that we need to wait until our target comes closer. Watching the dark outline, I carefully remove the rope from my pack. I face forward again and peer through the branches. I hold my hand up, ready to give the signal.

The man advances stealthily, obviously an expert at moving undetected. When he's as close as he's going to get, about six feet across from us, I drop my hand. We tear through our copse of trees.

I see a flash of his startled face the second before he turns to run. Richard is fast, tackling him to the ground with a loud grunt.

They struggle. The target stuns Richard with a solid blow to the face that sends Richard into a rage. Like some trigger has been pulled, he starts hitting him wildly. The target tucks himself into a tight ball, his hands shielding his head, pleading, his words gibberish.

"Richard, stop." I pull the gasping boy back. Richard glares down at him, his look murderous. Easily evidence of his HTS—*or* that his being here, training with a bunch of older, rougher kids, is making an impression. If you don't have any violent tendencies, chances are you'll leave here fully conditioned with them.

"It's just a game," I remind him in what I hope is a soothing voice.

Felix snatches the rope from my hands and works quickly to bind the target's arms. He wraps his upper body in the rope, trapping his arms at his sides and leaving a couple feet of rope for us to lead the prisoner—like a leash.

"C'mon." Felix rises and tugs him to his feet. "The sooner we get back to camp, the sooner—"

He never finishes his sentence. Another team bursts through the trees and forms a tight circle around us.

My skin pulls, awash with a thousand needle pricks as Jackson steps to the front of three others, two boys and Addy. A slow smile curls his lips. "And you even gift wrapped him for us. How thoughtful."

Richard steps in front of the target. "He's ours."

Jackson turns his smile on Richard and tries to ruffle his hair. The kid knocks his hand away. "Nice try, but sorry. We're taking him."

"No," I announce grimly.

Jackson's smile thins but doesn't evaporate entirely. "Are you going to fight me on this, Davy?" His gaze slides over me. "That could be fun."

"Yeah," Addy seconds. Even in this lighting, the pit marks and acne on her face stand out starkly. "That could be real fun."

My breath falls faster, chest rising with anger. Heat creeps over my face as I stare at the shadowy faces of Jackson and Addy. They're the same, I realize. Cut from the same cloth. They both think they can do whatever they want—*to* whomever they want. "*We* caught him."

"And I'm taking him."

Jackson steps past me, reaching for the rope. Before I can

even think about what I'm doing, I press the knife against his neck, just below his ear. It's a reflex. Like the way your leg jumps when your knee is hit just so. Even though it feels as natural as breathing, shock ripples along my every nerve that this is *me*. That *I'm* the one holding a knife to someone's neck.

He freezes even as Addy and the other two boys surge forward. I press the tip deeper.

"Stop," he bites out at them.

I flick them all a glance, satisfied none look ready to ignore his command.

Without turning to look at me, Jackson asks softly, "What are you doing, Davy?"

"Taking what's ours."

"You won't. You don't have the nerve—"

And maybe he's right, but I say, "Want to test me? It's only *your* throat."

"You'll regret this," he growls, neck stretched tight against the prick of my knife. But he doesn't call my bluff. He doesn't doubt me. And I guess no one would. No one does. Not here. Not among carriers.

Angling my head, I look back at the other three, my gaze lingering the longest on Addy, sensing she's the most dangerous. "Sit down. On the ground. All of you," I bark, making certain my voice rings with force.

They lower to the ground. I look at Richard. "Tie them up."

Eager to comply, he jumps to the task, smiling gleefully.

I look at Felix. He stares at me with wide eyes. I jerk my head at Jackson. "Him, too."

Nodding, Felix steps forward.

"You'll regret this," Addy snarls as her thick arms are bound.

"Make it tight," I instruct, ignoring her. "Don't want him getting loose."

Once Felix ties his hands with the rope, I ease the tip of the knife off his neck.

Jackson's eyes gleam at me in the gloom. "You're so smart," he murmurs as Felix forces him to the ground and starts tying his legs. "Right now, you've won. But what are you going to do when I'm free?"

I squat down and tap the knife to his nose. Maybe I shouldn't toy with him, but it feels so good to have the upper hand, even as his eyes flash murder. "I'm not worried about that." Not the truth entirely. But since I got to this place, all I've done is worry. I've been looking over my shoulder ever since Pollock showed up at my house. It's nothing new. Just another layer to my anxiety. To the constant fear. "I can take care of myself." I smile and eye his ropes. "Clearly."

He doesn't even wear the phony smile. It's like that has been cast aside for good. His lip curls over his teeth. "You won't see me coming."

A chill flutters across my skin in the warm night. "We're not supposed to harm each other, remember? This is a training exercise. My behavior will be forgiven, but you come after me in the dark some night . . ." I *tsk* and shake my head at him. "I don't think you want to get kicked out of here. Sent to a detention camp. Or worse."

That smile returns, slow and easy and hateful. I want to slap it off his face.

"It might be worth it. To watch you bleed . . ."

My throat thickens and the prickles are back, breaking out all over my skin. Thankfully, it's too dark for him to see me clearly. If my face is splotchy and red he can't tell. No way for him to know that he's getting to me.

"Come on," Richard urges, clutching the rope attached to our prisoner.

Felix takes the lead in front of Richard. Leaving Jackson and his teammates behind, I bring up the rear. No one else stumbles upon us, and we manage to make it back to the main grounds without further incident. Just as we clear the trees, our captive decides to put forth one more effort. He yanks hard on the rope, surprising Richard with a kick to the chest. The boy hits the ground. The target spins and lunges away, but I'm on him, tackling him to the earth.

He grunts and starts talking, his words all a hot mash of sound.

"Come on!" Richard grabs his rope and yanks him to his feet.

Felix offers me his hand. "Let's finish this."

Nodding, I accept his hand and rise. When the guards and instructors see us approach, they sound the bell, signaling the end of the game.

We deliver the captive to the waiting guards and watch as the rest of the carriers trickle back toward the main building, many grumbling and scowling. I can't help but stand proudly, my shoulders pulled back. Tully and the rest of our team join us, beaming and nodding in approval. Looking at me differently. With respect. After yesterday, this win is significant for me. I've proven myself.

I spot Sean and Gil. I breathe easier at the sight of them unharmed. Until that moment, I didn't realize fear for them had lurked in the back of my mind. Cut loose in the woods with forty-eight armed carriers, anything could have gone wrong.

Sean's eyes find me. He grins then, his lips curving in one of his rare smiles. Relief lights his eyes. He'd been worried. For me. Smiling back, I nod at the target, indicating that my team brought him in.

His eyes widen, understanding my meaning. He shoots me a thumbs-up, impressed. I blow on my fingers and brush them against my shoulder.

He rolls his eyes and shakes his head, mouthing at me: *show-off.*

I giggle. Richard looks at me strangely and I instantly sober, facing forward again as the guards take a head count and recount. And recount again. One of them turns to Harris and calls out, "We're four short."

"Well, what are you staring at me for? Go find them," Harris barks.

Felix, Richard, and I swap uncertain looks.

Felix clears his throat. "You'll find them that way." He points west.

Harris narrows his gaze on the three of us even as he

addresses the guards. "Go. Fetch them."

We wait in silence for the guards' return. Harris watches us as though we might make a sudden bolt for it.

Jackson, Addy, and their other two teammates walk ahead of the guards into the quad. One of the guards holds up severed rope for Harris to see. "They were tied up."

"But otherwise unharmed, I see." Harris looks back at us questioningly. After a stretch of silence, it becomes clear he expects an explanation.

I lift my chin. "They tried to take the target from us."

"And you weren't going to let that happen?"

"No, sir." I clasp my hands behind my back. "We did what we had to in order to complete the drill."

"What's your name?" He glances at Dusty rather than me for a response.

"Davina Hamilton," she supplies.

"Good job, Hamilton." His gaze flicks over my entire team, which now surrounds me, adding, "Good job, green team."

Harris's eyes widen at something behind me.

Curious, I turn, glimpsing the blur of a swinging fist. I jerk out of the way. Jackson's knuckles just graze my jaw. Pain radiates throughout my face, and I stumble back. Felix and Richard catch me, steadying me with their hands.

Looking up, I see Jackson still coming at me. The deceptively friendly mask he always wears is ripped free. In its place is simple hate. Hate for me. Clearly, I pushed him past the point of self-preservation.

I scurry back, but he's headed for me like a charging bull.

There's no breaking him from his course. Richard steps in his path, but Jackson knocks the smaller boy out of the way. Just as he's about to reach me, Sean cuts across my line of vision in a streak of movement. His body plows into him.

They twist and writhe on the ground. Sean gains the upper hand, pinning Jackson beneath him. The cracking sound of bone on bone reverberates on the air as Sean's fists connect with Jackson's face.

I shake my head. *Not again.*

Guards arrive, their hands seizing Sean by the shoulders and arms, pulling him back. I step forward and press one hand to his chest, trying to ease the tension radiating from him. It's like he doesn't see me. His eyes fix on Jackson with blood-hungry intensity.

"Sean," I hiss, shooting a quick glance over my shoulder at Harris, watching us like specimens under a microscope.

"Enough!" Harris shouts, pushing his way closer, his boots thudding over the ground. He looks at Jackson, bending over and spitting blood onto the ground—and what looks like a tooth—then back to Sean. As far as I can tell, there's not a scratch on Sean, but his face is wild, flushed red in fury. He'd like another go at Jackson. "The drill is over and I won't stand for any more fighting in the ranks. Understood?"

Jackson looks up, wiping a hand against his nose, leaving a dark streak of crimson against his face. He nods. Harris then looks at Sean. Sean grunts and offers up a nod as well.

Harris stares at Sean for a long moment as though he doesn't quite believe him. My fists curl at my sides, fearful that he will decide to punish Sean in some way. *Like by sending him away from here.*

"What's gotten into you, O'Rourke?" Harris demands.

Sean pulls back his shoulders, panting hard, saying nothing.

"They're from the same town," Dusty volunteers, motioning to me. Of course, she knows that. I'm sure Stiles included that in my file.

"Ah. Loyalty I admire, but I expect discipline." Harris looks back and forth between Sean and me, before narrowing his eyes on Sean, considering him in a way that is impossible to read. "And those who can follow rules."

Sean's own expression reveals nothing. "Understood," he finally says. He understands, but I can't help noting that he didn't promise to obey.

For a long moment, Harris and Sean stare at each other, the silence cloying and thick.

Nodding slowly, Harris turns his attention on me, studying me for a long moment. "Davina Hamilton. I won't be forgetting that name."

This camp serves one function. To teach killers how to obey and serve this country. If they can't be trained, they can't be kept around. Never forget that.

*—Correspondence from Dr. Wainwright upon Commander Harris's appointment to director of operations at Mount Haven*

# TWENTY-SEVEN

SWIVELING ON HIS HEELS, HARRIS RESUMES HIS place at the front of the group. From the corner of my eye, I mark Jackson's progress back to his team. Sean remains near me. Forty-eight of us stand, waiting as Harris stares out at us, assessing. I fidget impatiently, anxious to be released back to our rooms before anything else happens. Suddenly, this day feels endless.

"You are all here to prove that you are worth something. That you deserve a future with freedoms and privileges." His voice rings out over the pulsing night, floating across the stagnant air. "That you can be trusted, that you're better than your scum brethren in the detention camps. Carriers like him." He points to the target we captured.

My eyes widen. *He's not a volunteer then?* He's from a detention camp.

A guard shoves the man forward. He stumbles, catching himself. It's a wonder he doesn't fall. He's still bound with rope.

"This man has attempted several escapes from a camp in Colorado. He incited his fellow carriers into attacking and killing two guards in order to provide a distraction for his third escape attempt."

I assess the man, noting his thinness, his stringy, unwashed hair. It looks as though he hasn't had a good meal or bath in a month. A testament to life in a detention camp.

"There will be no fourth attempt for him . . . no more innocent guards killed. Mercy for him ends here and now."

Harris pulls a gun from his belt. I flinch at the sight of it even though I handle a gun every day during drills at the firing range.

My stomach bottoms out as he points the barrel at the target. The man stares straight ahead at all of us with unblinking eyes, his lips moving rapidly, saying something under his breath. I strain to hear. *Is he praying? Begging for his life?*

I glance around me. Everyone watches, transfixed, eyes glazed brightly.

I look back at Harris, tense, waiting for the sound of the shot. Instead, he lowers his arm.

Air slips out past my lips, relieved. Maybe he changed his mind.

He stares out at all of us, scanning the crowd until his gaze lands on me. "Hamilton," he calls.

Everything inside me seizes, my skin snapping with sudden cold. Picking up the target's rope, he walks toward me. Guards accompany him. My fellow carriers part until he stands in front of me. He's very tall. I have to drop my head back to look up at him.

His eyes assess me coolly. "I believe I mentioned a reward for the winning team. Since your team came out on top today, why don't you do the honors?"

I frown, hearing his words but not understanding.

Somewhere near me, someone gasps and I turn my head, looking for the source. I can't identify the person, but everyone stares at me with wide eyes.

Sean looks at me intently, his eyes full of something . . . sorrow, pain?

Bewildered, I look back at Harris. "I don't—" My words fade as I notice his hand. The gun that he now stretches toward me.

"Take it."

I shake my head.

He sighs in exasperation and grabs my wrist, pushing the gun at me. "Take. It." There's no flexibility, no room for argument.

My fingers close around the heavy metal. It's cold in my hand. Hard and unyielding metal. My least favorite part of each day is the firing range. The noise. The tension coursing through my body as I take my shots. I always feel faintly achy after leaving, my head shrouded in cotton.

I sense as much as see the other carriers back away from me like a receding tide.

"Stand close to him," Harris instructs, taking me by the shoulders and positioning me in front of the man. The target stares at me now, his brown eyes stark, defeated. No, not "target." A man. A human. A life.

Harris's voice rolls softly near my ear. "I know you've been practicing with the others, but I don't expect you to be an expert marksman yet. A simple shot to the head at close range is sufficient."

My breath falls in sharp little pants. My chest actually hurts. I look around desperately, as though a way out, an escape, is going to present itself.

Harris looks at me dully, like he's asking nothing from me.

Sean steps forward as if to reach me, but a guard stops him with a hand on his chest.

"I'll do it," he volunteers, his lips grim, his jaw set. He looks from me to Harris. Holding out his hand, he flicks his fingers. "Give it to me."

Harris glances at him, arching an eyebrow mildly. "I'm sure you would, O'Rourke. But Hamilton here will do it. Won't you?" He looks back at me, his eyes challenging . . . threatening. I'm expected to follow instructions, but how can I do this?

I stare at Harris, searching his face, looking for something in him that I might touch. Any softness that I might appeal to.

Nothing.

"Take aim," he instructs.

I lift my arm. It trembles so badly that I lift my other hand to grip my elbow and hold myself steady. Still the .45 shakes, but not so much that I'll miss. This close in range, there's no chance of that. I'm so close I can actually see the flecks of gold in the man's brown eyes . . . the pulse throb in his forehead.

"Safety's off. Fire when ready."

I curl my finger around the trigger. Like I'm going to do this. Like I can.

"Fire," Harris snaps.

*He's a carrier. Who knows all that he has done?*

*You're a carrier. You've done nothing.*

Until now.

Silence falls around me in a thick shroud. Everything slows. Almost like in a dream. No one makes a sound as they watch the scene unfold. I can feel Sean's eyes on me, hot and desperate, willing me to . . . to *what*? Shoot?

But I don't want to be that. *This*—the monster the world claims I am.

With a shuddered breath, I lift my trembling finger off the trigger and drop my arm. It's no use. I can't. I'm not a cold-blooded killer. They can't make me that.

Head bowed, I choke out, "I won't. I can't. Do your worst. Send me to a detention camp." I shrug weakly. "You can't make me do this."

Harris sighs heavily. "Very well."

I hear the slide of another gun from a holster.

I lift my head, frowning, wondering with an odd sense of detachment if he intends to shoot me. Maybe they won't even trouble themselves with sending me away. Maybe they're going to kill me, end it all right now.

Harris moves. I track his actions vaguely, still feeling as though I'm trapped in a dream. He stops directly beside Sean. And lifts his arm. Presses the gun barrel against Sean's head. Gasps ripple through the crowd.

He nods at Sean. "You shoot or I shoot him."

My chest constricts. "W-what?"

He digs the barrel into Sean's temple, forcing Sean to lean to the side. He tries to hide his wince, but I see it. It's as though I can even feel it myself.

I reach out a hand. "No! Stop—"

"You said 'do your worst,' Hamilton. Somehow, for you . . . I think this is it."

Hysteria bubbles up inside me. "Sean . . ."

His lips move, mouthing the words at me: *it's okay*. And he means that. His eyes look directly at me, accepting and understanding . . . *inviting* me to let this horrible thing happen to him.

It's *okay*? To do as Harris commands and put a bullet in his head? That will never be okay. Heat burns through me, followed by a wash of bitter cold. I will never be okay if that happens.

My lips tremble, tasting the saltiness of tears. I didn't even know I was crying. "P-please."

"On three," Harris announces, his eyes cool as ever. "One."

My heart lunges to my throat as his finger curls around the trigger.

"Please!" I shout even as I fumble to lift my weapon and aim once again at the carrier. I focus on his face for a split second. The brown eyes fasten on me, deep with resignation. And I realize that's always been there. Defeat. Resignation. Ever since I captured him, he's known this was inevitable.

"Two."

He's muttering those too-quiet words again . . . prayers or pleas, I don't know. I don't hear them. I can't hear them.

"No!" I scream, my voice rising up from deep inside me, shrill and wild as my finger squeezes the trigger.

The bullet bursts from the barrel with a loud crack, echoing on the night. My arm jerks from the recoil. The body drops in front of me. Dead weight. *Dead*. Just a body now. Not a life. I took that. Snuffed out his existence with the slightest touch.

My mouth parts on a sawing breath, and I take a halting step, peering down, my attention fixing on his eyes. Still open. Glassy. The life behind them gone, vanished. The color changes. Like a curtain dropped, the brown dulls into something flat . . . makes him appear mannequin-like.

Several carriers let out loud whoops. No doubt, *they* wouldn't have hesitated or required manipulation and threats to fire. They wouldn't feel the bile rising up in the back of their throats. They wouldn't have to bend over to empty their stomachs.

The gun slides from my hand and thuds to the ground as I

retch until there's nothing inside me to purge. Throat raw and aching, I lift my face.

Sean's there. So is Gil. Both pat my back. Sean makes small shushing sounds.

"See, Hamilton. That wasn't so bad."

I look up, breathing harshly, covering my mouth with the back of my hand. Harris smiles benignly, and it's a clawing swipe in an already bleeding wound.

I did it. I killed.

Exactly what he wanted me to do. Exactly what they all thought I would do. Everyone in here. Everyone out there in the world. A world so afraid of carriers, it makes killers out of the innocent.

"All right, people. Turn in your packs. Show's over for the night. Return to your rooms. Lights out in ten."

I rise and slide my pack off my back with numb movements, letting it drop where I stand.

"Davy," Sean and Gil both say my name. I ignore them. In my periphery, I glimpse Sabine, watching me, wringing her hands like she's too afraid to approach me. After what just happened, it's no wonder. They used Sean, threatening to shoot him if I didn't kill the target. Because they knew I cared about him. She's probably questioning whether being my friend is a good idea. I don't blame her.

Sean and Gil fall in step beside me. We start for the building, passing Sabine. Their presence is a comfort. At least I still have them. Right or wrong. For their well-being, I can't help thinking that it's wrong. Not that I can do anything about that anymore. It's too late. We're always together. Everyone knows I care about them.

I move one leg after the other, eager to close myself up in my room. To hide from what I've done—what I am. Even as this enters my mind, I know it won't work. I can't ever hide from this night. No matter that I did it to save Sean's life, I am what everyone always thought.

A killer.

---

HTS Detention Camp Code 11B:

Any child born to a carrier shall be tested for HTS at birth. Infants found positive shall remain in the detention camp of his/her birth. If found negative of the gene, they shall be remanded to the state for placement with relatives or an appropriate foster agency.

# TWENTY-EIGHT

I TAKE A QUICK SHOWER, INDIFFERENT TO THE ten-minute warning. I just killed a man. Those brown eyes are all I can see. I could have let him go over the wall. If I'd known who he was . . . what was going to happen. Yes. I could have let him escape. I would have given him a boost myself. If I had only known.

I stand beneath the spray of water, letting it beat down on my flesh, wishing—there I go again, still senselessly wishing—that it could wash away the day. Undo everything that happened. I search inside myself, reaching for the music that's always there.

Silence.

I try harder, struggle to find the familiar notes, lyrics, anything, some whiff of a song, a tune. It's no use. There's nothing except silence.

Dusty's voice inside the bathroom startles me. I lift my head from the spray. "That you in there, Hamilton?"

"Yes."

"It's almost lights-out. Get out of there now."

With a sigh, I turn off the water and step from the shower onto the cool tile, wrapping a towel around myself. I face Dusty numbly, gazing dispassionately at her sun-weathered face.

"That was good work today."

Winning the challenge. Taking a life. For her, it's one and the same. "Yeah. All in a day's work," I hear myself reply.

She frowns, and I'm guessing she doesn't care for my flippant tone. I should be properly flattered at the praise. I had wanted to do well and impress them so much before. Too late, I know the price of doing well in here now. She looks me up and down where I stand, dripping wet.

"I'll give you another thirty." Then she will lock me in my room for the night. Another cage.

I nod. "Thanks." She leaves the bathroom and I dress quickly. Going through the motions thoughtlessly. Clothes. Hair. Teeth. I pause at my reflection. The bandage is gone. I removed it while in the shower. All that remains is a short, jagged tear in my cheek. A bright scratch of red in my otherwise pale face. My dark blonde hair looks almost black plastered wetly to my head. I tie it in a quick braid, my fingers moving as nimbly as they once did over the piano or guitar strings.

Finished, I gather up my stuff. Stepping out into the hall, I cross to my room.

I'm at the door, turning the knob, beginning to push it open when I feel someone at my back. At first I think it's Dusty, but then I'm being shoved inside, propelled into the room.

I drop my things and whirl around, not about to get trapped alone with a carrier bent on hurting me. Today's been bad enough. I use my fists, whacking, slapping. Too tired to call up my recent training, my movements are wild.

My arms are seized, squeezed in an unrelenting grip. "Davy! Stop!"

I know the voice immediately.

Freezing, I glare up at Sean's shadow in the gloom of the room. "What are you doing in here?"

His hands don't drop from my arms as he shuts the door on us, sealing us in. He holds me from him. Looking me over in the near darkness. With one hand he flips on the light switch. His gaze scans all of me, setting my skin afire everywhere he looks . . . which is . . . *everywhere*.

"Are you all right?"

I lift up my shoulders and arms and throw off his hands. "Don't touch me. Please. I just can't have you touch me."

Because it's all I want. All I want and can't ever have. Not anymore.

His eyes cloud over, so full of anguish. "I'm so sorry, Davy."

I hold up a hand, closing my eyes and shaking my head. "Stop. We're not doing this."

"You didn't have to—"

"Stop! Don't say it." I punch him then, furious. I slap his arms and chest with both hands. "Don't say I didn't have to do it."

How can he think I had a choice? How dare he imply I could have let him die? The only thing I can cling to is the belief that I had to shoot that man.

"Davy." He snatches hold of my hands. "I'm sorry. You're right, of course."

Panting, I tug my arms free and wave toward the door, shaking. "Just go. You shouldn't even be here. This is the girls' floor. They're about to lock up."

He doesn't budge.

"I don't need them thinking we're closer than we are." I say this even though I know that doesn't matter anymore.

"They already know you'd kill to protect me. What difference does it make now?"

I swallow against the scratchy thickness in my throat. "I don't want friends around they can use against me."

"Well, too bad. I'm here." He steps closer. "You don't want to go through this alone."

*Want.* I close my eyes in an agonized blink, thinking about what I want. *I want this day undone. I want that man not dead.* "What I want hasn't mattered in a long time. This is what needs to happen." It's the only way I can live with myself.

"Look. I never imagined them making you do something

like that. . . . Using me . . ." His voice fades away and he looks down at his hands. I study his profile, the lines of his face stark and harshly beautiful in the unforgiving light.

"They'll do it again," I whisper, lifting my face, staring blindly at the ceiling tiles. Seeing only brown eyes. Hearing only the crack of the gun, the drop of the carrier's body on the dirt. That's it, all there is, the only sound in my head. No more music. Just this. "God, I can't do that again. There won't be anything left of me—" I stop with a choke, wondering if there's anything left of me now.

They were right all along. I'm a killer. The only hope I have now is to finish the program and get out of here as soon as possible. Get the imprint removed from my neck. Gain some semblance of freedom, of normalcy, for myself.

"You have to go. Don't come here again." I pause, take a breath, and swallow.

He looks up at me and just stares. "I can't pretend you don't exist for me."

I stop just short of jabbing him in the chest. Something about him, so large, so close, the aroma of night and wind still upon him, makes me keep my hand to myself. I make a small sound, part laugh, part moan. "Sure you can." I step past him to open the door for him to leave, but I don't get that far.

He grabs my arm and whirls me around, smacking me right against him. I strain to get away, arching my body. His eyes hold me again. It's always his eyes. The gray-blue so seductive, like smoke weaving its spell on me.

One of his hands cups the back of my head, fingers weaving

into the wet strands. Everything inside me stills, locks tight as his palm curves around the back of my skull. I can only look into those eyes. Watch him watching me. Stare helplessly when his gaze drops to my mouth.

His head moves down swiftly, stopping just a half inch from my lips. Our breaths merge, mingle. His hand flexes in my hair, as if testing the wet texture.

Then he closes the space between us. Kisses me finally. Sensation explodes inside me when his lips touch mine. It's not tentative or shy like most first kisses. The ones I've had anyway.

It's urgent and full of need. Hungry and desperate. The perfect force and pressure. I slide my hands around his neck, twine my fingers up through his hair.

I stretch onto my tiptoes. His hand on my arm moves to wrap around my waist, lifting me, plastering me against him.

"You smell so good," he mutters against my mouth. Feelings and sensations rush me, killing the misery, temporarily ridding it from my system. Later is soon enough to remember what I am, what I've become.

I make a small mewling sound, kissing him harder as he carries me to the foot of the bed. I'm glad for the small room. Glad to reach the bed so quickly.

His body settles over mine. I fist my hands into his shirt, clutching the fabric, hating it, wanting to tear it, shred it from his body as his mouth devours mine.

His hands move like the wind, soundless and sudden. Warm and caressing. His fingers slide over my skin, stroking, brushing everywhere. My hair. My face. My neck. Under my shirt. Against my stomach.

Wild pants break from my lips, spill into his mouth as his kiss consumes me. I let go of his shirt and slide my hands under the fabric, letting my palms test the expanse of his back and chest, touch skin.

With a groan, he pulls back, his hands going to the hem of his shirt. In one smooth move, it's up and over his head.

Then he's back. His mouth on mine. His bare chest pressing hotly over me. I wrap my arms around his shoulders, reveling in the moment—in *him*. Desire. Need. Connection to another soul again. In this, in him, everything else fades. The horror of earlier, a distant, faraway dream. Another life. Another girl. Another killer . . . not me.

Gradually, other sounds penetrate. The ding of the elevator, footsteps, doors opening, closing.

He says my name against my mouth, that deep voice vibrating against the sensitive flesh of my lips. "Davy? I have to go."

I drag my mouth away from his, my body limp, boneless on the bed. Everything inside me quivers with emotion . . . with longing and desire for another. And not just anyone. Sean. A carrier who can be the opposite of all predictions. Good. Principled. Heroic.

His eyes glitter, making the darker outside ring more prominent. "I have to go." I drink in the sight of him as he pulls his shirt back on over his head.

"Yes." I nod and suck in another breath, remembering myself. A proven killer. I have to beat this place. Survive it and get out. "You can't come here again. No more—"

He cuts me off. "Not that again." His gaze drills into me.

I hold silent, my heart palpitating to the point of pain inside my chest.

His thumb strokes down the side of my face, tracing the small cut there. "Let's leave this place."

"What?" My voice escapes in a croak.

"You heard me. Let's run."

The wild suggestion tempts me. My hand drifts to my neck, brushing the imprint there that forever brands me as the killer that I am. I'll have no way of getting rid of it if I run.

Sean continues, "I don't want to become what they're training us to be. I don't want what happened today to happen again, and it will. It doesn't matter if we ignore each other. They used me once to manipulate you. They'll do it again. Maybe next time, they'll use you to get me to do something." His eyes look pained. "And I'll do it. God knows I will."

Of course, he would. He volunteered to kill for me today—so I wouldn't have to do it. Not that Harris let him.

I moisten my lips. "Even if we could get away, where would we go? How would we not get caught?" My gaze skitters to the door, knowing we only have minutes before it gets locked.

He angles his head. His hair strokes his shoulders with the motion. I doubt he's cut it even once in the weeks since we first met.

"Can you trust me? Gil has been looking into it during Independent Study, and I've heard things, too . . . before we came here. There's an underground group out there offering shelter for carriers, helping us get to safety. There are places we could go."

*We.* He wants me to go with him. Run away into the dangerous unknown. My stomach does a flip. "Gil's going, too?"

"And you . . . I hope." His gaze searches mine.

"I don't know, Sean. If we're caught escaping . . ."

We know what would happen. Today taught us that.

"How can we risk it?" I finish.

"How can we stay here?"

His head dips and he's kissing me again, persuading me with lips that make me melt. It's unfair of him, but I clutch him close again.

A door slams nearby and I jerk in his arms.

Sean lifts his head. We wait, listening to the sound of receding steps.

I sag with relief. "Go. Now."

He climbs off the bed. "Think about it. We're working on a plan. Gil is waiting to hear back from a contact. It's gonna happen soon. This week."

*This week?* Sitting up, I swing my legs over the side of the bed. "You didn't just decide to do this today. How long have you been planning this?"

His expression hardens. "Let's just say after today I decided to put a rush on things." And I can see it in his eyes now. His pain. I'd only thought of my misery, but now I realize today destroyed a piece of him, too. I might have pulled the trigger, but he's the reason I did it.

"I won't be anyone's pawn again," he vows.

But he will. Or I will. Maybe next time the gun will be on me. As long as we're together, we can be twisted and manipulated. I could hurt him, Gil . . . to say nothing of myself. Some wounds are deeper than death. If nothing else, I've learned that.

He watches me, waiting.

"I'll think about it," I promise, trying to convince myself that out there we have a chance. That just maybe we could make it.

The conditions in the camp have reached crisis-level proportions. Disease, infighting, attacks on the guards. Escapes are more frequent, and we haven't the manpower to give pursuit. We request immediate relief . . . more guards, more supplies, more temporary buildings. Perhaps the dismantling of the camp altogether is necessary. Something needs to be done or I fear the carriers shall soon overrun us. . . .

*—Correspondence from director of Camp 4 to Dr. Wainwright*

We haven't the supplies or manpower to spare at this time. Your foremost priority is to maintain control of the camp. I cannot stress how crucial this is. Exterminate any agitators that threaten your command and do not waste food or medicine on the gravely sick.

*—Reply from Dr. Wainwright*

# TWENTY-NINE

I WORK EXTRA HARD THE NEXT DAY. EVEN STILL sore from my sparring match with Tully, I push through the discomfort, ignoring the twinges in my ribs.

I avoid Sean and Gil, needing time to think, to process. I feel them looking at me several times throughout the day. I'm sure Sean recapped Gil on our conversation in my room—leaving out the make-out session. I know I left Sean with the impression that I would consider running away with him, but in the light of day I'm not sure of anything. I can hardly think about that. Flashes of that carrier falling to the ground play over and over in my mind. The weight of the gun in my hand.

The recoil as I pull the trigger. A living nightmare.

My feet pound the earth. Sweat trickles down my spine. I breathe through my nose as I follow the winding jogging trail. I push myself until my lungs start to ache, welcoming the punishing pain, deserving it.

Sean lies in wait at the water fountain stationed in front of the gym. It's my second pass in front of the gym on my run. I've been jogging with a half dozen others over the dirt path snaking through the buildings and looping around the woods. I'm sure there are kids in front of me and in back, but I've been solo for a while now. Sometimes, Sabine keeps me company, even though she's a lot faster than me, but she's nowhere around today.

"Hey," he calls.

Immediately, my face burns, thinking about all the kissing we did last night. I pause for a quick drink at the fountain, wiping at the icy water dribbling down my chin, gathering my composure. "Hey." I bend down for another drink. It's hot and I'm thirsty, but I'm also desperate to look casual in his presence. I can't just stand and gawk at him with my heart in my eyes.

"Give any thought to what we talked about?" He stares at me, his eyes intent, pinning me where I stand.

I swallow, my throat now cold from the water. "I don't know. . ."

He glances left and right before looking back at me and leaning closer. "You can't want to stay here."

Staring at his face, at that earnest gaze, I want nothing

more than to go with him. I want to believe there could be something better out there for us. For a killer like me. A place I could go with him and be safe. A place where the world is safe from me, too. The thing is . . . I can't imagine that place really exists.

"Sean, I . . ." My voice falters and I step back, putting more space between us. My gaze dips, and I get distracted looking at his mouth, remembering the taste of it. The shape and pressure of it against mine. Maybe that's why he kissed me. To addle my thinking and get me to go with him.

Shaking off the thought, I snap my attention back to his eyes. "I can't do this right now. I'm supposed to be running." I step around him.

"Tonight then?" He grabs my wrist, stalling me. "We'll talk then." I look down at the long, tan fingers wrapped around my wrist. His voice curls around me, too. Just as enticing. And I don't deserve that. I shouldn't feel anything *good* after what I did yesterday. "I can find you after dinner."

His hand reaches for me like he's going to touch me. My breath hitches. With a quick glance around, remembering himself and where we are, he drops his hand back to his side. The air deflates from my chest, and I know then how much I wanted to feel his hand on my face. It's the only thing—*he* is the only thing—that eclipses the horror of yesterday for me.

Sadly, *wrongly*, I do want to see him again. I want him to come to my room, but not to talk about his crazy plan. I want to forget about that and just be with him again. Like before but more. More of his lips. More of his hands . . . his warm skin against mine. I want to hold his face and look into his eyes and see compassion and caring and empathy . . . all the things I haven't seen, haven't felt in far too long a time. Those things that remind me I'm a human and not just the killer I've become.

Edging away, I say, against my better judgment, "Yes. Come."

His lips stretch in a slow smile.

I'll explain my position to him then. That it's too risky. How far can we get with imprints on our necks? My best chance is to stay here until I've earned the right for them to remove my imprint. Then I can slip away.

I set out again, the image of his smiling face etched in my mind.

But it's not long before yesterday returns to haunt me. Shame sinks its teeth into me. I pump my arms harder. I wish I'd said no. Seeing him again, being with him, tasting his kiss . . . I don't deserve that.

My feet pound the trail, legs working fluidly. I'm so busy with my thoughts that I don't even feel the ache in my body anymore. Running has just become automatic, the simple repetition of my steps as I wonder about the man I killed—who was he before the Agency showed up to drag him away? Did anyone mourn him? Would they even know he died?

I catch a blur of movement to my left and think it's another runner joining me on the trail. It's only a split second thought though. It flees the instant a body rams into my side like a vehicle butting another one off the track.

Caught off balance, I fall onto my side. Hard. My shoulder throbs. Wincing, I roll onto my back, wondering if I might have dislocated it. I don't make it to my feet. I don't have time to examine my shoulder. I don't have time for anything.

Someone grabs my ankles and drags me off the trail and deeper into the woods. I open my mouth to scream, but another body is suddenly there. He slides his arms beneath my armpits, slamming one hand over my mouth. I'm mute. I bite down on salty fingers and am rewarded with a sharp cuff to the ear.

My vision blurs, graying for a moment. Dizziness swamps me. The world jerks and heaves as I'm carried. I blink, fighting past the light-headedness.

We squeeze through thick brush. Branches and leaves scratch at my arms. Suddenly, I'm unceremoniously dropped to the ground. I take the brunt of the fall on my hip and I cry out, certain a bruise will form there within an hour.

Swallowing my wince, I look up. Jackson stands over me, and I know true fear. Two boys I don't know hover behind him—I've seen them, of course, but I've never spoken to them. Jackson probably appealed to their interests . . . torture, sadism. I don't have to have done anything personally to them to make them want to hurt me. They're carriers. There doesn't have to be a reason for them to inflict pain on others.

Everything in me tenses, ready and alert for the first chance to break away.

I eye the three of them, trying to assess them. Jackson is fast. I've seen him sprint. I doubt I can get away from him, especially after already running for nearly an hour now. He'll be on me in a flash. The lanky one beside Jackson doesn't look necessarily intimidating. The third one is thickset, reminds me of Tully. He's one of the few I outrun in the mornings.

Still, there are three of them. And one of me.

"That was easy enough," the stocky one pants, his face glistening with sweat. Yeah. I could definitely outrun him.

"Not so tough now, huh?" Jackson rests his hands on his narrow hips and leans closer. "Where's your boyfriend? He hardly ever lets you out of his sight." Jackson smiles slowly. "It's just us now."

I swallow. My gaze flicks to each of them. I feel like prey crouching beneath them. Any moment, they'll pounce and devour me. Simply because they can. It's what predators do. Hunt and destroy.

"You think you'll get away with this?" I ask.

"Who's gonna find out it was us?" Jackson smiles. "And if they do, so what? The weak don't make it in here."

"Yeah." The lanky one nods in agreement. "Like Tully. He's out of here."

"What are you talking about? He was here yesterday—"

"They came for him last night thanks to you and your boyfriend." Jackson looks annoyed about this for a moment, but then he smiles again. "After we're done with you, they'll ship you out, too. Assuming there's anything left of you."

My stomach sinks. He's right. If they don't kill me right now, I'm gone from here.

Gone from *Sean*.

This realization hits me hard. I don't want to lose Sean. To never see him again . . . It's worse than the fear of ending up in a detention camp. It's almost as bad as I felt when I pulled that trigger on the carrier. I shiver and Jackson's smile deepens. I hate that he sees this weakness in me. That he's getting to me. *That I'm terrified.*

I scan the crowd of trees, the thick brown-and-green tangle of brush, the outline of mountains rising in the distance. The foliage will only muffle my screams.

We move simultaneously. Jackson starts for me as I bolt. I take off. Laughter rings in my ears as he catches me and lifts me off my feet, his arms steel bands around me, trapping my arms.

He hugs me tightly, crushing me, squeezing my ribs and pushing the air from my lungs. A strangled cry escapes me.

"That's right," he goads. I feel his face nod alongside of mine, his hair brushing my cheek. "Scream."

And that's when I know it excites him. He gets off on my fear. My pain.

I arch my neck, straining from him. My gaze sweeps the sky. Leaves sway above. The two other guys call out encouragement.

I lower my head and bring it back up. I don't make contact with his nose, but I hit him, knock him somewhere around the eye. He howls and his arms loosen around me. I drop, stagger to my feet, my hands briefly scraping the ground.

I don't wait. I don't look back. My feet pound the leaf-littered ground. I dodge limbs, bushes, trees. I run wildly, zigzagging. I've lost sense of my location, but I'm convinced I'll hit the joggers' trail or one of the buildings soon. The instructors aren't going to let them brutalize me right out in the open. I just have to make it out of the woods.

The things they could do to me if they catch me race through my panicked thoughts. I run, keep moving, thrashing through the woods. Instinct drives me.

"Davy," one of them calls nearby in a singsong voice.

I stop, drop low to the ground and freeze, every muscle in me locking tight. I listen, heart hammering a loud tempo in my ears. Crouched, I inch back, away from the sound of the voice. I don't think to watch behind me.

One of the guys, the stocky one, shouts gleefully as his hands come down on my shoulders. "I got her! I got her! Jackson! Over here!"

I whirl, at least relieved it's not Jackson. He's more formidable to me. More dangerous.

Twisting around, I face the boy holding me. "What about when Jackson turns on you? When he decides to use you for a punching bag? Remember what he said? There will only be a few left standing at the end of this."

"Yeah. And I'll be one of them."

"If he's picking off the weaker, you look like a good target."

"Shut up!" He shakes me.

I kick him hard in his shin and slam my heel down on top of his foot, grinding deep.

He cries out, releasing me. I'm up and running again.

Only I don't make it three strides before I'm caught in the

face with the sharp crack of a branch.

I fall on my back, my skull throbbing from the hard collision. My face stings. I gingerly touch my nose, my cheek, fingers roaming, testing, brushing over my lips. Wetness coats my fingers. My bottom lip is split and bleeding profusely.

Jackson stands over me, a long branch in his hand. He slaps it against his other palm. "Oh, man. That looks like it hurts." He points to his puffy eye. I guess I did that. "This doesn't feel too hot, either, bitch."

I lower my hand from my mouth, mumbling, "Now we're even."

"Oh, this isn't about what's fair. It's about fun. My fun." He cocks his head. "At your expense. Sorry."

Of course, he's not sorry. I see that in his gaze, in the hard, brittle eyes. My pain, my fear, thrills him.

He crouches in front of me. I draw back, watching him survey me consideringly, his gaze lingering on my bare legs. He's still slapping that branch in his open palm. By now the other two guys have arrived, breathless, behind him.

When he brings the branch down on my thighs I'm almost expecting it. I flinch. A hiss of pain escapes through my teeth.

He lifts his arm and lets the branch fly again. Pain rips across my flesh. My leg shoots out reflexively. I kick him in the jaw, sending him flying backward.

I scramble to my feet and run.

"Get her!"

I ignore the hot agony in my legs. My feet work, legs eating up ground.

Heavy feet pound behind me. A hand grazes my shoulder, slowing me. I stumble and then he's on me. We tumble and keep rolling. Screaming, I claw, I hit. Jackson's curses burn my ears. He punches me in the stomach. I moan. Grabbing a fistful of his hair, I yank until I feel the roots tear loose.

Shouting, he loses his grip. I scurry frantically to my feet, using my hands for leverage.

I'm not running as fast as I need to be, but that punch in the gut still has me winded. My breathing is loud and harsh, crashing over the humid air. I swipe at low-hanging branches.

I hear him behind me.

I don't look back, too frightened at what the split second glance will cost me. I push harder.

He grabs my shirt, seizing a fistful. I screech and whirl around, swinging even as hot sobs scald my throat. My knotted hand catches him against the side of the head even as I brace for a return blow, the pain to come.

Dimly, it occurs to me that I've known more pain in the last month than ever before. In my entire life. Is this all I will know now? Will pain become everyday? As natural as drawing air?

"Davy! Stop! It's me!" I register his voice at the same time I realize I'm not being attacked. He's carefully holding me by the arms. Familiar blue-gray eyes drill into me, searching, touching that part of my heart I'd tried and failed to lock away.

"Sean?" I sag against him, relief pouring through me.

"What happened? You're bleeding." He brushes my

mouth with his hand. Scowling, his gaze drops over me, examining me.

Remembering we're not alone out here, I look around us, still panting. "There are three of them—"

His face hardens. "What did they do?"

"Nothing." I cover his hand with my own and squeeze reassuringly. Nothing the instructors will look twice at when they see me anyway. I don't need them pondering how I got slapped. They'll probably think my split lip was from yesterday's drill. "Which way to the trail?"

"This way." He starts to guide me through the dense woods. "Who did this?"

"Some guys. Jackson."

He looks over his shoulder like he wants to go back for them. Rage brightens his eyes.

"It doesn't matter," I choke out, and then swallow, clearing my throat. I force my chin up and stuff away the part of me that wants to crumple, break, and fall into tears. Weakness can't exist in me anymore. When I try again, my voice rings stronger. "I'm starting to think there's a reason for locking up carriers. We really are animals."

We step out onto the dirt-packed trail and I exhale, looking left and right, almost expecting the other three to be waiting, but it's just us.

Sean stops us from going any farther. Color burns beneath his tan. "Is that what you are? An animal? Is that what I am?"

"I didn't mean us," I say, but I'm not sure. I know what's inside me now. I tell myself that I had to take that man's life.

For Sean, I had to. But it doesn't change what I did. Or what I am. It stays with me, haunts my every thought and sickens me.

"Don't lump us with them." His eyes glitter brightly. He grinds his hand against his chest for emphasis. "I know I'm different from them. So are you. That's why I won't stay here for another day." His lip curls up over his teeth with disgust. "I'm not playing their games anymore. Whatever they have in store for us, I'm not going to be a part of it." His lips flatten tightly, clearly waiting for me to say something.

I stare up at him, barely breathing, thinking what it would be like to stay here, living through more of this. Leaving here would be a dream. Only I've given up on dreams.

I nod down the trail. "We better get going."

He holds my arm, stopping me from moving on.

"Davy." The sound of my name is full of desperation. "They made you kill a man."

I flinch. He doesn't need to remind me. When I close my eyes, the man I killed is all I see. I draw a ragged breath. I shake, thinking of brown eyes, vacant and glassy. Empty. The sound of a body hitting the ground.

He dips his head to look evenly into my eyes. "Can you trust me? Can you let go enough to do that? I have a plan, Davy."

I release a shaky breath, the plea in his eyes affecting me. I laugh weakly. "You told me not to trust anyone but myself. Remember? Were you excluding yourself?"

"Oh, no. I meant me, too."

"Then what changed?"

"That was before."

"Before what?" I ask.

He takes his time answering. "Before you got under my skin. Before you killed someone to save my life. Believe in me, Davy. In *us*." He pauses. Hunger stirs in me as I watch him. The tendons in his throat work. "Let me save your life now. Because you have to know that if you stay here, you're dead. Promise me you'll come with me."

"If I go with you," I whisper, swallowing, "there's nothing waiting for us. No chance of anything." And if we're caught . . . what then? I don't say it, but the words, the fear, hangs between us.

Something rustles in the trees nearby and Sean tenses. I follow his gaze, holding my breath. No one emerges.

Sean looks back at me. "I'm leaving with Gil. Tonight. I was going to tell you in Independent Study."

I suck in a sharp breath. *So soon?*

"We'll be long gone before roll call in the morning. Gil has made arrangements. He's got a guy that's going to pick us up who—" Sean stops, shakes his head. "Doesn't matter." His voice is flat, the words falling with finality. "Next time there won't be anyone around to come looking for you and pull you back onto the trail." He brushes fingers against my cut lip. A shiver runs through me. "I can't stay and watch you get hurt here."

I exhale, shaken. My stomach twists sickly. He drops his hand and starts walking. I fall into step beside him.

I want to tell him I'll be all right without him, but it's

a long time since I've felt confident that I'm ever going to be all right. After yesterday, I doubt that I'll ever feel fully right again. I'll never go back to the girl I used to be who hears music in her head. But this. Here. *Without him.* It's impossible.

We walk together, side by side but not touching, on our way back to the compound. Every nerve ending tingles, alive and awake with him so close beside me. An ache suffuses my chest to think of him leaving. Gone.

I notice Jackson and the other two in the distance by the dining hall. Their body language conveys their fury. One of them points at me, but they don't approach. Not out in the open like this. Not with my alleged boyfriend by my side. I glance at him and my chest tightens painfully.

*God, I don't want you to go.*

At first, I don't realize I've uttered these words aloud until he looks down at me with a frustrated expression, his eyebrows pulling tight over his eyes.

"Don't make this harder than it is, Davy. If I stay here, they'll kill us both. Maybe not physically, but what's left of us . . . our souls. I'm not sticking around to watch that happen. You could ask me for anything, but not that."

"I won't. I'm not asking that." Then I hear myself saying, "I'm coming with you."

For a moment he just stares at me like he doesn't understand—or believe—my words. Then his expression lightens and a smile lifts his mouth. "You mean that?"

I nod.

He inches forward like he's going to hug me but catches himself with a quick glance around. "You won't regret it, Davy. We're going to make it. You'll see." He gives my arm a slight squeeze. "I'll come for you tonight." I nod again, hoping he's right and that we won't regret this.

The number of US carriers fleeing across our border has become of grave concern. As much as the CBSA has tripled its efforts, we simply cannot impede the illegal influx. The merging of so many displaced and volatile individuals among our citizens has yielded deadly consequences. Such a threat cannot be ignored. At this time, until the US carrier population is better managed, all visitors from the United States shall be refused entry into Canada.

*—Correspondence to the US secretary of state from the Canadian envoy to the United States of America*

# THIRTY

SITTING ON THE EDGE OF MY BED, MY FINGERS tap an anxious staccato against my thighs. I focus on my impending escape, concentrate on this. A difficult task when glassy, dead eyes keep intruding on my thoughts. I wonder things. *Who was he before someone studied his DNA under a microscope? What was his name?* Shaking my head, I shove away the crippling thoughts. I can't afford them tonight.

I tell myself that escaping here won't land us in a bigger mess, in more danger. I close my eyes and rub the bridge of my nose. Not that I can change my mind now even if I wanted to. Sean is coming for me. I'm going with him. I promised. And I *want* to go.

My chest tightens, clenches and squeezes with the desperate hope that we make it out of here. Rising from the bed, I walk to the window and stare out the blinds. Perimeter lights edge the building and grounds. I hear the purr of an ATV before I see it roll across the lawn. It's the only sound in the night. The building is as quiet as a tomb.

No alarms have gone off, and I can't help wondering how we'll get out of the building. They lock us in at night. Security sits downstairs.

A faint click sounds behind me. I spin around, staring first at the door and then everywhere else all at once. Dim light pours into the room, saving me from total blackness, and I identify Sean as he steps inside. The fear ebbs, replaced with a new kind of tension.

"Sean," I whisper, my heart pumping harder.

He shuts my door behind him and leans back against it. In the gloom, I can detect the rise and fall of his broad chest. Like he just ran several flights of stairs.

Nervously, I brush a strand of hair from my cheek. My gaze darts around before coming to rest on him again. Of course I can't help replaying the last time we were alone in my room. I swallow against the sudden dryness of my throat.

I moisten my lips. "You made it."

He moves, closing the distance between us, advancing with steady strides, eyes gleaming and dark. His hands slide along my cheeks, lifting my face to his. He kisses me, hard and swift. His hands move from my face to my back. Fingers splayed wide, he pulls me against him, wrapping me up in his warmth.

Warm tears roll down my cheeks. He's the only one. Since all this happened to me, he's the one who's been there for me. The one to make me feel like I'm still a person. Not a pariah. Not the monster in the dark. He's never told me what I am. He's just assured me that I'm not anything I don't want to be.

Our lips fuse hotter, more urgent. I throw my whole weight against him. Off balance, he staggers, arm looping around my waist. We fall back on the bed, me sprawled over him.

I kiss him like it's the last time. Because who knows? It could be. If we're caught, we'll at least have this. I work my hands beneath his shirt, skate my palms over his flat stomach, revel at the quiver of his warm flesh under my hands.

He thrusts me from him, his fingers scoring through my hair, holding it back from my face so that he can see me. "Davy. We don't have much time. Gil's waiting downstairs, hiding in the stairwell."

I take a bracing breath. "Yes. Of course." We're really doing this. "Let's go."

The door creaks open and we fly apart, Sean pushing me behind him.

"Hey." It's Gil, his dark eyes shining behind his lenses. "We've got to go if we want that head start. The guards change shifts in a couple hours."

I grab my backpack. Sean takes my hand and we're moving. Walking through the door and out into the silent hall without a backward glance. There's no sight of anyone on my floor. We take the stairwell, my heart pounding so hard I'm afraid it can be heard a mile away. At the bottom floor, Gil eases the door open and peers out.

At first glance, the guard looks asleep at the desk, but then I notice his complete and unusual stillness and the odd way his head rests on the surface. Sean creeps toward his desk and deposits the keys there that he apparently used to open my door. We start to slip past him, but suddenly I stop. On impulse, I move back to the desk, my pulse now a feverish throb in my throat. I snatch up the keys, motioning Sean and Gil to wait, and race back up the stairs. At Sabine's room, I unlock the door. She's already up, standing tensely beside her bed, her small frame trembling. Her fearful expression eases somewhat when she sees it's me but remains wary.

"I'm getting out of here," I whisper. "You can stay or come with me."

She hesitates only a moment before grabbing a pair of pants and slipping them on over her shorts. She stuffs her feet into her shoes, not bothering with the laces. I don't have to warn her to be quiet. She follows me soundlessly down the stairs, past the unconscious guard and outside.

Sean and Gil are waiting by the door, their expressions anxious until they spot me. Their eyes widen slightly at the sight of Sabine behind me. Pushing open the door, Sean motions me to hurry. My steps quicken and together we dive outside. The air hasn't cooled off much and I'm immediately doused in the humid evening. I look left and right, scanning our surroundings. My heart pounds a frantic rhythm. We take a left. I listen for sounds as we move along. Nothing. Not even the purr of the ATV patrolling the grounds.

We hug the shadows, rounding the refectory, heading west. The same direction the carrier had taken last night in his dash for freedom, where the perimeter wall is at its lowest. A pang sharpens my chest at the memory, at the bitter, bitter wish that he had made it.

Sean guides us behind the thick hedge bordering one side of the refectory. The four of us crouch down. I look at the boys curiously. Sean shakes his head at me and motions for me to stay silent. He looks back out at the quad in the direction we just came. I follow his gaze. Nothing. I look back at him questioningly. He motions to his lips, mouthing the word: *wait*.

Then I see her, muttering under her breath as she stomps a hard line. I'd know that walk anywhere. It's hard and swift, more like a man's stride. I catch some of her words. ". . . know she went this way . . ."

I peer through the spiny leaves and observe acne-scarred Addy's face. Even in the dark, I can detect the wildness in her eyes.

She stops and looks around, her narrow face drawn tight. Sighing, she props her hands on her hips and calls out, "I saw you! I know you're out here! I saw you and that twig leave the building. Come out, Davy!"

My heart squeezes to hear my name on her lips. I exchange looks with Sean and Gil, trying to convey my regret that I earned this girl's wrath so much that she followed us.

"I'll wake everyone up," she continues in a loud whisper. "Have fun explaining what you and Sabine are doing out of your rooms!"

I motion that I should go and appease her . . . keep her from making good on her threat. Sean shakes his head fiercely at me, mouthing *no*. Gil is the opposite, nodding and gesturing for me to go ahead. Sabine holds silent, like a little mouse next to me, probably debating the wisdom of joining us.

I tear my hand free from Sean and step out from the hedge before he can stop me.

Addy's gaze lands on me. "Hiding? Bit wimpy. Thought you were tougher than that. Where are the others?"

I ignore her question, crossing my arms over my chest. "What do you want?"

"Was just returning from a meeting with one of the instructors when I saw you slip out. Yeah," she sneers. "You aren't the only one they think has potential. Turns out I'm excelling so much at Spanish that they've started tutoring me in Russian, too." She takes a single step closer, her shrewd gaze narrowing on me. "*Where* are you going?"

I stare at her a long moment, weighing my answers.

"I'm getting out of here." I settle on the truth. She already suspects as much. It would be foolish to lie. "Running away."

She considers me thoughtfully. I do the same, trying to read her expression and glean something from it. Maybe she wants to leave, too. Who really wants to be here, after all? Surrounded by guards with their electric prods? Instructors with their judging eyes. The threat of detention camps and death hanging over us.

I exhale. Only one way to find out. "Come with me."

She snorts. "Oh, that's funny. Nice joke. We wouldn't last ten minutes out there. Especially with that imprint you're sporting. No, thanks." She crosses her thick arms, a smirk on her lips. "But you know what I will do? I think I'll just go ahead and rat you out. Score me some points with the powers that be. Could always use the advantage."

I point to my face. "It won't help you. They're going to keep pitting us against each other, thinning us out until we're just a few. Your ratting me out isn't going to save you. You should come with me."

She shakes her head. "No."

"Then at least give me a chance. You don't have to tell anyone you saw me. Just go back to your room."

No emotion registers on her face. "Go ahead. It will take me about five minutes to alert the staff. That can be your head start." Turning, she starts to walk away.

Something inside me snaps. I only see her back walking away from me, on her way to destroy me. To destroy Sean and Gil and Sabine. This twists inside me like a hot poker. I can't let her do that. I can't let her go.

I don't even feel myself moving, but I'm aware that I'm running, launching myself at her, landing heavily on her back. The bigger girl hits the ground with a sharp cry. She doesn't take it without a fight. She bucks beneath me. I try to stay atop her, squeezing my thighs around her hips.

I grab a fistful of her hair and pull her head back to growl into her ear, "You're. Not. Telling." I pull back my arm to strike her.

"Davy!" Suddenly, my arm is caught in an iron grip. I try to pull it free, but there's no budging. I look at the hand on my arm. My gaze skips up to Sean's concerned face.

I look back down at Addy, my hand twisted in her hair. I release her and climb off. She flips over, her acne-mottled face red and seething. "You'll pay for that." Her gaze moves to Sean. "Your boyfriend, too." She opens her mouth to scream, but suddenly a rock strikes her in the head. She topples over.

My gaze swings. Stops on Sabine. She stands with her hand poised in midair, as if still pitching the rock.

"Sabine," I breathe.

She blinks at the sound of her name. "She was going to tell."

Addy stays down, motionless. "Oh, God. Is she . . ."

Sean checks her pulse and shakes his head. "She's still breathing."

I exhale heavily. I wanted to hit her. Hurt her. Sean had to stop me. This frightens me maybe the most.

"We need to go." This from Gil, his gaze scanning the grounds.

I shake my head, staring from Addy to Sabine. She looks so small, so innocent. For the first time I wonder what I really know about this girl.

Sean grabs Addy's ankles and drags her into the bushes, out of sight.

Then he's back at my side, seizing my hand and pulling me

along after Gil. "C'mon. We have to go while she's still passed out." There's no time to talk. And no going back. Sabine follows us. I can hear her light tread under the heavier beat of our own. Sean's running fast. I keep up, panting beside him. We break off the trail and head into the trees. It's dark, but Gil whips out a flashlight from his backpack, guiding us through the grasping press of foliage. We stop at the perimeter wall. I blink, feeling dazed, my head fuzzy like it's wrapped in cotton.

I glance over my shoulder into the dark woods behind us, wondering if I'm leaving the place where I truly belong. I am a killer, after all. Maybe Sabine, too, for all I know. She didn't blink an eye using that rock on Addy.

I'm lifted off my feet as Sean swings me over the wall. Sabine drops down without any help. She's like a jungle monkey. Sean follows, landing lightly on his feet. A car waits, rumbling in the dark. The headlights flip on and we're bathed in the sudden flood.

"He's here!" Gil exclaims, rushing ahead, waving excitedly to the person behind the wheel. No stranger to him, apparently.

The guy is in his forties, plain and unassuming looking. Nervous. His gaze darts everywhere all at once.

"Who's that?" I pause warily beside Sean, watching as Gil and the driver step close to talk.

Sean faces me, his features cut in harsh lines from the glow of the headlights. "The guy that's going to get us out of here."

"Oh," I murmur as though that explains everything. But I don't press. I'm still reeling from the last few moments. From what I'm actually doing. From all that I've done. All that might happen yet.

He turns me to face him. "Don't start questioning yourself now. We're doing the right thing. We have no other choice."

I nod. I don't want him to worry about me or that I'm about to break, crumple to bits and pieces in front of him. "I'm not."

"Hey." He tilts my chin with one finger, his eyes mesmerizing me. "You trust me, right?"

This time my nod is sincere. "Yes." I do. I trust *him*. It's just me I doubt. Glassy brown eyes keep flashing in my mind. A reminder of what I am, what I've done. The peace that will never be mine. A painful lump rises in my throat.

Gil and the driver get in the front of the car. Sean pulls me into the backseat. Sabine follows. Sandwiched in the middle, I settle alongside Sean's solid warmth. His arm wraps around me. I take comfort in his embrace. Security, however imaginary. Gil looks back at us with a reassuring smile.

Sean leans closer. His warm lips brush my ear. Goose bumps break out over my arms. "We're going to be fine."

I absorb these words and try to believe them, but I'm not sure what "fine" is anymore. Everything feels desperate and hopeless. Everything is "have to." Every time I close my eyes, I see the face of a dead man and know that I'll kill when cornered. I guess that makes me no different from any other wild animal.

I lace my fingers with Sean's, squeezing tightly, looking for something to hang on to, something warm and beautiful and precious. Something that brings meaning in all of this.

Anything to slow my descent.

I wake to sunlight. I can even smell it. Warm and rich as loam on the air. The small room is bathed in its warm rays, making the white walls appear even whiter, a colorlessness that seems to stare back at me, waiting for my next move.

I stretch on the bed with a noisy yawn, luxuriating in sleeping so late, enjoying my body's sense of languor. Right or wrong, for the first time in months, I feel safe. Logically, I know I shouldn't lower my guard. We could be captured at any time. My hand brushes the sheet beside me, the indentation from Sean's body still there. I smile slowly. For now, I feel free. If I've learned anything, it's that now—this moment—is all that matters.

Rising slowly, I dress and brush my teeth in the trailer's single bathroom across the hall. Clothes hang over the shower rod to dry. Yesterday, Sabine and I washed our things in the sink, figuring that even wrinkled, clean was clean.

Walking out into the main room, I find Gil and Sabine at the small kitchen table, playing cards. Ever since Gil's contact dropped us here three days ago with instructions on how to cross the border, we've played cards a lot to amuse ourselves. With nowhere else to go and no television or books to pass the time, there's not much else to do as we wait.

Sabine munches on dry cereal. "Hey," she greets after swallowing her mouthful. She looks different since leaving Mount Haven. With the lines of her face less strained, she's pretty in a way I had never noticed before.

Gil offers me a distracted wave as he studies his cards intently.

"Hi." I take an apple off the counter.

I nod to the trailer door. "Sean outside?"

Gil flicks his gaze away for a split second. "Yeah. The usual spot."

I take a noisy bite from the apple and slip on my shoes sitting beside the door.

Stepping outside, I blink against the glare, holding a hand over my eyes. It's not too hot yet, at least in the mornings, but the promise is there, in the day to come, in the weeks ahead. I move over the broken ground, skirting patches of mesquite scrub and small cacti. I pick my way to where Sean sits, his back to me.

He's parked on an outcropping of rock, looking down with binoculars at the valley below. Sunlight shines off his hair, gilding the long strands a brilliant shade of dark gold.

He lowers the binoculars as I take a seat beside him. "Morning, sleepyhead."

I shrug. "What can I say? It feels good to sleep in."

Smiling, he leans across the space between us and kisses me. Slow and lingering. It's like this now. Kisses. Touches. All freely given and taken. In just three days, being with him has become as necessary as breathing. It's like being here, time suspends. We forget Mount Haven and everything that happened there. The outside world is gone.

I nod to the valley below. "How's it going?"

He follows my gaze. "I think I have their patterns figured out."

I take the binoculars from him and study the river, a thick serpent amid the sloping mountains, the water more brown than blue. "It looks quiet."

"A patrol just went by. Like every day at this time."

"What about the construction crews?" My gaze narrows on the orange flags and stakes, indicating where the wall will go to divide Mexico from Texas.

"No sign of them in two days. I think we have some time while they're surveying and setting the rest of the pins along the border north of here."

I nod and lower the binoculars. "So when do we cross?"

"Well, according to Gil's guy, they pick up on Mondays on the other side, but I think it's safer to leave Saturday around four a.m. Our chances should be good then. We'll just have to lay low and camp out one night." He touches my cheek, his fingers a whisper-soft brush on my skin.

A night with him under the stars? I could handle that. I lean into his caress, looking from him to the river below and the wild stretch of land beyond. Where we're headed. Where our future awaits.

"I'm ready."

Dear Reader,

Any time you flip on the television, you see horrible crimes reported on the news. It always leads to one question. Why? Why does violence happen? What makes people do horrible things? Can it be stopped?

When I began writing *Uninvited*, I knew right away that I was dealing with some tough themes. Inexplicable violence among teens and children is not the easiest topic. As a mother, when I look at my young children, I find it especially difficult to consider. Yet it is a reality within our world. Once Davy, Sean, and Gil appeared so fully fleshed in my mind, I couldn't shy away from their story. Davy, especially, was a voice I couldn't silence. She is me. She is my mother. She is my niece. She is my daughter. She is every girl I ever knew. Reader, she is *you*. She's what could become of any one of us if the world of *Uninvited* ever came to pass.

The role of nature and nurture has been a long-standing debate. Long before true-crime TV and DNA coding, philosophers debated why people behave the way they do. Plato believed human behavior arrived innately. Aristotle took a different view, speculating that humans were born a "blank slate"—that environment determines actions. This discussion is nothing new. When horrific things happen, the world seeks answers. When fear rules us, we are quick to point fingers in the quest for truth, in the hope for answers. And so, the world of *Uninvited* isn't such a far-fetched scenario.

As you close this book on Davy's journey (for now . . .

because Davy's story isn't over yet!) and go about your life in this remarkably fast-developing world of science and technology, never forget that we are more than genetic code. We can be more than the labels applied to us. We can be more than what others whisper behind our backs or shout in our faces. Free will exists. We need to *choose* to be the best we can be, and we need to help others do the same.

Believe in yourself.

Warmly,
Sophie Jordan

DAVY'S STORY CONTINUES IN

DAVY'S STORY CONTINUES IN

---

**Presidential Proclamation**

Section 1. Funding for Detention Camps

a) Within forty-eight hours of the issuance date of this memorandum, and in conjunction with the Department of Treasury and the Office of Management of Budget, a sum of $1.27 billion shall be released to the Wainwright Agency for the express purpose of the administration and expansion of all detention camps for the continued harmony and protection of this country against the threat of HTS carriers, whose genetic mutation predisposes them to commit violence. . . .

# ONE

THE MAN I KILLED WON'T LEAVE ME ALONE.

He comes to me at night. The first time he intruded on my dreams I thought it was an isolated thing. A sudden troublesome nightmare that would fade with the night, never to return.

But it does. *He* does. And I begin to realize he's never going away. Brown eyes. Bullet hole. Black-red blood. He will always be there.

The knowledge sinks slowly, awfully, like an animal's teeth biting down and holding deep and hard into my muscle. I can't pull away. Can't shake it. I'm caught. Pinned in its jaws.

Strangely, I thought being labeled a killer and losing everything—my future, family, boyfriend, friends—was the worst thing that could ever happen to me. It's not. Finding out they were right? Finding out that's exactly what I am?

That's worse.

He's just a shadow in the corner of the room tonight. A dark, motionless shape, the edges of him blurred like smudges on paper.

I sit up in the bed, drawing my knees to my chest. Sean lies beside me, chest rising and falling softly, unaware of our late-night visitor. And I guess he's only *my* visitor really. Nothing haunts Sean. For him the past is just that. Something left behind, and I envy his ability to move on. To accept himself. To simply accept what is.

My gaze slides back to the dead man. I feel his familiar eyes crawling over me. Watch him watching me while cicadas drone a steady lullaby outside the trailer. Looking at him, I remember everything. That moment when the director of Mount Haven forced my hand and demanded that I kill. Oh, Harris gave me a choice. I guess. If letting him kill Sean was a choice. Either I killed a stranger—an anonymous carrier—or Sean died. That was my choice. No matter what, someone would have died. Either way, my fate was decided.

Sean sleeps on, blissfully unaware, his body like something sculpted from marble, the dark ink tattoos on his arm and neck standing out starkly against his lighter skin. I try to use this—the familiar, comforting sight of him—to make me feel better. He's why I killed that man, after all. So Sean could live. But it doesn't work. Unable to look at him, unable to bear the reminder, I turn away.

And that's what Sean has come to be. A reminder of the most horrible moment of my life. I don't regret saving him, but it doesn't change the fact that I'm a killer now.

When we first fled Mount Haven and arrived at this trailer practically sitting on the US-Mexican border, everything was great. Sean. Me. *We* were great. Holding hands, touching, kissing. Like two teenagers who had just discovered each other. In a way, I guess we were that. We curled around each other every night, our bodies like two spoons. There was no pressure beyond whispered words and lingering kisses. Just the scent of him, his skin warm and solid next to mine, was enough. Being with him filled me with a giddy sense of hope—a belief that everything was going to be all right. Was that only days ago? How quickly things disintegrated and dissolved to dust.

My nails dig into my palms, indenting the flesh with tiny half-moons. I embrace the pain, taking the punishment. Rolling on my side, I pretend that the figure in the corner isn't there anymore, watching me. Brown eyes. Bullet hole. Black-red blood.

I pretend Sean hasn't become someone I can't bear to see or touch or love.

Closing my eyes, I tell myself pretending will eventually work. That it will become real.

***

I'm the first one up. I feel achy and tired all over, and I take an extra-long shower, bowing my head and letting the water beat down on my neck. It doesn't help that I never really went back to sleep, too afraid of a repeat visit from Brown Eyes himself. I used to treasure my eight hours of sleep every night.

Back home, Mom had to shake me awake two or three times every morning. I loved my bed. The down-filled comforter. The surplus of pillows and stuffed animals from my youth. The way the morning sunlight would filter through my pink-and-green diaphanous curtains. It's strange how much you miss all those little things. What I wouldn't do to hug one of my old stuffed animals. To be that girl again. Sometimes on Saturdays Mom would make French toast and sausages. The savory aroma would fill the house and lure me from bed. It's hard to accept that those days are gone. Even lunches at my old private school, Everton, had been delicious. Not that I appreciated it at the time. I miss the salad bar and the made-to-order stir-fry.

Gil pops up on the couch, his hair sticking out in every direction. He rubs his eyes as I pour cereal into a bowl. No milk, but I'm already used to eating it dry.

A book slides to the floor. He must have fallen asleep reading it. It's an old, yellowed, dog-eared copy of *The Hobbit*. Last night he told Sabine the general plotline. She sat before him like a little girl, holding her knees and rocking in place, her eyes wide as he painted a picture of hobbits, dragons, and all manner of fantastical creatures. Sean had listened, too, his smile rueful as his eyes slid from them to me.

"Sorry." I wince as I set the box back down on the table. "Didn't mean to wake you."

Blinking, Gil reaches for his glasses sitting on the upside-down crate serving as a coffee table. No longer blind, he zeroes in on me. "Nah, I needed to get up anyway."

I resist asking why. It's not as though we have that much to do. Sean monitors the comings and goings at the river below. Gil occasionally joins him or relieves him. Right now we're just waiting until Sunday, when we'll make our crossing. Along with a copy of *The Hobbit*, we discovered a box of checkers on the dusty shelf in the corner of the trailer. We play that a lot, even though Gil always wins. There's the challenge, the hope that we might beat him, that keeps bringing us back. That and boredom.

I munch noisily as Gil removes a stale bagel from a bag and takes a huge bite. Our food choices are limited. The place was supplied with minimal groceries when we first arrived. Nothing fresh. Mostly items that won't expire or grow mold anytime soon.

"Didn't think I could miss anything about Mount Haven," he mutters, dry crumbs falling from his lips.

I nod, understanding. "The food."

"I never ate that well before. Unless you count jumbo slushies and bags of Cheetos from the gas station."

I nod like I agree. Like I didn't eat well in my old life, too. Except I did. We ate out at the best restaurants. Sushi. Chinese. Italian. And Mom was a good cook, even if she only bothered once, maybe twice, a week. She made a lasagna so deep you could lose a fork in it. Dad would groan at the sight of it. My chest tightens, an uncomfortable ball forming in the center. I wonder if I'll ever see them again.

Sean and Sabine join us. We all move around in companionable silence, preparing our unappetizing breakfasts.

Sabine isn't a morning person. You're lucky to get a word out of her before ten a.m. She rips the foil packaging off a Pop-Tart and sits across from me at the table. Shaking long brown hair back from her face, she manages a smile, biting into the pastry. Crumbs fall to the table, and she brushes them onto the floor.

Sean uses one of the jugs of water to make some coffee, and soon the rich aroma fills the trailer. He offers me a mug and I accept. After the first bitter swallow, I reach for the sugar and add a generous spoonful. Then a second. Maybe someday I'll enjoy a latte again. Maybe they have those where we're going. Maybe. My life is full of maybes. Even more than the maybes are the "never happening agains."

I sigh against the ceramic rim, grateful for the surge of caffeine to my bloodstream.

"Good?" Sean asks.

"Yeah. Thanks."

Sabine's gaze darts between us. There's silent inquiry in her eyes. Speculation. I know she's wondering what's up with us. Well, with me.

Sean gathers up his well-worn map and binoculars and the spiral pad he's been using to take notes. The map in his hand crinkles as he says, "I'll be back later." His gaze sweeps the room, lingering on me the longest. "I wouldn't mind some company."

I nod, and the motion feels jerky, unnatural. "Sure. I'll be out in a little while." Like I have something keeping me inside the trailer.

The trailer door shuts quietly after him.

Gil rises. "Hope you don't mind, but I'm gonna borrow one of the beds and go back to sleep. That couch sucks."

He heads off, the weak linoleum creaking under his bare feet. I've been here almost a week and still can't stand walking barefoot over the gross floor.

"So what's up with you and Sean?"

My gaze whips up. Sabine has moved on to the second Pop-Tart. She chews primly.

Despite our less-than-stellar diet of Pop-Tarts and dry cereal, she looks good. Better than she did when I first met her at Mount Haven. There's color in her cheeks now and her gaze is bright.

"What do you mean?"

She rolls her eyes. "You can barely look at him."

Is it that obvious? We're all getting along. Smiling. I put on a good show. At least I thought so. "We're fine. Nothing's wrong," I deny. Because it can't be. Whatever this is, I'll fix it. We'll be fine. I'll be fine.

"Right." The corner of her mouth lifts. "When we first got here, you two couldn't keep your hands off each other. It was like being stuck with a couple of honeymooners."

My face warms. "It's nothing. I'm just focused on getting across. I'll relax once this is over and we've made it to the other side."

She shrugs a slim shoulder. "We'll either make it or we won't. I'd think you'd want to get in as much quality time with Sean as you can before we leave. Especially since we might be caught or killed. Carpe diem and all that." She says it so matter-of-factly. Our life has become this. The subject of our potential demise commonplace. *Caught or killed.* At this point, they're one and the same.

Her smile slips away and she stares at me evenly, a sharp glint in her eyes. Almost like she's annoyed with me. How can I explain to her what's going through my head? That since we settled in here, I'm having a hard time coming to terms with killing that guy. Being close to Sean is . . . difficult.

Rising from the table, I murmur something about making the bed and head to the back of the trailer. One thing about being stuck in an eight-hundred-square-foot space is that there is nowhere to hide. Not from one another. Not from ghosts.

I wake with a jolt again that night. Opening my eyes, I sit up and immediately look for him. The man I killed. He's not here. A relieved breath pushes past my lips.

"Davy?" Sean's there, sitting up beside me. I blink at the empty space surrounding us and lower my body back down on the bed, clutching the sheets to my chest in knotted fists.

I gaze at the ceiling, focusing on the web of spidery cracks in the vinyl-covered ceiling.

Sean settles beside me. His hand curls around my arm in a loose touch.

"Bad dream?" His deep voice rumbles through the dark.

I nod. It's easier than explaining that I woke because I was afraid a manifestation of the guy I killed might have decided to come visit me again.

"Are you okay?"

My voice scratches across the air papery-thin. "Yes."

"Why do I feel like you're just telling me that because you think it's what I want to hear?"

It's what *I* want to hear, too. It's what I want to be true.

I face Sean in the dark. He's so close but feels far away from me. It's as if I left him in the past. Back at Mount Haven, where they were grooming us to be something more than the killer stamped onto our genetic code. Something worse. Except he isn't gone. He's here. "I don't want you to worry about me."

"I'm always going to worry about you, Davy. That's called caring."

"I know. I care about you, too." *I'm just not sure I can be with you anymore. Not like this. Not the way you want me to be. Not the way you deserve.*

After a moment, his hand slips from my arm and some of my tension whispers free, and I hate this. Hate that I've pulled away from him and he knows it. Sabine noticed. He'd be a fool not to notice. If it wouldn't be so awkward, I would move into Sabine's room across the hall. But that would only be like waving a red flag that something is wrong, that I'm broken.

"Good night, Davy."

"Good night," I return.

I'm going to be okay. We're going to be fine. Broken things get fixed all the time. I'll stop being so weird around Sean, and everything—the world included—will work itself out.

# DAVY'S STORY CONTINUES IN

# UNLEASHED

## FATE MADE HER A MONSTER, BUT THAT WON'T BE HER DESTINY.

HARPER TEEN
*An Imprint of HarperCollinsPublishers*

www.epicreads.com

FORBIDDEN LOVE.
HIGH-STAKES ACTION.
HEARTBREAKING CHOICES.

Don't miss any of the books in the sizzling Firelight series!

**HARPER**

*An Imprint of HarperCollinsPublishers*

www.epicreads.com